A̲s̲ ...

gl̲ ...

I hurried ... take a step back. The carcass of a turkey vulture, hideous to look at, blocked the path. This particular specimen, a putrid odor from its bones, had ended up as carrion itself. Maybe that was what had upset Armistead.

I turned and hurried after her again, but no sooner had I stepped around the dead vulture than I began to notice an even more powerful stench, an all too familiar odor that stopped me in my tracks once more. Inching toward the shade beneath the poplar, straining to make out what lay there, I prayed that my first impression was a mistake.

But there was no mistake. You could tell it was a body now, or at least what was left of one. Not this, I thought. Not here. Not now—the memories of working homicide were dark apparitions I had worked to expunge. . . .

A
Witness
Above

ANDY
STRAKA

A SIGNET BOOK

SIGNET
Published by New American Library, a division of
Penguin Putnam Inc., 375 Hudson Street,
New York, New York 10014, U.S.A.
Penguin Books Ltd, 80 Strand,
London WC2R 0RL, England
Penguin Books Australia Ltd, 250 Camberwell Road,
Camberwell, Victoria 3124, Australia
Penguin Books Canada Ltd, 10 Alcorn Avenue,
Toronto, Ontario, Canada M4V 3B2
Penguin Books (N.Z.) Ltd, 182–190 Wairau Road,
Auckland 10, New Zealand

Penguin Books Ltd, Registered Offices
Harmondsworth, Middlesex, England

First published by Signet, an imprint of New American Library,
a division of Penguin Putnam Inc.

First Printing, May 2001
10 9 8 7 6 5 4 3

Copyright © Andy Straka, 2001
All rights reserved

REGISTERED TRADEMARK—MARCA REGISTRADA

Printed in the United States of America

PUBLISHER'S NOTE
This is a work of fiction. Names, characters, places, and incidents either
are the product of the author's imagination or are used fictitiously,
and any resemblance to actual persons, living or dead, events, business
establishments, or locales is entirely coincidental.

BOOKS ARE AVAILABLE AT QUANTITY DISCOUNTS WHEN USED TO PROMOTE
PRODUCTS OR SERVICES. FOR INFORMATION PLEASE WRITE TO PREMIUM
MARKETING DIVISION, PENGUIN PUTNAM INC., 375 HUDSON STREET, NEW
YORK, NEW YORK 10014.

ACKNOWLEDGMENTS

William Hoffman, Virginia novelist and farmer, says you don't write books—you grow them. I have found his words to be true, even for a first-timer's little detective story. I've also found trusted readers can provide soaking rain and abundant sunshine when needed, and I owe many thanks to the friends and colleagues who supported me in the creation of this book.

Frank McCraw and Ellen Whitener suffered through whole drafts or early chapters, as did fellow authors and writers Deborah Prum, Ken Elzinga, Mike and Sarah Dowling, Lucy Russell, Jennifer Elvgren, and Kate Hamilton. Jane Rafal pointed me in the right direction. Bob Brackett helped with some of the forensics. Police chaplain John Kuebler provided great insight into the psychology of officer shootings and their aftermath. Jon Davey gave valuable input about legal issues. I also appreciate the early assistance of the British School of Falconry in Manchester, VT, and the Falconry and Raptor Education foundation of White Sulphur Springs, WV, for allowing me to spend time with their falconers. Thank you to Lee Chichester for her insights into hawk husbandry. Thank you to special friends Dr. Randy and Carolyn Bond, Birch Martin, Dr. Bill and Cam Hammill, Bro and Dr. JoAnn Pinkerton, Michael and Meggan McPadden, and screenwriter, novelist, and buddy Michael Martin for all their prayers and support. I am particularly grateful to falconers extraordinaire, Mark and Lorrie Westman, who read the manuscript and provided crucial technical input; grateful as well to a wonderful

Acknowledgments

agent, Sheree Bykofsky, who not only lent her insight to the writing but encouraged me through an important revision. Finally, my editor, Joe Pittman, and his assistant Annette Riffle, deserve commendation for making this a much better work in the end.

I wish to dedicate this book to my family: to twin brother, John, for his early encouragement of my stories; to Chris and Kelci for loving and believing in their dad; and most of all, to Bonnie, whose love, vision, and devotion, not to mention superhuman grammatical expertise, help sustain me through it all.

Our soul is escaped as a bird
out of the snare of the fowlers:
the snare is broken,
and we are escaped.

Psalm 124:7

Prologue

Either homeboy had wigged out on us or forgotten his blue-faced, oyster shell Rolex. Better yet, rather than finger one of his own for murder, he had decided he preferred to perpetuate his still young life.

The snow could have been confetti the way it swirled in the glow from the streetlights and skittered across the hood of the unmarked. I blew on my frozen hands to stave off the numbness. Toronto, on the passenger side, nursed a tepid foam cup. We both stared down the street at the upper-floor windows of a darkened two-family, its sagging porch clashing badly with the well-tended look-alikes on either side. The block was out of our jurisdiction, off North Avenue in New Rochelle. Son of Sam territory from a decade before, a mixed commercial and residential neighborhood, tony section of Pelham a few hundred yards over the hill.

"It's getting colder. You wanna call it a night?"

Jake Toronto looked more like a club bouncer than a detective. Short but linebacker broad, his ample shoulders shaped his turtleneck beneath an unbuttoned Knicks jacket. Narrow cheekbones looked out of proportion to the rest of him: a Roman nose, close-cropped black hair, and deep-set eyes. An aura of menace mixed with Old Spice seemed to surround him. He left you with the impression something boiled just beneath the surface with which you would not wish to contend.

I didn't answer.

"Game's on from L.A.," he said. "I could still catch the second half."

I still didn't answer.

We had been chasing down leads about a series of drive-bys, thought to be gang-related, one of which had, perhaps mistakenly, taken out a popular Bronx school principal and her son. The young man we were supposed to be meeting called himself Jazz, although his real name was Jesse. He lived in the house with his mother and was supposed to know one of the shooters. We had already rung the bell and peeked through the curtains. Twice.

"C'mon, Frank. You think these guys keep day-timers? This kid ain't gonna drop no dime tonight."

"What about the mother? She said they'd both be here."

"The sister's probably out smoking juju somewhere, doesn't even know what year it is."

"Maybe." But I kept staring at the house. Toronto's instincts had proven accurate on more than one occasion, but sometimes if you pushed a little harder, stayed a little longer, and asked a little more . . . "Let's give it five more minutes."

He sighed and leaned forward with his hands cupped around his coffee as if in prayer.

The wind picked up. A wheezing sound vibrated through the glass and for a moment I thought I heard another noise, distant and indistinct. I looked at Toronto, who remained still, his eyes focused on the house down the street. A minute later, the radio suddenly squawked.

"N-Y-P-D, New Rochelle."

"What now?" Toronto rolled his eyes then buried his face in his hands. Normally, we might not have taken the time to inform the locals of our presence, but we had suffered a little incident out on the Island the month before and didn't want a repeat performance. I picked up the mike.

"Go ahead."

"Officer needs assistance. Three blocks east of your location. Shots fired!"

The line of expletives from Toronto was a mile long, but I was too busy re-starting the car and jerking it into an improvised three-point turn to pay attention to what he said.

"Copy, New Rochelle. We're on our way."

The engine growled. I got the beacon out and attached it to the roof. Toronto's talk morphed into stony silence. Out of the corner of my eye I noticed him check his weapon and, with his other hand, pulverize what was left of his empty cup.

We passed through two intersections with their signals glowing red, but luckily no cross traffic. Ninety seconds later we screeched to a halt in front of a New Rochelle cruiser double-parked outside a vacant brick apartment house that appeared to be under renovation. The driver's side door of the patrol car hung open and an officer crouched behind the fender, his weapon pointed at the building.

Two large Dumpsters, filled with construction debris, stood between the empty structure and the street. The power appeared to have been cut off to the area—the lighting was no good. But it was good enough to make out the officer's partner lying on the pavement in a growing pool of blood.

A couple more rounds went off and the patrolman behind the fender returned fire into the dark. Ducking low, I followed Toronto out his protected side. We shuffled over to the officer.

"Pavlicek and Toronto, NYPD. What do you got?"

"Shooter's in the building. Looks like two of 'em. I couldn't tell for sure."

"What happened?"

His look stayed fixed on the building. "We saw a deal going down. Chased 'em down the street into here. They took out my partner."

He was a Frigidaire of a man, older than either Jake or I—clearly no rookie. For a patrol officer he didn't look to be in the best of shape. His coat was unbuttoned.

Steam flared from his nostrils. His jaw was rigid and he wiped his brow with the back of his hand, almost seemed to be fighting back tears.

Jake and I made our way over to the prostrate figure. "Jesus," Jake said under his breath. The downed officer's name badge read: Singer. He had taken a shot or two to the face and appeared to have stopped breathing. One of us would need to start CPR, not that it looked like it would do much good. Plus, we had the immediate threat from across the street. Sirens could be heard in the distance, and it would be at least a couple more minutes before their arrival.

The building had gone quiet now. Maybe the shooters were reassessing their odds.

I scrambled back to the other officer. "What kind of firepower we up against?"

His name was Cahill, according to the tag. He breathed heavily, sweat dripping from his nose despite the cold, and kept his weapon pointed at the dark.

"Fuckers got automatics," he said. His own gun was a Glock. "I picked up this little number myself. Backup to the mags they give us. 'Bout goddamned time someone evened up the odds out here."

I couldn't have agreed more. A guy like him, working dogwatch, needed to protect himself. I had made the switch to a semiautomatic myself, not wanting to wait for official sanction. Toronto still preferred his monster .45—if it came down to it, he'd need only one clear shot to put somebody down.

I hoped it wouldn't have to come to that, but we were living every cop's nightmare: An officer wounded. Hostile armed suspects. In the dark.

Toronto took up position at the back of the cruiser while I moved around behind the unmarked. The sirens in the distance grew a little louder. We could wait it out until help arrived—we still weren't really sure what we were up against—but Singer's life was clearly ebbing away.

Another burst of shots *pop-pop-popped* from the building. Several cut branches in the tree limbs hanging overhead.

"You're outgunned now," I shouted toward the building. "Let's not make this any worse than it already is."

Silence.

"Drop your weapons and come out with your hands where we can see them."

Still nothing.

I thought I saw a shadow of movement between the Dumpsters. Then, at the side of the building, where the light was a little better, two figures turned and started to run.

I had the better angle. "Stop where you are and put your hands in the air!"

They kept going. I fired a warning round over their heads. One of the figures ignored the shot and darted into the shadows, but the other one stopped without raising his hands—he kept them at his side as he turned to face us. There was something dark and metallic in one of them—it looked just like one of our Glocks; not surprising since the gangs had them before we did.

"Drop the weapon!" I said.

Toronto was moving into position beside me. Cahill took another shot at the still-fleeing suspect but missed.

"I said, drop the weapon!"

He took a step into better light, a black teenager wearing a sweatsuit with high-top sneakers and down vest, wide-eyed in fear.

"Don't do it, my man," Toronto muttered beneath his breath. "Don't do it."

But his weapon arm rose, clearly pointing in our direction.

The strange thing was, the actual act of pulling the trigger felt no different than pumping rounds into targets on the range. Toronto and I had trained for a moment like this, been prepared for that horrible instant when a decision must be made—kill or be killed—but when the time actually arrived, the response was more knee-jerk than contemplative. We fired almost simultaneously. The teen slumped to the ground.

No time to think about what had happened. Officer Cahill was already out in front, hot-footing toward the downed shooter, a ballsy move since the kid was still armed.

"I'm on the runner," I said to Jake. "You better start CPR."

My best chance was to cut around the side of the building and try to head the kid off before he made it back to the avenue. I sprinted around the front and swam into darkness on the other side, tripping over a pile of torn insulation. One streetlight illuminated the fence at the back of the lot, which allowed me to catch a glimpse of him just as he hurdled the chain-link. This one looked to be bigger than his companion, probably faster, and he looked like he knew where he was going. I was in decent shape, but I would need every bit of stamina I owned to have any chance of running him down.

The supine image of Singer drove me—it could have just as easily been me lying there. I didn't care who the runner was, where he came from or who his parents were. I didn't think about what socioeconomic rung he or his family or friends were hung up on, or the prejudices, real and otherwise, mounted against him.

I was at the fence in a few seconds. On the other side a poorly-lit parking lot backed a small commercial building. There were houses lining the rest of the street, however, lights blazing in a few windows: people awakened, no doubt, by all the shooting, phoning 911 or just sitting tight waiting for something to happen, not wanting to get involved. The snow blew almost horizontally now, mixed with sleet that stung my face. The rest of me had gone numb.

I sprinted across the lot. Too slow. The shooter was maybe a hundred yards distant now, knifing between parked cars in front of a row of bungalows. My last glimpse of him came as he ducked between bushes across someone's back lawn. The place was almost totally dark; he could have gone any one of three different directions from in there.

Reaching the spot, I watched and waited a few minutes for any sign: footfalls, a clothesline rattling, a dog barking. Nothing. Within a quarter hour uniforms and cruisers would be crawling all over the area, beaming bright lanterns and interviewing neighbors, all to no avail.

Back by the Dumpsters, support had begun to arrive in force: three or four NRPD squad cars, an ambulance and paramedics leaping to the pavement. Jake, blood soaking his turtleneck, was still working on Singer with another officer assisting. Cahill limped toward me, looking anxious—for the first time I noticed he had been wounded in the leg.

"How's your partner?" I said.

"Don't know. It don't look good. Singer's got a . . ." He stared blankly into the sidewalk.

"I'm sorry."

He didn't move for a few seconds. Then he looked up and refocused on me. "I don't know, but listen, detective, we got problems."

"What do you mean?"

Another officer, a woman, tried to approach and enter the conversation. "Cat, we've—"

He waved her away. "Give us a second, will you?"

"But, Cat—"

"Give us a goddamned second!"

She stared at us then retreated to go help with Singer.

Cahill lowered his voice. "What I mean is, I know this kid you guys put down. He's from the neighborhood, only fourteen."

I nodded, only half-listening.

"What I'm trying to say, this was a good kid . . . and . . . well . . ." He handed something to me. "This is what I found in his hand." It looked like a piece of drainage pipe, the inside stuffed with nickel bags.

"Where's the Glock?" I said.

"What Glock?"

"The kid's."

He shook his head. "No gun."

My gut tightened. I stared at him. "But I saw him raise the weapon. Jake must have seen it too. We . . ."

He pursed his lips and shook his head again.

My head began to swirl and I closed my eyes. Why hadn't I listened to Toronto? Why did I always have to push things? Jake could have been watching his game right now, or maybe we could have stopped for pie and coffee at the Thruway Diner. Why hadn't I just taken us home?

"Hey, listen, detective—it's Pavlicek, right? You said your name was Pavlicek."

I nodded dumbly. An ambulance was arriving now, siren screaming.

The big man's eyes blazed with a sudden intensity. "It may be too late for Singer, but you all saved my ass. I got a throw-down in the car. You fellas say the word and it's done."

I continued to look at him, but my mind was reeling now, somewhere else, away from this madness, somewhere safe and warm. Down the block a TV van was already turning into view. There was a big empty billboard attached to a building on the corner with words that read: APPLE MACINTOSH. THINK DIFFERENT.

Cahill clutched my arm. But his big hand was frozen and fell away. His voice seemed to come from another world. "Detective?"

The snow was changing now to larger flakes that had begun to cling like bits of cotton candy to the cars and the bodies. Soon the sidewalk would be covered, then the block, the whole city, maybe the entire world.

"Listen to me, will ya? All you gotta do is say the word. . . ."

1

Thirteen Years Later

That September Friday I took the morning off to enter
my hawk; even though the foliage was still too thick
for decent hunting, the weather not ideal and the red-
tail barely out of moult. Armistead's bells, bewit-
attached to her pounces, trailed jingles over my head
as she shadowed me through the muddy glare. I had
squandered the night before keeping tabs on a Charlottesville architect whose wife wanted to know why her
husband had started to come home so late, the idea
being the good woman would continue to pay me, particularly if I uncovered genuine philandering for once.
With Armistead the idea was simpler: build fitness for
tackling game, maybe flush a tidbit or two across the
stubble of an unused field so her instinct might draw her
to a stoop.

It would be the big raptor's second season out. She
was a survivor—no doubt about that. When I had
trapped her as a passage bird the year before, she had
borne deep gash marks across her breast and flanks,
probably from a life-or-death tussle with an owl. Most
of her wild cousins had already succumbed by now to
disease, man-made blight or been taken as prey themselves. After a few years with me, Armistead would have
a better chance.

We reached a tangle of downed trees. Virginia pine—
over the top of their bonsai branches, Old Rag Mountain

9

towered before the line of the Blue Ridge like a displaced canine tooth. Armistead followed on, easing ahead to settle in the limbs of a nearby oak. When her bells went quiet I realized what was happening: her hunter's eyes sweeping the terrain, absorbing every detail in a millisecond. The anticipatory quality of her movements suggested a knowing preamble to flight.

The wiregrass cracked with sound. A cottontail burst into view running. Armistead did not disappoint. I caught sight of her against the sun, already rearing at the pitch of her climb.

It was over fast. The hawk dropped with such speed her talons struck like hammers. In one smooth motion she snared her prey and drove it to the ground, spreading her wings wide to hide the catch. Good girl. But suddenly she wheeled skyward again, no rabbit limp in her grasp.

Keeee-rr-rrr . . . Keeee-rr-rrr . . . The red-tail's plaintive cries split the air.

I could hardly believe what I had seen. She must have somehow missed what should have been an easy meal. Or worse, she had actually knocked the creature into the overgrowth in a flutter of dust and squeal, wounded. The last thing I needed right now was an incomplete kill: the cottontail suffering a prolonged death since the force of the strike would have damaged vital internal organs. I fingered the sharp awl I carried to dispatch quarry if it became necessary. There was no alternative. I would have to go in to finish the job myself.

I jogged along the edge of the field to the spot where Armistead, still screeching, swooped back and forth. No sign of Mr. Bunny. The place reminded me of an instance, a few weeks before, when I had brought my daughter along for Armistead's first outing of the fall. Nicole, loquacious and impulsive; just turned eighteen and with the same spectacular looks as her mother, minus the duplicity. She was a senior in high school, preparing for college, and she loved to go hunting with me since I had taken up falconry. It was one of the few things we shared since her mother and I had divorced years before and I had left her to be fathered, for all intents and purposes and despite my regular support payments, by a now-deceased stepparent, a man who had provided a much wealthier backdrop than I would've ever been able to afford.

Unfortunately, our most recent trip had turned out quite differently than expected. Armistead had acted skittish all day and kept flying off for long stretches, forcing us to chase her over the rolling terrain. The land we were on belonged to an uncle of Cat Cahill, none other than the same Cahill I had first met on that fated night so many years before. The farm had been passed down from his great-great-grandfather, an officer in the Army of Northern Virginia. It was Nicole, not myself, who had finally coaxed Armistead out of the tree where the hawk had perched for over an hour that day. I was only an apprentice falconer, after all, and though my daughter was no practitioner herself, she and the red-tail seemed to enjoy a certain understanding. A girl/girl thing, Nicky explained.

"Ho hawk!" I blew my whistle now and held up my arm with a piece of meat to call Armistead to the glove.

No response. If anything, she made even more of a racket. Like most birds of prey, she could take to the ground after a wounded catch, hopping and flitting about, and she would come to my call when hungry. But not this time. Maybe it was the girl thing again. Maybe she was embarrassed. Maybe I ought to give up anthropomorphic psychology.

I stepped over a pile of rocks into the weeds where the rabbit had disappeared. Armistead suddenly decided to follow, scolding, as if I were the one to blame for her miss.

"Pipe down. If you hadn't dropped your lunch, we wouldn't be in this predicament."

But as if to spite me the great bird extended her wings

and glided several yards ahead. She stopped at the edge of the woods to hover above the base of a large tulip poplar, staring down and calling toward the ground. Maybe she had rediscovered her prey.

I hurried to catch up. Only to stumble then take a step back. The carcass of a turkey vulture, hideous to look at up close, blocked the path. This particular specimen, a putrid odor from its bones, had ended up as carrion itself. Maybe that was what had upset Armistead.

I turned and hurried after her again, but no sooner had I stepped around the dead vulture than I began to notice an even more powerful stench, an all-too-familiar odor that stopped me in my tracks once more. Inching toward the shade beneath the poplar, straining to make out what lay there, I prayed that my first impression was a mistake.

But there was no mistake. You could tell it was a body now, or at least what was left of one. Not this, I thought. Not here. Not now—the memories of working homicide were dark apparitions I had worked to expunge.

I pulled out a handkerchief to cover my nose and mouth and rocked back on my heels. Sweat dripped from my temples. Blood, the color of oil and coated with flies, saturated the clay. Armistead, having shown me what she wanted me to see, retreated to the sky to ring effortlessly over the field.

I looked over the remains. They appeared to be those of a young black male: dark blue Filas; a green hooded sweatshirt; baggy, filth-stained jeans. An attempt had been made to conceal the body beneath a pile of brush, which had failed, obviously. The corpse lay facedown, arms akimbo. The right posterior of the midsection bore a gunshot injury, a wide starburst splitting of the skin, evidence of a contact entry wound. There didn't appear to be any defense wounds on the hands, which had blown up like swollen gloves, but something glinted in one of them—a thin silver chain affixed to a rosewood cross.

I swung at the air. The flies that had scattered at my approach now returned with aggravated ferocity. I was about to walk away—this wasn't my problem, after all; I just had to notify the proper authorities—when I noticed a flap of brown leather protruding from a clump of leaves. It appeared to be the side of a wallet, flecked with mud.

I picked up a stick and prodded it open to peer inside. Some damp, folded money became visible, lots of it. However the young man had died, he hadn't been robbed. Probing at the seams of a fold-out section, I flipped through photos of a middle-aged woman, a family with brothers, no sisters or father in evidence. And there, in the centerfold, the dead teen's driver's license.

The picture gave new form to the half buried body at my feet. He had been a grinning youth with a look of worldliness beyond his years. Puffy face with waxen skin, brown almond eyes, tinged by a trace of sadness. I bent down as close as I dared and read the name and address: Dewayne Turner, 1215 Lockbridge Court, Leonardston, VA.

My eyes stung. I squinted and read it again, just to be sure. It was, after all, the town in the Allegheny highlands near where I had settled with my ex-wife and child after moving south. Camille and Nicole still lived there, not to mention Cat Cahill, who had grown up in the region, and even my ex-partner turned master falconer, Jake Toronto. Coincidence? Maybe this was my problem after all.

I was about to turn away again, when something even more curious caught my eye. If I hadn't pushed against the wallet in a certain way, I might not have noticed it at all. One of the bills was stuffed inside at an odd angle. Along the end of the single was a string of numerals and dashes in blue ink. The moisture had caused them to bleed, but it was still possible to decipher them. A phone number. Not just anyone's. She had a private number, separate from her mom's.

Here is where—and I'm ashamed to recount how easy it was—I decided to break the law. Holding the wallet upright with the stick in one hand, I reached into the leaves and picked out a sturdy twig. Now I possessed a crude pair of chopsticks, with which, after a considerable number of tries, I was able to extract the bill by its edge just far enough that I could grab it with my falconer's glove. I folded the piece of evidence and stuffed it in the pocket of my jeans. Almost as an afterthought, I did the same with the cross and chain.

The flies kept up their assault. I spat at them, but it did little good. My shirt was soaked by now. A wave of nausea seized me. Bent over double, I moved the wallet back into its original position and covered it with dry leaves, broke the twigs into several pieces, and tossed them into the woods. The smell still clung to everything, miasmic over my hands, in my clothes. My legs almost buckled and I fell to my knees.

The kid was too young, but weren't they all? More memories. *A current under sea/ Picked his bones in whispers/ As he rose and fell/ He passed the stages of his age and youth/ Entering the whirlpool,* Eliot wrote. Something like that. I would have to find the passage when I got home, on my shelves where I kept literature between the *National Geographic*s and hunting magazines.

I stood and backed into the field where I could make out the rocky summit of Old Rag again through the haze. Its climb had grown so popular of late that on summer weekends it was almost impossible to find a parking space at the trailhead; the park service collected a fee and you were as likely to be climbing through gum wrappers left by some scout troop as through pristine woods.

I wondered if any hikers, standing in the right place now with a good pair of binoculars, could focus on my figure at the edge of the field three thousand feet below. Or if any would have suspected that nearby, among the woods and cropland stretched out like a hard-spun quilt, the remnants of Dewayne Turner festered in the heat.

Feeling better, I took a few steps into the grass.

"Okay . . . okay," I said, and blew the whistle again loudly enough for Armistead to hear. But she still kept her distance, as if to measure my response.

I groped for a piece of meat from my falconer's bag, placed it between my thumb and forefinger, and held it up where she could see it. I must have stood like that for a long time. Eventually, the hawk's weight trembled my arm.

No fury was left in her eyes, no remorse either. She ate slowly, not greedily but with precision while I secured her jesses. When she finished, I hooded her to begin the walk out. Thunder rumbled, angry clouds appeared, and rain began.

We both forgot the cottontail.

2

We were drenched by the time we reached my truck. I settled Armistead inside her cage. Next I used the cell phone to call the state police. I also called Cahill's uncle, who worked a day job and leased out most of his acreage for others to farm.

The first to arrive was a fresh-faced state trooper, careening to a stop behind my truck, beacons spinning on his navy-and-gray Crown Victoria. The rain had stopped. I hoisted myself from the pickup.

"You the man who called about the body? Mr . . . Pavlicek, is it?"

He was tall, maybe six-foot-three, with a square jaw that angled over a wide neck. His crew cut made his ears look oversized. He donned his campaign hat as he approached.

I was still wet and disheveled, clad in blue jeans and a dirty T-shirt. The shirt had been given to me by a woman named Marcia D'Angelo and it bore a drawing of a crocodile that read: *Life in the slow lane Boca Grande.*

"That's me."

He surveyed my rig, two-tone green F250 with flared fenders and a little mileage on it. Didn't swagger or act suspicious. Just examined it all with the clinical thoroughness you would expect. He paused to look in at Armistead on her ring perch.

"You out here hunting?"

"That's right."

"Like to see some ID, sir, if you don't mind."

I pulled out my wallet and slid my driver's license from its sleeve for him to scan.

"Thank you," he said and handed it back. "What do you do for a living, Mr. Pavlicek?"

"I'm a private investigator."

"S'that so?" There was no change in his expression. "How'd you come across the body then?"

"I didn't." I nodded toward the cage. "The hawk did." It wasn't worth giving him the whole story about the rabbit.

"You a bird hunter or something?"

"Falconer."

He nodded.

"My apprentice license is in the truck if you'd like to see it."

"Won't be necessary," he said. "How far from here is the body?"

"Half mile or so, but it's rough going."

"Any way to get a vehicle in there?"

"Not right now. If you cut some of this scrub out, maybe."

Another car appeared around the curve. A Madison County sheriff's unit, brown with mustard star. Unlike the trooper's vehicle, its windows were wide open and I could hear radio chatter in the background. It came to a stop and two deputies jumped out.

The trooper excused himself and approached the new arrivals. The three held a low, official-sounding conference, before opening the trunk of the sheriff's vehicle and lifting out a set of orange plastic saw horses to turn away traffic. Then they turned their attention back to me.

The trooper still did the talking. "Mr. Pavlicek, could you lead us to the body so we can cordon off the area?"

"Sure."

"Did you see anything else unusual near the body?"

"Not much." I shaded the truth, figuring they could

find the wallet just as easily as I had. "There was one funny thing though . . ."

"What was that?"

"A dead turkey vulture."

"Okay," he said. "One of us will stay here to manage traffic. . . . Your own bird going to be all right?"

"My truck's in the shade. She'll be pretty quiet as long as her hood is on."

"Good," he said. "Let's go."

I led them to the spot. It took about fifteen minutes of hot, silent walking. The foliage was mostly bear oak and a few scattered cedar. A thin vapor coated everything— the sun had already begun boiling the moisture out of the ground. The trooper carried a handheld radio and a roll of fluorescent orange surveyor's tape. About every thirty yards he stopped to tie a piece to a branch or a rock.

When we got close enough to notice the smell, the deputy produced a set of surgical masks. We all slipped them on.

"Which way exactly?" the trooper asked.

I pointed to the base of the poplar. He and the deputy continued on while I hung back. I watched as they almost stumbled over the vulture, just as I had. They approached the body and made a big circle around it, rolling out the marker tape as they went. They pulled latex gloves from their pockets and snapped them over their hands, examining the area. Eventually, the trooper reached down and prodded at what looked to be the wallet in the same way that I had.

He said something to the deputy, and picked it up. He produced a white paper bag from somewhere, and dropped it inside. A few feet away the deputy bent over and picked up a few other objects.

They spoke quietly for a minute. The trooper said something into his radio and they waited while he listened for a reply. Before too long, he held the device close to his ear. He pulled out a small notebook and began writing. When he finished, he and the deputy took one more look around, then turned and walked back to where I stood.

"Well Mr. Pavlicek, looks like you found yourself a body all right," the trooper said. He didn't elaborate. The three of us retraced our steps along the trail of tape.

By the time we made it back to the vehicles, four or five more state police and sheriff's cruisers had arrived. A small band of troopers and deputies stood around, and a van was parked alongside my pickup, with two men unpacking equipment.

"That's some bird you got there, mister," the deputy who had been left behind said.

"Thanks." I looked in on Armistead who, despite all the commotion, remained aloof beneath her hood.

They asked me to sit tight while another group went out to examine the site. I had already wasted most of the day anyway, so why not? Maybe, while I cooled my heels, I could devise a way to bill the state or local municipality for my time. Might even gain a new air of respectability—Pavlicek, government contractor PI.

I waited in the truck with the windows open. A lunch of tuna sandwiches, an apple, and some chocolate chip cookies lay packed in a cooler on the floor. I drank some water and ate the apple. In the glove box I found an old notepad, wrote the name and address from the dead teenager's license as best I could remember it on a slip of paper, and tucked it between two twenties in my wallet.

More police arrived. The medical examiner with an assistant. I watched them unpack some equipment while I listened to an oldies station out of Front Royal.

Finally most of the second group of cops returned. I stepped back outside, into the sun. A stocky man, almost bald, approached, removed his sunglasses and showed me his shield. He had a pasty face, a bulbous nose that had seen a hard life of broken capillaries, and squinty eyes that looked like dark beads. Rivulets of sweat eddied down his neck to stain his white collar and loose tie. He wheezed like a steam engine.

"Mr. Pavlicek"—he pronounced it Pavli-sek—"thanks for waiting. Humid, ain't it, for this time a year? . . . I'm Special Agent William Ferrier, state police."

We shook. "It's Pavli-check," I said.

"Rhymes with that basketball player—who'd he play for, the Celtics?"

"Yeah."

"Must be from up north."

"Used to be. I've adapted."

"Good. Well, if you can spare us some more time, I'd like to ask you a few questions."

"No problem. What happened to the local sheriff?"

"Department's a little understaffed here right now." He dabbed the back of his neck with a handkerchief. "We're with the Violent Crimes Unit out of Richmond. Been up in Culpeper on some other business lately anyway. So they asked us to come over and help out."

"Okay."

"Why don't we sit in my car where it's cooler? I could use some water. How about you?"

"Already had some in my truck, but I wouldn't mind some more."

I followed him to a pale, unmarked Caprice that bore official state plates, its engine running. A younger man, also wearing a tie, sat in the driver's seat sipping Pepsi from a can and rocking almost imperceptibly to some silent song. Ferrier and I went to opposite sides, opened the rear doors, and climbed into the cool of the back.

"Chad, this here is Mr. Pavlicek. Mr. Pavlicek, this is my partner, Chad Spain."

His partner bobbed his head in greeting. He was much thinner, with slick hair and a pockmarked face and wore aquamarine sunglasses. Ferrier pulled two containers of bottled water from a cooler on the floor and handed one to me. The backseat smelled like shaving cream.

"Thanks," I said, twisting off the top.

"Trooper tells me you're a PI from Charlottesville." He took a long swig from his bottle before refastening the cover.

"That's right."

"Wouldn't happen to have your license, would you?"

I extracted it from my wallet and handed it to him.

He look it over and handed it back without comment. Then he asked: "And you were out here . . . what . . . hunting?"

"That's right."

"It's out of season, isn't it?"

"Yes," I said. "For firearms. But falconers can hunt with their birds anytime. As long as the bird kills only for its own consumption. Out of season, whatever remains has to be left where it lies . . . just like in the wild."

"Learn something every day. See you also got a permit to carry a concealed weapon."

I nodded.

"What kind of investigations you involved with down there in Charlottesville?"

"The usual," I said. "A few skip traces, the occasional runaway, several divorce situations. Haven't ever heard from V.I. Warshawski. Seems like I spend most of my time on the computer these days."

He grunted. Probably never heard of Warshawski.

"Ever work a murder case before?" he asked.

"Not as a PI."

"Oh?" His forehead wrinkled. Curious.

"I specialize in greed and lust, not lethal malice."

"Sometimes one can lead to the other," he said. "What'd you do before you went private?"

"Homicide. Up in New York."

His eyes bore into me for a second or two. If he was surprised, he didn't show it. "That a fact? How long ago?"

"Thirteen years."

"Hear that, Chad? . . . Homicide . . . Thirteen years

ago in New York . . . Pavlicek." He paused. His mind seemed to be searching for something. ". . . Wait a minute, I remember you. . . ." The eyes softened. "You're one of those fellas got in trouble over shooting that colored kid up there. Trial was all over the news for awhile. Ain't that right?"

His question hung thick in the cool air for a second, awaiting an answer.

I took the occasion to look out the window. A group of deputies and troopers accompanied by a photographer and a technician were starting back toward the site.

"I always wondered what became of you guys," he said. "There were three of you, weren't there?"

I nodded.

"I heard two of you had moved down this way. What was that other fella's name? Indian or something, wasn't it?"

"Jake Toronto."

"That's it—Toronto. He live around here too?"

"Actually, we both ended up a couple hours west of here. Out in Leonardston. Cahill, the officer who went on trial with us, grew up around there. We all got to know one another pretty well during the trial. He sold Jake and me on this place. I moved down with my family almost as soon as everything was over. Toronto came down later. Even Cahill moved back after he retired."

"Retired?"

"He stayed on the force for a couple years after everything was over."

"That's right," he said. "He was the one they let off the hook."

"Right. Mandatory early retirement with full pension."

"Sure."

"How'd you end up pee-eyeing out of C'ville then?"

I shrugged. "Found a job peddling prescription pharmaceuticals for awhile. But I couldn't stand cow-towing to doctors. My marriage broke up. She got our daughter."

"Sorry to hear that," he said.

"It happens."

"That when you moved back over here?"

I nodded.

"And got your private license."

"Yes."

"A few steps down from homicide, ain't it?"

"You might put it that way."

"Funny, the three of you from New York all ending up in Leonardston for awhile." He stared at me. But he didn't bring up the coincidence of the dead Dewayne Turner being from there.

"We had our fifteen minutes of fame," I said. "Not the kind I would have picked."

"I'll bet . . . well, for what it's worth, a lot of us figured you guys got a bum rap. Be honest though, I'm a little surprised they give you paper to carry concealed."

"Another state. Another time. I guess distance heals."

"Maybe. Wilson Abercrombie's an acquaintance of mine. You know him?"

Abercrombie was the chief of the Charlottesville City Police, and right now, not a very popular one. He was an acquaintance of mine too, but I didn't want to get into on what terms.

"We know each other."

"Un-huh." He took another swig of water, smacked his lips. "So you were out here hunting. How'd you find the body?"

I repeated what I'd told the trooper.

He listened without expression. Then he said: "Falconry. I was interested in that when I was a kid. Had a book that told all about knights and nobility, shit like that. They rode around on horses with those big birds on their arms, didn't they?"

"Right."

"Like the look of your animal too. What kind is he?"

"*She* . . . is a red-tail hawk."

"*She* got a name?"

"Armistead."

"Armistead," he said. "I like it. Named her after one of Lee's general's, did you?"

"To tell you the truth, I just liked the way it sounds."

"Huh. Well, I'd love to come out with you sometime. You know, see you and your hawk do some work. She must be some hunter."

"You want a master falconer, the guy to see is Toronto. I'm still an apprentice. He's my sponsor."

"S'that right? You two still buds then?"

"You could say that."

"He work with you?"

"Not officially. Sometimes he lends a hand."

"So you're over in Leonardston a lot."

I could see where he was going. "Some," I said.

"How about the other guy. What's his name—Cahill? You still pals with him too?"

"His nickname's Cat. We keep in touch. But if it's falconry you're interested in, Jake's your man. He's been into it for awhile. Flies a goshawk—much faster bird than my red-tail. A fierce hunter. You ought to check it out."

He nodded vacantly. "I may just do that . . ." he said.

"You see the turkey vulture out there near the body?"

"Was that what that was? I was going to ask you about that."

"A lot of people, when they see them soaring, confuse them with hawks. But there's a big difference. Vultures feed on carrion. That's probably what this one was doing."

"Weird, huh? Ugly thing too. But I suppose it's a good thing we have 'em around. What do you think killed it?"

"Don't know. My guess would be disease. But if I were you, I'd have a vet or the folks from the wildlife hospital over in Waynesboro take a look at it."

"Thanks for the tip," he said with a tinge of sarcasm.

I waited for him to write down the information.

"You know the owners of this land?" he asked.

"I'm out here with permission. It's been in Cahill's family for a long time. Belongs to an uncle of his, an insurance agent up in Warrenton. I phoned him after I called you guys. He should be showing up soon."

"Good," he said, handing me back my licenses. He pulled out a clipboard with a form attached, and started to write again. His partner in front, still rocking, clicked the keys on a laptop propped against the dash.

I looked out the window again, thinking about Nicole. Had she been friends with this guy Turner? I had never heard her mention his name. Leonardston was still a small town. Jake or Cat or her mother might know.

George Rhodes, Nicole's stepfather, had been killed in a tragic boating accident a couple of years ago. Say what you will, at least George had been there for Nicole when she needed a daddy. I was more like an alien, picking up my daughter for brief visits one weekend a month.

Ferrier finished his notes. He said he had written up a summary of my statements, handed the paper to me, and asked me to read it. I did.

"If you agreed with everything, sign at the bottom of the form," he said. I signed with a pen he had given me and gave it back along with the notes.

"So you've been out here hunting before?" Ferrier said.

"Couple of times."

"When was the last time?"

"Two, maybe three weeks ago."

"See anything suspicious at the time?"

"Nothing I can remember." I was glad he assumed I had been alone.

"From the condition it's in, body's been out here at least a week," he said absently. "That would put the murder sometime around the middle of the month."

He leaned over the seat to his partner. "Well I think that's all I've got for you right now, Pavlicek. How about you, Chad? You got any questions?"

Agent Spain shook his head.

"We've got your statement then," Ferrier said. "But I'd like to get your work and home phone numbers in case something else comes up."

I pulled out a business card and he attached it to his clipboard. I gave him my home number, which he wrote on the back. Then he handed me a card of his own with his home number penciled in next to the state police line.

"Since you're a colleague," he said, "or at least a former one, you need anything, anything at all, just give me a call."

"Thanks. Do you mind if I ask you guys a question though?"

"Sure, go ahead."

"How can you be certain this was a murder?" I was hoping that hole in the young man's side might somehow have been self-inflicted. Since there was no weapon that possibility was as remote as a snowstorm appearing. But I was still hoping.

Ferrier shrugged. He glanced at his partner, who handed him the paper bag I had seen the trooper use earlier at the crime scene. "Corpse had a wallet with ID on him. Rare, but it happens. If everything else checks out with Forensics, which I'm pretty sure it will, no doubt we're gonna call this a kill. Already checked with the local sheriff's department where the boy's from too . . . Kid was a known drug dealer, name of Dewayne Turner. Reported missing a couple of weeks ago. Way things are now, between D.C., Richmond, and Norfolk, seems like we get a few like this every month."

A dealer. Did that mean Nicole was into drugs?

"He could have driven out here to do himself in," I offered, trying not to sound too eager.

"Unlikely. No weapon. And I doubt if they'll find any residue on his hands either. Something else out there make you think so?"

"No. Just speculating out loud, that's all."

I looked at my watch. Time for me to leave.

I pushed opened the door and a saunalike heat washed over me. In that split second I saw Ferrier reach between the front seats to replace the bag containing the wallet. His hand drew my attention to another, as-yet-to-be-sealed bag, lying in the same spot, its open end facing me.

It must have been the other object I had seen the deputy pick up near the body, something I had missed. They were in bloody pieces now and with such a brief glance I almost didn't recognize them. A pair of clear broken sunglass frames with metallic lenses that had popped off. Oakleys, the same style and color as the ones Nicole had been wearing on our hunt the month before.

I stepped out and leaned against the door, looking back into the car.

"We appreciate you showing us where to find the body and waiting around to answer our questions," Ferrier said.

"Only wish Armistead and I hadn't been the ones to find him."

"I know how you feel . . . Oh and Pavlicek, next time you go hunting with that bird of yours?"

"Yeah?"

He smiled. "Let's hope she finds smaller prey."

3

You begin to doubt yourself in front of lawyers. Men whose livelihood—often it seems, whose very existence—depends on every twist of word. Who could stand before the real bar of justice, if there were one in this sorry world? Not I. Not anyone I have ever known.

"So you say, Detective Pavlicek, that it was dark?" The attorney with the Brooks Brothers' suit rested his wing-tip on the dais beneath the stand.

"That's correct."

The unarmed fourteen-year-old Toronto and I shot to death was named William Balazar. He had been a straight-A student at New Rochelle High School. His grieving parents hired New York's most flamboyant, telegenic lawyer to torture us with what would be a protracted lawsuit for wrongful death.

"But not dark enough that you could not see what you thought was a gun?" the attorney continued. He looked perfectly comfortable in this environment, his eyes clear and unyielding behind his tortoise-shell glasses, his demeanor respectful but probing, immaculate in his colorful tie.

"Yes."

"And could you not also discern, in that light, that the figure standing a mere twenty yards away was an African-American?"

"Yes."

He paused for a few seconds, as if to let the impact of this supposedly grand revelation sink in.

Cahill had never dropped the throw-down, of course. My career and Jake's were effectively over, despite the fact that Officer Singer was dead and a police review board, as well as the D.A.'s office, had cleared us of any criminal wrongdoing. With tensions boiling everywhere at the time, the last thing the NYPD needed was a couple of detectives branded as trigger-happy racists. It didn't help matters any that even with a sterling solve rate, Jake and I had managed to develop something of a checkered reputation within the department.

Even Toronto's mixed heritage couldn't save us—at various times he had described himself as part mulatto, part Indian, and he didn't care, he said, to find out what else. The city's leading minority activist stated publicly we both looked white to him.

"So I ask you now, Detective Pavlicek, to tell the court—I am sure you and Detective Toronto have searched your souls on this—would you have made the same decision? Would you have still pulled the trigger if William Balazar had been white . . . ?"

Agent Ferrier chuckled as I nodded and closed the door. I turned and began walking in the direction of my truck. A dreamy heat rose through the fumes from the line of assembled vehicles. The medical examiner was gone, already headed with his entourage toward the site. Cat's uncle, the farm owner, showed up as well, and I spoke with him briefly, explaining what had happened, before pointing him in the direction of Ferrier's car. A van from a Charlottesville TV station pulled up to the barricade. I checked on Armistead again and hopped into the truck.

Rehashing the past with the state police detective had reminded me of a copy of a letter I'd left folded in my glove compartment several weeks before. I reached in among my pile of road maps and pulled out the envelope.

It was from an old acquaintance in New York, a diminutive ballistics expert named Rashid Fuad, who had worked with Toronto and I on a few cases long ago. Addressed to Cat Cahill on NYPD stationary, it said Fuad was writing to inform Cat that the department, after all these years had managed to make a tentative link with what they thought might be the weapon used to gun down his old partner. Seems the boys in Fuad's department had been messing, on an experimental basis, with a kind of hot-shot, state-of-the-art imaging software, where the computer was supposed to analyze and compare digitized photos of gun barrels and evidence taken from crime scenes, looking for matches. They had been diligently going about the laborious task of archiving all their old black-and-white images into their computer when, lo and behold, in the years-old Singer/ Balazar case, the machine had spit out a match.

Not that it amounted to much. All the brilliant program told us was that a bullet fragment taken from Singer's body matched the barrel of a nine-millimeter Glock that had been test-fired in an unsuccessful attempt to match it with evidence from a completely unrelated case the year before Singer's death. The handgun in question was even legal. It had been registered to a now-deceased lackey who had worked for one of the major dope pushers in New York, a greasy slob named Boog Morelli. No one had a hard time speculating that the shooter who'd managed to disappear the night of Singer's killing, an eighteen-year-old pimp and sometime crack dealer from the Bronx, had links to one of Morelli's goons.

Not too surprisingly either, the pimp himself had ended up dead a few months after offing Singer, the victim of an overdose. Bronx homicide had I.D'd him as the likely perp in the patrolman's murder, based on rumors from the street and a footprint of a rare Armani loafer, size 10, found in the frozen mud behind one of the Dumpsters in New Rochelle. They were the same shoes the pimp had been wearing in the cheap hotel room in Queens where'd he'd taken his last wild ride with Mr. Rock.

Sometimes I wonder if, with all our technology, we acquire more information than is good for us. No one had even considered reopening the case.

I folded the letter and put it back in among the maps. The TV crew was starting to roll film now. A deputy let me past the blockade and I pulled away from the scene as quickly and inconspicuously as I could.

I cut down Route 231 through Banco, crossed the Robinson River, then on to the town of Madison. I veered through the village onto U.S. 29, its southbound lanes bending toward Charlottesville and home. Twenty-nine ran roughly parallel to the famous Skyline Drive twenty miles to the west and offered panoramic views. It had yet to deteriorate into one of those sleazy strips, lined with cheap hotels and flesh bars, that other highway corridors nearer bigger cities had become.

I wasn't enjoying the views, however. Not today. I needed to talk to my daughter pronto, but I was afraid to use the car phone—call me paranoid. I turned on the radio and picked up Roy Orbison on the oldies station out of C'ville.

Traffic was already picking up with weekend tourists. C'ville is an overgrown college town with roots to the founding of the republic, Thomas Jefferson, the Rotunda, Monticello, and all that. A city where old brick and old ways clash with hip thinking. Development had recently mushroomed from the central lawn of the university, where Edgar Allen Poe had his old room enshrined, to a seemingly ever-expanding panoply of shopping venues, expansive farms and upscale neighborhoods that dotted the piedmont hills like jewels all the way to the distant Blue Ridge. Hard to imagine that on those same streets and country roads slaves were once kept and traded like cattle, a few even by old Tom Jeff himself.

I pulled into my own driveway just as the sun was beginning to drop below the treetops over on Rugby Avenue. It was a relatively quiet neighborhood, far enough from the university and downtown. The smell of charcoal and the sound of Dizzy Gillespie emanated from somewhere on the next block. Most of the houses were simple ranches or split-levels. My landlord, Walter Dodd, sat on the front stoop of the two-story frame-over-brick he and his wife shared with me; it had separate entrances and two interior layouts that were mirror images of each other.

"How was the hunt?" His bony fingers worked methodically to coil an orange power cord he'd been using to trim the hedge.

"Okay."

"Okay?"

"Well, we had a little incident."

"Incident?" He finished spooling his cord.

If I ever had to be away for a day or two, I could leave Arimstead in the care of Walter and Patricia. The Dodds, retired, were an odd pair, but peerless as far as landlords go. They had been married almost as long as I had been alive, and didn't ever seem to regret it. They had even allowed me to construct a mews for Armistead in the backyard. Walter had kept a Cooper's hawk himself, growing up on his family's farm in Tennessee, long before the feds started requiring their sanction for such things. Arthritis made walking long distances difficult for the couple, but whenever possible I took them hunting with me to watch "our" hawk in action from the truck.

I gave him a thumbnail sketch of all that had happened.

Walter used to manage a lumber yard in the city, still met regularly for coffee with a group of pals at Spudnut's Donut Shop, still devoured the local newspaper every day. He had lost most of his hair, but retained the demeanor of the classic Southern gentleman—unhurried, unruffled, at times seemingly unconcerned. None of it fooled me. He had been an MP in the army during Korea, had seen his share of dismal news.

"I thought that hawk looked a little different," he said. "Thing like that can affect an animal. . . ."

He was right. I probably should have been paying more attention to Armistead, but right now my mind was focused on Nicole.

"The police say how they thought the body got there?"

"They're pretty sure the young man was murdered."

"Murdered?" Walter's expression said he was impressed. He had the idea most of the cases I took weren't sexy enough for a real-life private eye.

"Come on, Walter, that's what the cops are for. This isn't some dime store novel. If the kid were a drug dealer, this kind of thing happens all the time."

"Hrmph," he said. "You used to work homicide, didn't you? Still pack a gun too, I've noticed."

I said nothing.

He helped me unload Armistead and her paraphernalia from the truck and settle her on her perch in the mews out back.

"Thought you might be going out again tonight with that gal of yours," he said.

"Really? Why?"

"She called about your date."

"Date?" I stared dumbly at him.

"The one you were supposed to have with Miss Marcia What's-Her-Name. She called about over an hour ago. Wanted to know if we'd seen you around."

I slapped my palm to my head.

Marcia D'Angelo was the schoolteacher I had been dating since we'd met at a Christmas party the winter before. Our situation had grown a little complicated. We were ripe with possibilities, short on consummations. I was supposed to have met her at the Barnes and Noble on Barracks Road at four. The rendezvous was to include coffee and talking, then maybe onto dinner and a movie afterward, if the talking went OK.

"Did she leave any message?"

"Yup. Said you could reach her on her cell phone

when you got in. Said she was going out to dinner and a play with some friends."

Funny how friends could materialize when you'd stood someone up on a date. Some of Marsh's amigas were great, but others I could do without. Who was I to be picking her friends anyway? Did I let her pick mine?

"Guess I better call her."

Walter nodded in reply. Then he pulled out his tobacco pouch and said he would sit with Armistead for awhile. Armistead's mews was one of the few places Patricia still let him smoke. I suppose the smell of his hickory pipe was as responsible for Armistead's manning as anything I had ever done. The red-tail looked to me as her source of food, which was the only reliable bond that kept a raptor with any falconer. But sometimes with Walter, and even once or twice with myself, there had been a glimmer of a deeper trust.

The apartment, closed up for the day, smelled a little musty but at least was nice and cool. I went to the fridge, popped open a beer and stood in the middle of the kitchen to dial the phone.

Marcia answered on the third ring.

"Oh, hey. Forgot about me, huh?" Her tone told me she was in the presence of others.

"I'm sorry, Marsh. Boy, am I sorry."

"Okay, but you don't realize what you missed."

"Really?"

"Really." Playing it cool. Camouflage the hurt.

I tried humor. "You mean you were finally going to let me take you home and ravage you?"

"Not quite, but it's a thought. Jason's staying overnight at a friend's."

I waited. Another opportunity down the drain.

"Is that all you have to say for yourself?"

"I was thinking about your thought," I said.

"Men . . ." I could almost see her rolling eyes. "So what happened? You just out hunting and forget?"

I heard her whisper something away from the receiver.

Some of her friends opposed hunting, period. Even falconry. They thought something as natural as a tree barbaric.

"Yes," I said.

"Lose Armistead again?"

"No. Not this time."

"What then?"

I paused to give my words more impact. "We stumbled on some remains."

"Remains? . . . What kind of remains?"

"Human. I spent a good part of the afternoon dealing with the state police."

There was an appropriate moment of silence while the information was being processed, passed on, perhaps even discussed. She came back on. "Frank? Are you there?"

"I'm here."

"You're serious, aren't you?"

"Unfortunately."

"You okay? You want me to come by?"

I could tell she wanted to, and if it hadn't been for the long conversation I was expecting with my daughter, I would have said yes.

"No. Thanks, you go ahead and go on to your play."

More whispering ensued from her end. "Frank, listen, I'm sorry. It must have been awful . . . like back when you . . ." She stopped, maybe realizing she didn't want to bring up some specter from the past.

"It's all right, Marsh."

"The play should be over by eight-thirty. Can you meet me afterwards at Sloan's?" Sloan's was a home-grown fern bar, not one of those cookie-cutter outlets of a national chain. The place was almost always packed on weekends.

"Sure, I—"

"I want to hear all about it," she said, "I'll be waiting at a table. If I'm not there first, you do the same."

"All right."

"I really am sorry, Frank . . ."

"Me too. I should have called you."

"Yes."

After we hung up, I moved through the foyer with the cordless handset, into the spare room I had turned into a library. A Mennonite carpenter, grateful for the information I had provided him about a general contractor with whom he had some concerns, mainly because the man hadn't paid him in six months, had lined the walls for me with bookshelves made of pine. Nothing fancy, just practical. I didn't own a degree from a prestigious university or some snooty little liberal arts college to tack on the wall. What I had were novels, a number of historical texts, and books of poetry. Several hundred of them in fact.

Cummings to Twain, Dostoyevsky to Steinbeck. Shakespeare to James Joyce and John Gardner, Rita Dove to Doris Betts and E. Annie Proulx, James Ellroy and Raymond Chandler, even Beckett, Salinger, Vonnegut and Frost. Literary, historical, mysteries, thrillers, interspersed with short stories and poems with some of the most creative use of language around. You didn't get that kind of education in detective work, but I had decided scholarship was more a matter of passion and discipline than of breeding and the opportunity to sit in the finest schools.

I settled into my favorite reading chair, the big recliner with the pulsing waves of heat massage and stereo sound that hadn't worked in more than three years. My back stuck like Silly Putty to the leather. I was badly in need of a shower.

Nicole's phone rang several times. Her voice eventually answered, an upbeat recording that said please leave a message.

I said: "Nicky, this is your dad. It's Friday about suppertime. I'm at home and I need to talk with you about something important. Please call me as soon as you can."

I could think of nothing else to safely say. I didn't

know who else might listen to her messages. There was no other way of getting in touch with her, either, except through her mother, who'd been about as friendly to me, of late, as your average rattlesnake.

I decided I better call Cat Cahill too, before his uncle got to him, not that he could do anything about the situation from over in Leonardston. He knew my daughter, of course—sometimes she even referred to him as Uncle Cat—but I wasn't about to share my suspicions with anyone until I had talked with her myself.

I tried his restaurant first, but they said he had taken the night off. Must have been my night for answering gizmos. After his wife's cheery electronic greeting, I rattled off a cursory summary of my discovery on their home machine.

Images kept flashing through my mind—gray skin fragments, what could have been a toenail, smooth edges of exposed skull. If I let them, Dewayne Turner's remains might even fit into some larger pattern for my life, one I was still trying to decipher. It seemed a whole lot easier to picture them as a mere extension to the detritus of the forest floor.

Sloan's was packed, as usual, by the time I arrived. A crowd of men and women in their twenties and thirties, dew-eyed and dressed to romp, hugged the bar. An Orioles/Yankees pennant race game on the big screen held a lot of people's attention in the main dining room. A glass block wall divided the drinkers from the rest of the restaurant, which was peppered with university sports memorabilia and photographs.

Marcia sat at her agreed-upon table, doing her best to remain inconspicuous. I watched her for a minute from across the room. She was not the most beautiful woman in the world, if you go by what the fashion magazines show—her nose was a little too big, her lips perhaps a bit too thin. But she had something great models almost always possess: a photogenic magnetism that sprang from her eyes.

She was also a recognized expert on the Civil War, namely the role that women played in the conflict, had even authored a book on the subject. I often wondered what her students thought of her—she taught history at Albemarle High School—whether or not there were any schoolboy crushes.

Her face brightened when she caught sight of me. She was wearing black pumps tonight with a dark blue sheath dress; someone might have made this particular blue just to match her eyes. I moved toward her through the throng.

"You sure you're okay?" She stood up to give me a peck on the cheek. "I felt terrible after we talked earlier. Here I was all ready to jump down your throat . . . And the play was just . . . well, I couldn't stop thinking about what happened to you."

"I should have kept our appointment or at least called. You want another chardonnay?"

She covered her glass. "I'm driving. Better switch me to club soda."

I got the waitress's attention and ordered two club sodas.

Her hand reached over to cover mine. "So tell me what happened out there today."

I shrugged. "Like I said on the phone, I found a body." Just your average everyday corpse. What could be more blasé?

She saw through me in an instant. "Then what happened?"

"Let's see. I called the state police. They came and cordoned off the area. A couple of detectives questioned me for awhile. That was about it."

"Who was it?"

"You mean the body? I don't know. Some black kid I'd never heard of. They said he was a drug dealer."

"Oh."

Marcia knew all there was to know about my past. The irony of my discovery could not have been lost on her. I thought of my wallet with the slip of paper and Dewayne Turner's name and license number written on it.

"But something else seems to be worrying you," she said.

I hesitated. If I told her too much I risked drawing her in as a witness to my illegal collection of evidence.

"Kid was from Leonardston," I said.

"Leonardston? You mean where you used to—?"

"Right."

"And?"

"I saw something around the body, something that caused me to be suspicious."

"Suspicious? Of what?"

"Of someone who went out to fly Armistead with me at the same farm not too long ago."

She said nothing for a moment. She ran her finger around the rim of her glass, thinking. "Did you tell the police anything about what you saw?"

"No. Not yet."

We stared at one another. "Couldn't you get into trouble?"

"Potentially. Look, it may just be a coincidence."

"Did you talk to your daughter yet?"

I shook my head. "Left a message on her machine."

"Don't you think you ought to try her again? When was the last time you two spoke?" She was warming to the challenge.

"I don't know, two, maybe three weeks."

"How long ago did you say you'd been out there with her?"

"It was earlier this month."

"Would that have been long enough for the body to have ended up in the condition you found it?"

"Probably."

The waitress brought our club sodas. I could sense Marcia sifting through the possibilities.

"I don't know much about police work, but might I make a suggestion?" She stroked the side of her new glass with her little finger.

"Couldn't hurt, I suppose."

"You don't wait for Nicole to call you back. You go over there and find out in person right now what's going on."

"You mean to Leonardston?"

"Uh-huh." She squeezed her lime into her glass and took a sip. "You're over there all the time anyway, aren't you, to visit Jake?"

"Yeah, but that's different."

"It's also more reason for you to go—you're familiar with the area. So I say, go now. Get to the bottom this. You can be there well before midnight."

Any visions of romance for the night vanished. "I'm not sure it's so simple, Marsh. Other than hunting once in awhile, Nicky and I aren't exactly close. And anyway, the state police are involved. They'll want to talk to me again for sure, if she's a suspect. It's not like people down there don't know she's my daughter."

"Jason and I are leaving early Sunday to go to Williamsburg for a couple days. Remember? It's his history club's field trip to Yorktown. If you have to be out of town, it's the perfect opportunity for you to go."

"Look," I said. "There'll be a story on the news tonight or in the paper tomorrow about the body. A TV van was just pulling up when I split the scene."

"Really? I suppose as long as they don't mention your name in the reports, no one else will be able to connect you with the body," she said.

"Connect *me* with the body? . . ." The folks at the next table cast us a sidelong glance.

Marcia lowered her voice. "Well, from what you said, you already have a connection, whether you like it or not."

"But I wasn't out there looking for a dead body."

"Maybe you were meant to."

"Now you're beginning to sound like Walter."

She placed her hand over mine again. "You're the detective, Frank. You'll figure it out."

"I suppose you're going to tell me something like, 'She's your daughter,' too."

She nodded. Her smile created a little dimple in her chin that I would have given anything, at that moment, to lean over and kiss. Instead, I slipped both my hands around her fingers and stared at them. They were slender, graceful even, soft to the touch.

"Anything else I can do?"

I thought about that. "Well . . . there is one thing . . ."

She smiled and rolled her eyes. "You are nothing, if not persistent. Did you call Jake and tell him what happened?"

"Not yet."

"How about your ex-wife?"

"You kidding?"

Marcia's own ex-spouse was a big-shot executive who, after fifteen years of marriage and a child, had simply informed his wife that he no longer loved her, that he had been carrying on an affair with one of his firm's vice-presidents, an attractive twentysomething blonde.

"I did call Cahill though," I said. "The land where I found the body belongs to his uncle."

"He's the one who owns the restaurant in Leonardston, isn't he?"

I nodded.

"What did he say?"

"Nothing. Only got his answering tape too."

"Doesn't that make you frustrated, another machine?"

"Yes."

"Even though your finding whatever you found is only a coincidence."

"Okay," I said. "You win."

4

Which was how I happened to find myself two hours later drifting toward hills that could have passed for the moonlit humpbacks of subterranean blue whales. Out here on a winding state highway in the sawtooth Alleghenies, the land grew pockmarked with the remnants of twenty-six-inch coal. On the seat beside me sat my cell phone and a S&W .357 Magnum, secure in its Kramer holster. It was already after eleven P.M., and I had no plans to stay the night.

As I said, during the long period of investigation and legal action over the New Rochelle shooting, Cat Cahill had regaled Toronto and me with stories of growing up in western Virginia before moving to the Bronx. Without skipping to Montana after the trial, it sounded like the perfect place to escape New York. Even my heritage argued for such a move. My father had been a Czech bureaucrat who had managed to defect after Prague spring—Pavlicek was not our real name. But my mother heralded from the mountains of Tennessee. Growing up, whenever they took me to visit Mom's relatives, Dad told me the Appalachians reminded him of the Krkonose near Jablonec in northern Bohemia where he had hiked as a young man.

Never mind that the reality of Leonardston, Virginia, hadn't quite lived up to Cat Cahill's embellishments. Oh, it was beautiful enough all right, but we had only lived there a year when the arguments between Camille and myself began to escalate. I was a loser who spent too much time on his new job and had now blown everything. I didn't make enough money, didn't know who she really was. The move to a new environment and a new type of job, I had hoped, would be the balm the marriage needed to survive. Instead, it proved to be the irritant that tripped us into oblivion. By the time George Rhodes entered the picture with his big house and horses, we were already sleeping in separate beds.

Around a curve the lights of Leonardston appeared.

"Hey partners! Lasso yourselves up a great deal at Bartman Motors! In downtown Leonardston, right across from the Taco Bell!" the local FM station barked in surround sound. Next, came a pale imitation of running horses, followed by music: ZZ Top.

The seat of Affalachia County rested in a narrow valley along the banks of the Tungsten River, and despite a fortune that had waxed and waned, clung to its existence like an elderly survivor. Currently, things were on the uptick. A large civic club sign marked the entrance to town. There was a new elementary school, three modern bank branches on Main Street, and a supermarket shopping center with a big parking lot. All closed, of course, at this hour.

At least I knew where I might find Nicole. At the end of Main Street, Cahill's Restaurant sported a new maroon awning in front. Beer neons glowed through the windows. The lot was packed, but a car was just leaving. I flipped down the visor as I took its spot.

In the vanity mirror's reflection my face looked altered by age: cheeks that had long ago lost the gauntness of their youth, skin around the eyes that had begun to sag. The nose, broken twice, seemed more crooked. The once jet-black hair and heavy brows were beginning to gray. I clipped the visor back where it belonged.

I got out and walked toward the door. Three cars down from my truck, inside a rental car with Maryland plates, a man sat smoking. For a moment I thought he might be watching me, but then I thought I must have imagined it.

I slipped in through the front of the building with an eye out for Nicole. She was nowhere to be seen, so I edged through the crowd toward the bar. I recognized, vaguely, a waitress hurrying past with a load of drinks.

"Nicole Pavlicek? Seen her come in?"

She stopped and eyed me for a moment. "Ain't you her father?"

"That's right."

She tilted her head toward a far corner. I followed her gaze, someone moved in the crowd, and I caught a glimpse of my daughter seated in a booth with another young woman.

"Thanks."

I was already ensconced in Charlottesville by the time Cat Cahill retired from the New Rochelle force, moved back to Virginia, and opened his bar and restaurant. A few years years before, Jake Toronto too, after bouncing around the country, bought some land and settled not far from Leonardston. It seemed like poetic synergy: the three of us—Jake, Cat, and I—coming to rest in nearly the same orbit.

Unlike me, Cahill had enjoyed a long and, by all appearances, happy marriage. He had even become a grandfather. In the same way I was drawn to the stability of Walter and Patricia Dodd's home, I suppose, Jake and I were pulled into Cat's sphere of influence. Maybe the Leonardston native felt some guilt for having indirectly gotten us into the situation that ended our careers. Either way, it was hardly surprising that Nicole had become enchanted by his magnanimity too.

I weaved through the crowded tables toward Nicole. She was intent on talking with the girl seated across from her, and hadn't seen me yet. A few feet away from her clumps of young men hovered around a couple of pool tables. As I neared the booth she looked up at me with a start.

"Daddy?"

"Hi, Nicky."

"What are you doing here?"

"I came to see you."

She didn't look pleased. "I'm sorry, but I'm trying to have a conversation right now. You should have called."

"I did. Earlier this evening. Left a message, in fact."

"Well, I didn't get it."

"It's important, Nicky."

She stared at me for what seemed more than a minute, but must have been only a few seconds. God, her pretty face reminded me of her mom's from a couple decades before. Her hair was different, of course, dark and cut short, somewhere between a crewcut and a bob. She wore shorts, sandals, and a tank-top blouse; eyeliner, blush, and black cherry lipstick. Her friend, a tired-looking blonde, had a harder edge to her.

Nicole sighed. "I guess. If we have to. Give me a minute, will you, Regan?" She swung her long legs up and out of the booth.

The other girl nodded and pulled a cigarette from her purse. But before she could even put it in her mouth, Nicole grabbed it from her hand. "Ah, ah-h-h. Remember what we said? You've got to give it up."

She turned to me and took my arm. "I've only got a couple minutes. Let's go sit at the bar."

I couldn't help feeling a small bit of pride. "What are you now, the tobacco police?"

She said nothing. The self-assurance of youth.

We crossed the room and found two empty stools. I ordered us both club sodas.

"Well?" she said.

"Nice to see you too, honey."

"C'mon, Dad. You come barging in here unannounced. What do you want me to say?"

The drinks arrived and I took a sip. "I don't want you to say anything. Just tell me about Dewayne Turner."

Her own drink remained untouched. She crossed her

arms and bit her lip. "Is that what you came to talk to me about?"

"Did you know him?"

"What are you up to? And what do you mean, *did*?"

I told her about the find I'd made while hunting.

She listened for several seconds. Her hand suddenly seemed to quiver as she picked up her drink. She glanced back at her friend across the room, then interrupted me in mid-sentence. "I can't talk about this right now, Daddy."

"What do you mean? Why not?"

"I just can't, that's all. I'll call you later this weekend."

"But—"

"I'll call you. I promise."

A commotion broke out in the back of the place. Two sheriff's deputies in tan uniforms and hats had appeared and were in the process of arresting a black teenager who'd been playing pool. The officers were both white. One had a mustache and the other's skin was badly sunburned. A small crowd had gathered. The bartender came out from behind his counter and went over to get a better look. I turned from Nicole and followed.

The arrestee, a skinny youth, decked out in blue jeans and a muscle shirt, while not resisting, didn't appear too happy about the situation. "I didn't do nothin', man. What you goin' and hastlin' me for?"

But the deputies were efficient. One of them twisted the kid's arm up against his back as if it were a pretzel.

"Hey! That hurts, you know."

I stepped a little closer.

They had him up against the wall and the cuffs on him. The deputy with the mustache took something from one of his pockets and whispered something only the youth could hear. Then he reached for his nightstick.

"Excuse me, officers," I said. "But I didn't see this suspect resisting arrest."

The deputies turned to look at me. The one with the

stick in his hand stared at me as if I'd stepped off another planet. "Who the hell are you?"

"Name's Pavlicek. I used to be a cop myself."

With that he visibly relaxed. Must have been worried I was an attorney. "Just makin' an arrest, buddy. You'd best be about your business."

"Yeah, well I would, except—"

"Except what?"

There was a stir in the room and I turned to see another man approach, a muscular type with sandy blonde hair and a sculpted waist. He wore a golf shirt and khaki slacks with a gold star and a gun attached to his belt.

"I'm Sheriff Cowan," he said, extending his hand to me. His grip was too strong, either out of habit, nervousness, or wanting to make an impression. His face jogged a connection in my mind, as if that terminus had just been waiting there for those features to show up to activate the circuits. It was handsome and unblemished, except for a nasty scar above one eyebrow. The chin predominated, enough to make you wonder how he would do in a fistfight. The man was practically Hollywood material—Affalachia County conjures up its vision of the all-American peacekeeper.

"I understand you may have a problem with the way my deputies are making this arrest."

"Yes, sheriff, I do."

"Would you like to file a complaint?" His eyes bore into mine.

"No. I just thought your men might be using excessive force."

"Says he used to be a cop," the mustached deputy said. He and his partner were beginning to lead the youth from the restaurant now. The partner was reading the kid his rights.

"Is that right?" the sheriff said. "Well, Mr. . . . ."

"Pavlicek."

"Pavlicek. Yeah, well I'm awful sorry you see it that

way. But, as I'm sure you all can appreciate, police tactics can sometimes vary from locale to locale."

I said nothing. What, was this guy running for a new term?

Surveying the room, he crossed his arms and lowered his voice so that only I could hear. "Look here, this kid's a gang-banger. Sold some crack to a couple twelve year-olds an hour ago."

I nodded.

He tapped me on the shoulder and nodded as well, then wheeled around to follow his deputies out the door. A couple of the kid's friends shouted taunts at them and made as if to follow, but didn't. There were some swearing and shaking of heads from the group, but it didn't take long for most of the others in the restaurant who had witnessed what happened to go back to their drinks and talking. I thought Nicole might have gone back to talk with her friend too, since she wasn't at the bar when I turned back to talk with her.

But when I looked across at the booth where the two had been sitting, they were gone.

5

Late the next morning the telephone jarred me awake. I cleared my throat and answered on the fifth ring.

"Pavlicek."

"You sound a little out of it, Frank. Rough night?" It was Agent Ferrier of the Virginia State Police.

"Sorry. I was up late."

"Oh?"

"It's not every day I come across a dead body."

"Sure . . . Let me ask you something. You said your bird's the one led you to the spot where you found the body?"

"Right. Like I said, she'd taken a rabbit."

"What happened to the rabbit?"

"I don't know. It was probably wounded. My guess is it might have made it to a burrow."

"Uh-huh. You know, I been checkin' up on you."

"Yeah?"

"You and your partner were pretty famous there for awhile."

"More like infamous."

"Right. Since you used to live in Leonardston, you ever come in contact with Dewayne Turner before?"

"Never."

"How about his family? Turns out he has quite a few relatives in that area."

"Nope. Not that I know of."

There was a pause while he seemed to be shuffling

some papers. "Let's see. Your licenses are clean. You even pay your bills."

"Nice to know someone cares."

"I even talked to a couple of your old supervisors up in New York. They said you sometimes like to push the edge, but as far as they were concerned, when push came to shove, you were a pretty straight shooter."

"I pay them to say that." All this praise was starting to make me nervous.

"Yeah, well, that's why I'm having a hard time trying to figure out why you would tamper with a crime scene."

I let his insinuation hang for a moment while I thought of what to say. "Who says I did?"

"Someone did. Not too long before we went over the site either. The vic's wallet looked like it had been disturbed. There was fresh soil broken near the body. Right now my prime suspect is you."

Stupid. Stupid, stupid. I figured they would be on to me sooner or later. I just didn't count on it happening so fast. I thought back to my aborted conversation with Nicole the night before. Though I was treading on thin ice here, I wasn't about to lay my cards on the table until I knew more of what was going on.

"How many of these kind of killings you investigate every year, Ferrier?"

"Too many. The whole state's seeing more trafficking these days. Coke, heroin, meth, you name it. You know the way the whites and middle-class blacks fled the cities? Now even the dope dealers are doing it."

"What's your solve rate?"

"Why do you want to know?"

"It could've been anybody," I said. "Could've been kids just messing around who found the body and were too scared to turn it in. Maybe someone who just didn't want to get involved."

"That mean you're denying you deliberately contaminated potential evidence?"

"Not exactly."

"Not exactly . . . That the way you want to play it?"

"If I were trying to hide something, why would I have called you guys?"

"Who are you working for?"

Now there was a good question. Was I working for Nicole, or myself? "I'm not working for anybody."

"Okay. Look, Pavlicek. Since you used to be on my side of the table, I'll spare you the bluster. You know as well as I do, most in our business don't think too highly of you people on the private side. I like to keep an open mind, though, judge each person on their own merit. You know what I mean? And I gotta tell you, you ain't started off on the right foot."

"Sorry."

"I'll give you a couple days to think things over. Tomorrow's Sunday and not much is going to happen then anyway. But come the end of the day Monday, at the latest, I want to hear back from you as to exactly what you were looking for when you went over my crime scene, you got that? Otherwise, you'll have more than your license to worry about."

"Would you buy professional curiosity?"

"I don't buy shit, Pavlicek. You push too hard and you're not going to like what happens."

He hung up.

Just peachy. Not only was I playing cat-and-mouse with my daughter, now I had to fend off the official gumshoes. I couldn't really blame Ferrier. Guy was just doing his job. But, hey, Nicole said she'd call me back well before his deadline, and I'd get a better idea where we stood. If need be, maybe I could even turn up the charm and keep him at bay a little longer than he'd indicated. But something told me that might be easier said than done.

No call came from Nicole the rest of that day. Cat Cahill did call me back, however. He said he was sorry he'd missed me the night before, that it was probably a good thing I had been the one to make the discovery of

Turner's body, rather than his uncle, whose ticker might not have survived the experience.

Saturday's *Charlottesville Daily Progress* carried a single quarter column on the front page of the inside regional section about my discovery of the late Dewayne Turner. The only mention of me in the article was that "a hunter" had discovered the body. Cat's uncle and Special Agent Ferrier were quoted. The dead man had been a drug dealer all right, according to the sheriff's office in Leonardston. The shooting was thought to be gang-related.

That afternoon I caught Toronto at home. He lived on a small farm surrounded by neighbors who allowed him to fly and hunt with his birds on their land. He had managed to sock away enough in various investments that he was able, supplemented by the occasional nebulous "security consultant" assignment, to support his Spartan lifestyle. I had tried his number twice earlier— Jake didn't believe in answering machines.

"Yo, my hawk-man," he said.

I told him all about what had happened, using the same approach I had employed with Marcia when it came to the part about Nicole.

"I was over there too last night," I said. "A quick trip to see Nicky at Cahill's. I managed to talk to her, but she wasn't exactly forthcoming. Promised to call me back before the end of the weekend though."

"You see Cat?"

"No. They said he was taking the night off. I just talked to him on the phone this morning though."

"Hey, maybe the dead kid you found had a crush on Nick, something simple as that. She's a fine-looking young thing."

"Don't get any ideas."

"I'm just saying, that's all."

"Yeah, well it's almost time for season. How's Jersey?"

"Primed," he said. "The ghost of the forest will be ready."

A WITNESS ABOVE

Jersey was a three-year-old goshawk, the only raptor Jake was flying at the moment. Not being one to waste any resource, Jake, during season, would usually take what was left of Jersey's bagged quarry after the bird had eaten enough to maintain her weight. He made rabbit stew, cooked squirrel, possum, and even fashioned clothing out of some of the skins, and necklaces out of song bird feathers. Hard to believe from a guy who grew up in Elmhurst, New York, whose father had been a cop, and until he was twenty-seven years old had wanted nothing more in life than to be a detective. He said it was the Indian coming out in him.

When he first told me he was taking up falconry, I thought it a little odd. Why would anyone spend so much time just to train and take care of a big bird? But my first trip hunting with him convinced me otherwise. It wasn't the same as hunting with a gun. It was working in concert with something wild and precious. Most of the time, it didn't seem like hunting at all.

"So when you bringing Armistead over?" he said. "I need to get a look at that red-tail and make sure you aren't abusing her."

"Soon."

If only I'd realized then how soon it would be.

6

Sunday morning I tried, unsuccessfully, to sleep in. Too anxious to stay in bed. I had gone to Marcia's house for dinner the night before. She lived in a nicer part of town, a neighborhood of grand colonials nearer the university. We didn't talk much about my abbreviated trip to Leonardston. We talked instead about a new book she was writing that dealt with the role of women in the South during the Reconstruction. We talked about the play she had seen Friday night, even a little about how the university's football team was faring. She fed me salmon, baked potatoes, and yellow squash, and we stayed up late on the couch in front of a black-and-white rerun of It *Happened One Night*. We kissed a few times during the movie, but then we stopped. This incident with the body and Nicole wasn't exactly doing wonders for my love life.

Walter and Patricia made their usual noises when they left for church around eight. I laced up my running shoes and put in four miles, along Rose Hill Drive to Preston, across to Rugby Road and down through the university, then back up Emmet Street to Barracks, returning on Rugby Avenue.

Back home, I padded barefoot into the kitchen and downed half a quart of orange juice. Then I got out the frying pan, three fresh brown eggs, a mushroom, and a block of sharp Cheddar cheese. I made myself an omelet, poured myself a cup of coffee, and sat alone at the kitchen table while I leafed through the Sunday paper, searching for any more mention of the murder of Dewayne Turner. There was none. Still no message from Nicole either.

I spent most of the afternoon working with Armistead again, doing some jump training in her outdoor enclosure where I had her weathering. I should have gone into the office afterward to catch up on paperwork, but couldn't bring myself to climb in the truck. Monday promised overdue reports and a series of telephone calls. I rented office space in an old converted warehouse near the downtown mall, one of those places where you share a receptionist, a copier, fax, and coffee machine with other economically underprivileged businesses. I didn't employ a secretary, just my five-year-old word processing software, which could crank out eighty words a minute when I got up to speed.

Still no word from Nicole. Early that evening I went out back to check on Armistead. The waning light shone pale on the backs of the houses along Rugby Avenue as I entered the wooden structure beside the fence. The red-tail stirred a little.

"Hello, queen," I said. She did look rather regal on her perch. "Had a good workout today, didn't we?"

She came fully awake and tilted her hooded head toward the sound of my voice.

"If I don't hear from that daughter of mine you like soon, we might have to take a little trip. Over to Jake's—you'll probably remember."

She shifted her feet.

"It's business, girl. Remember that rabbit the other day? . . . Well . . . It's turned into an even bigger problem than I thought."

Afterward, I was lying in bed with a bead on Tom Clancy's latest opus, but I couldn't concentrate. Was I going to have to call Nicole or go back over there to find her again? I was just about to pick up the phone on the lamp stand when it rang. Nicole breathed heavily on the other end.

"Dad?"

I breathed a sigh of relief and swung my legs off the bed. "Yes?"

"I'm glad I caught you in."

"Me too, honey."

"Yeah. I'm sorry I didn't call back sooner, but things have gotten sort of crazy over here."

"You sound like you've been running."

"Running? You mean like working out?" Her laugh sounded cynical. "Not really . . . I've come into a little trouble though."

"Trouble?"

"Yeah."

My gut tightened. I could hear a hollow scraping in the background, like the sound of a desk drawer being pulled open, an echo that could have been reverberating off cinderblock walls. Someone in the background coughed.

"What's going on, Nicky?"

She didn't answer right away. She was still breathing hard, and I could tell she was trying hard not to cry, so I waited.

"Well, for one thing, I'm in jail," she finally said.

7

For the second time in less than forty-eight hours I arrived in Leonardston, Virginia; this time with my overnight bag packed and Armistead riding securely in her hawk-box in back. The place had all the appearance of a quiet Sunday night in a small Southern town. If I weren't so worried about Nicole, I might even have been entranced by the bucolic splendor.

Near the school something flashed in the corner of my eye. Just in time for me to slam on the brakes as a group of four or five kids on mountain bikes sailed across the road in front of me. None of them looked my way—they seemed oblivious to the accident they had almost caused. But before they disappeared over an embankment, the last one in line acknowledged my presence for all of them: he flipped me the bird. So much for bucolic splendor.

A recently built municipal building bore an impressive sign for the sheriff's department and, I knew, the jail. Aerials and satellite dishes protruded from the roof. Gray walls matched a flagstone sidewalk. Inside was a small reception area with a Formica-topped counter. A deputy with skin the color of mahogany and a uniform that appeared almost ready to burst apart at the seams, stood his post. He studied me, eyes flat and expressionless and dark as coals.

"Can I help you?" His voice was a deep bass.

"Yes. I'm here to see a prisoner, if that's possible. Her name is Nicole Pavlicek."

"And you are?"

"My name is Frank Pavlicek. I'm Nicole's father."

Some flicker of recognition seemed to enter his mind. He squinted, shifted his feet, and put his thumbs inside his gun belt. "It's after regular hours. Wait here a second," he said and started to turn away.

"Before you go, better let me check my weapon," I said. I smiled and slipped off my jacket, undid the holster, and handed it to him.

"You a cop or something?"

"No. But I used to be."

He nodded, slid open a desk drawer, placed the holster inside, and locked it. "Thank you, sir. I'll be right back."

People up north tend to think hicks from small Southern towns are either ignorant, naive, or both. I had made the same mistake when I first moved to Virginia, misconstruing civility for stupidity or weakness. I didn't anymore.

In less than a minute the deputy was back. A door opened at the side and he came through it followed by none other than Sheriff Cowan.

"Well, hello, Mr. Pavlicek. We meet again." His smile was almost an accusation as we shook hands once more.

"Working late, aren't you, sheriff?"

He shrugged. "Comes with the job. Why don't you all come on back to my office and we can talk before we take you back to see your little girl."

The last time I'd thought of Nicole as little was on her ninth birthday, but I said nothing. I followed him through a door and down a corridor that smelled faintly of disinfectant.

"Coffee?" he asked as we passed a machine.

"No thanks."

"You trek all the way over from Charlottesville again this evening?"

"Right."

"Pretty drive at sunset. Where you staying?" Casually curious.

"With a friend, Jake Toronto." Before leaving home, I had called Toronto who'd merely grunted affirmatively when I told him I was heading his way with Armistead, and that we might have to stay a few days. I'd also called Marcia in her hotel room in Williamsburg to let her know what was happening and that I'd be gone.

"Toronto. Sure, the bird man. You two used to be partners, right?"

"You seem to know a lot about me," I said.

"I like to know about people, especially those that walk into my jail."

We arrived at his office. It was a spacious corner room with a window that looked out the back of the building on some shrubs and beyond to a brightly lit lawn. Built-in bookshelves lined one wall, though he didn't seem to have much reading material, mostly training or procedural manuals. The plush carpeting was easy on my feet. The sheriff settled into the leather chair behind the desk.

" 'The Cambridge ladies who live in furnished souls are unbeautiful and have comfortable minds,' " I said.

"Say what?"

I took an arm chair opposite. "Nothing. Poetry. e.e. cummings."

He snickered and picked up a piece of paper on his desk. Reading. "Let's see, now. You used to work Homicide in New York. Lost your position under, ah, special circumstances. . . ." We both knew what circumstances he meant. He looked up at me as if waiting for me to offer more of an explanation, but I didn't.

He went on: "Private investigator—you didn't tell me that the other night. Been doin' it quite awhile. Says here you got a permit to carry. License is up to date."

"I would've run for office too, but I'm not good-looking enough."

He didn't see the joke. Great guy to work for. Perfect and humorless.

"You know why your daughter's been arrested, don't you?"

"She said you found drugs in her car."

"That's right. And you were talking with her Friday night when we, ah, first met."

"Uh-huh."

"Come over here to Leonardston often, do you, Mr. Pavlicek?"

"Occasionally."

He reached into a stack of papers on his desk and pulled out what looked like a fax. "I was reading a report from the state police on a different case this weekend—not your daughter's, you understand—and I come across somethin' interesting. Your name, in fact. I even spoke with an agent"—he scanned the fax—"Ferrier. Special Agent William Ferrier. He says you're the one found our late great Dewayne Turner dead."

"Unfortunately." This was starting to get uncomfortable.

"So let me understand here. You happen to be the one who finds a body way over there in Madison County. Vic happens to be a drug dealer from Leonardston. Then you show up that night in my town talking with your daughter in a bar." Cahill's was more of a restaurant than a bar, but I let it pass. "Then, just a couple nights later, your daughter's arrested for possession with intention to distribute. I got it right so far, Mr. Pavlicek?"

I nodded.

"Don't all that seem a little unusual to you?"

"A little."

He smirked. "Your daughter was pretty close with Dewayne Turner, you know."

I didn't, but I refused to give him the satisfaction of knowing that. I nodded.

"If you're dirty, I'm gonna nail you." Just like that. John Wayne.

"I'm not dirty."

His jaw worked hard at a smile. "Your denial is

reassuring. . . . You know, Ferrier didn't exactly say this, but if I was in your shoes, with your background and all, and I was privy to some, let's say, privileged information about my daughter, I might be inclined to come over here and poke around a bit." He stared at me for a long second.

I shrugged. I needed to at least try to neutralize this guy. "Next, you can tell me this isn't New York . . . this is official police business . . . I'd do the same if I were in your shoes. But look, sheriff, the way I see things, we're all on the same side here."

"Oh, really? I'm glad to hear you say that." He leaned back in his chair and folded his hands behind his head.

"Nicole says she's innocent."

"Don't they all?"

"You okay with me talking to her then?"

He waved his hand and sat forward again. "All right. I won't stop you from trying to help your daughter."

"That's decent of you." I meant it.

"I got to tell you though, I've got another problem. And you coming up with that body right now doesn't exactly help."

"Oh?"

"We had Dewayne Turner in custody the night before he disappeared, a few weeks back. . . . Picked him up for loitering."

I wondered if they'd strong-armed Turner the way they did the kid in Cahill's the other night.

"Turner used to be a player in the drug trade around here. Served some juvie time when he was still a minor. Some folks are saying he got churched, that he hadn't been dealing for awhile, but I'm not so sure I buy into all that. Anyway, we didn't find anything on him that night. Questioned him but we had to turn him loose."

"Where's your problem then?"

"Problem is, we can't find anyone who saw him again after he left our jail." He stared at me for a long hard second.

"Which leaves you trying to explain why a black teenager, last seen in your custody, disappears and eventually turns up dead a hundred miles away."

"You got it. What's worse, Turner's older brother is a newspaper reporter. Already threatening to bring in the NAACP to investigate and God knows who else."

So the Affalachia County Sheriff's Department had a public relations problem. Unless the sheriff wasn't laying all his cards on the table either. Maybe there was a cover up. Maybe Cowan was the dirty one. Maybe we were just two dirty guys together.

"How did you arrest Nicole?"

"That was different. Call came in on the Crimeline yesterday. You know, one of these deals where we offer a reward for information and all. 'Cept this caller wanted to stay anonymous. Nothing unusual about that. A male. Claimed he knew where somebody was hiding a stash of powder. Said the Pavlicek girl had it in her car, a red BMW convertible. Inconspicuous, right?"

"So you stopped her."

"Of course. But not before she give us a good chase. Doin' about ninety. We figure she must have panicked. Deputies pulled her over outside her mama's place. Found the coke under one of the wheel wells."

"How much?" I said.

"Couple of keys."

"Decent dollars."

"Yeah. And your daughter ain't exactly known to be desperate for money." He looked at me skeptically. "How about you?"

"I'm not broke, but I might have a hard time scraping up enough to finance a couple keys of coke on a moment's notice."

"Uh-huh." Cowan stood. Now that we were buddies, he turned and surveyed the night view out his window. "You want to know something? That girl of yours has had a better chance than most around here to make something of herself. Her stepdaddy, you know—nothing personal now, Frank—he was like a rock for that kid. But you take George Rhodes out of the equation . . ."

"Sounds like you know the family well."

He shrugged, sat down again and put his big black walking shoes up on the desk. " 'Bout as well as I know everybody around here, I guess." The all-American cop thing again. "Your little girl's been hanging with the wrong crowd, I can tell you that."

"Anyone in particular?"

"Turner for one. That kid was trouble. I don't care what those church people say. There's a girl too, a year or two older than yours. Name's Regan Quinn. We've busted her for possession a couple times. Went to high school with Nicole but never finished. Works down to the White Spade now."

"I know the Spade." Quinn must have been the young woman talking with Nicole the other night.

He shrugged. "Some things don't change."

"Nicole been arraigned yet?"

He shook his head. "Still trying to piece our facts together."

"How about a lawyer? Her mother hire one?"

"Right," he said. "Shelton Radley. I believe he also handled George's estate."

Shelton Radley had been practicing law in Leonardston for over thirty years, had been George Rhodes's attorney. He was honest, as far as I knew. Except for his affair with the bottle, he might have been a decent lawyer—if there were such a thing.

"You still get along with your ex-wife?" he asked.

"We're not on each other's Christmas card list, if that's what you mean."

"You fly hawks, don't you, like your pal Toronto?"

"One. A red-tail."

"Big bird," he said. "You boys get off on it when they kill something?"

How could you explain working with a bird of prey

to someone like this? You couldn't—not really. "She has her moments."

"Your daughter mention anything to you about having problems? Anything to make you think she'd be usin' drugs?"

"Nope."

"Well her mama don't seem so surprised."

I decided I'd risk probing a little more. "Ferrier mentioned that the drug trade's picked up down this way."

He glared at me. "Some." Now I was stepping on his toes.

"How are you dealing with it?"

He waved his hand and suddenly looked tired. "How else? Best we can. Most of these new operators, gangs and whatnot, they're pretty sophisticated. Know how to come and go and all the back roads and places where they can slip across state lines. DEA came in a couple years back and mounted an operation. That made some dent. But it's like the moonshiners. If we brought in enough manpower and equipment to really do the job, people'd start complaining we was running a police state."

"Land of the free," I said.

He grunted again.

"So what's your working theory on the Turner murder?"

"My workin' theory?" He chuckled. "Simple. What goes around comes around."

"It was over drugs then?"

"Ten to one."

"If you don't mind my asking, I assume you have a tape recording of the anonymous tipster."

"We do."

"Mind if I have a listen to it?"

He stuck his chin out, thinking it over. "Don't see why not. . . . You can come by tomorrow and I'll listen to it with you myself."

"I'd appreciate that."

His face hardened. "But listen, you mess with my case and I'll come down on you so fast it'll make your ears spin."

"As long as I can still listen to Frankie Vallie." Might as well try the humor one more time.

He still didn't get it. "Shit, I know you're not even tellin' me half of what you know right now."

I said nothing. Silence had to be safe.

One last grunt, standing to usher me out. "I'll have someone take you back to see your daughter," he said.

8

As jails go, Affalachia County's must have ranked higher than most. The corridor walls were coated with fresh paint. Sterile light shown on a clean concrete floor. The lock-ups themselves enjoyed no air-conditioning, of course, but the usual odor of sweat, urine, and old Jim Beam was missing.

I waited in a small room used for questioning. No windows, a wooden table, three folding metal chairs. No video camera, I noticed, either. But I couldn't be sure what might be hidden. The light came from a single row of fluorescent fixtures embedded in the ceiling.

Nicole, led by the same deputy who'd greeted me earlier, baby-stepped into the room clad in a blaze-orange jumpsuit, shackles, and handcuffs. Standing, she was tall, only a couple inches shorter than myself. Gone was the makeup she had worn the last time I had seen her. She looked scared.

"Daddy," she said when she saw me. Her brown eyes brimmed with tears.

I stepped toward her and we hugged. "I'm here, Nick-ita. You doing okay?"

She didn't answer. She sat down in one of the hard-back chairs. The deputy removed the shackles and closed the door behind him as he left.

"They treating you all right?"

She nodded, wiping a sniffle with the back of her hand.

"Can I get you anything, a soda?"

She stared blankly at the floor. "Maybe a tissue."

"No tissues, but will this do?"

I pulled a handkerchief from my pocket, she nodded, and I handed it to her. She dabbed at her cheeks.

"You sure you're okay?"

"I'll be all right. Just give me a minute," she said.

I waited.

"Probably shouldn't have even called you."

I shifted in my chair. "Why not?"

She let out an exaggerated sigh. "I don't know. I just didn't know who else to call."

We could start with her mother, but I let it go. "You and your friend cut out on me the other night."

"I know. I'm sorry. We had some important things to talk about."

"It must've been a shock to hear about Dewayne Turner. You knew him, didn't you?"

She said nothing.

"Okay. We'll come back to that. You want to fill me in some more on what happened today?"

She nodded. "Like I told you, they stopped me out on the road. I know I shouldn't have tried to get away, but I thought they were going to give me another ticket for speeding and I've already got too many points on my license. They had their guns out, waving them in the air like I'm some kind of criminal. Made me get out of the car." She closed her eyes.

"What happened then?"

"They made me turn around and put my hands on the car. One of the cops felt me up."

I looked at her skeptically.

"Well that's what it felt like, Dad. Like he was violating me or something. I know. I know . . . they've got to check for weapons and stuff."

"What happened after that?"

"They started asking me questions. Where was I going? Where had I been the last couple days? They had one of those dogs with them, you know, that, like, sniffs for drugs and they started searching through the car."

"Was that when they found the drugs?"

"The dog must have found it. They were poking around under the car by one of the back wheels. I saw them pull something out. It was wrapped in white paper and plastic. I'm telling you the truth, I had no idea it was there."

"You ever seen cocaine before, Nicky?"

She shrugged to indicate she had. What she'd seen though had probably been the sugarlike dust snorted or smoked by users, not the uncut pure stuff that had been hidden beneath her car.

"You heard from your mom?"

"Yeah, right." She rolled her eyes. "She came down a couple hours ago and made a big deal about how shocked she was. She and her stupid boyfriend. I don't think she even believes me."

"I take it you two aren't getting along."

Another shrug. "You don't want to know."

"That's a lot of equity for someone to have stashed under your car. Where were you going when they stopped you?"

She instinctively tried to fold her arms but was unable to with the cuffs on. "Same place you found me Friday. Over to Uncle Cat's to play pool."

"I didn't know you played pool."

She shrugged. "It's a decent way to meet guys."

"What time did all this happen?"

"I don't know. Maybe four o'clock."

"And you knew nothing about the drugs under the car?"

"How many times do I have to say it? No."

This was not the same Nicole who had helped me train Armistead to the lure a couple weeks before. We were on her home turf. Most parents, when faced with such uncertainty, at least had the advantage of working through prior difficulties, maybe some positive memories of happier times they could try to draw on. All I had were snatches of visits, a put-on happy face, a put-on smile. Nicole, in my mind, had somehow jumped straight from innocent honesty to the wary, dissembling adult seated before me. Absence had caused me to miss the in-between.

"I'm in no position to lecture you, Nicole," I said. "But don't you think you have better things to do than hang out in a place like Cahill's and shoot pool?"

She clenched her teeth and chewed on a nail. "No."

"Your lawyer been in to talk with you yet?"

"Sure," she said. "With whiskey all over his breath. What a creep."

"What did he say about your case?"

"Whatever. He was worse than Mom, trying to preach to me about the law, put the fear of jail into me. Wanted to know how something like that could be in my car and me not know anything about it."

"You tell him what you told me?"

"Of course."

"What did he say then?"

"He said he would work on it. Then before he leaves, this black woman comes in, says she's like, the commonwealth's attorney or something, some big deal. Says it's her job to try to find out what happened, but I don't have to talk to her if I don't want to."

"Did you talk with her?"

"Some. Radley was there too. What difference does it make? I didn't do anything. I was like just driving down the road minding my own business. What else am I supposed to say?" She pushed her chair from the table and stood up.

"Look," she said. "Thank you for coming, but this is like just some big mix-up or something. No emergency."

"You don't figure a potential life sentence to the women's correctional facility up in Fluvanna constitutes an emergency?"

"Life?" She looked at me warily and sat back down. "What are you talking about?"

I scanned the room again for hidden cameras, microphones, anything. "I had to talk to the state police and the sheriff about Dewayne's body. Do you know where Armistead and I found it?"

Her eyes closed. She bit her lip, opened them again, and looked through me at the wall. "Where?"

"The same place you and I went hunting a few weeks ago, up at Cat's uncle's farm."

She shrugged.

"You don't have any idea how his body got there?"

"You must be kidding, Daddy. You don't think I had anything to do with what happened to Dewayne, do you?"

"You tell me. What did happen to him?"

"How should I know?" she said. "He disappeared." She ran her fingers through her hair.

"He had your phone number in his wallet, Nicole."

"So?"

"How did you two know each other?"

She stared at the wall for a moment as if she were thinking about something else. ". . . From school. He was on the guys' team back when I was playing basketball."

"Would you call him a friend?"

"No. Yes. I don't know. Maybe."

"More than a friend?"

"That's none of your business." She smiled. "Maybe he was going to ask me out," she said.

"*Did* he ever ask you out?"

"Sort of. Not really."

"The police also found a pair of sunglasses with his body. They look just like the ones I saw you wearing last month."

She shrugged again. "They aren't mine. Mine are in their case. Go look in my top dresser drawer at home."

"You sure?"

"Yes, I'm sure. He had a pair that looked just like them and so does Regan."

"Regan. The girl you were with the other night."

"Yeah, right. She's a friend."

"Okay. You have to admit though, Nicky, the place where he was found and the fact that you were there with me is quite a coincidence."

"Look, if you want to go playing Sherlock, why don't you start by talking to the people around this place? Dewayne was arrested the night before he disappeared. I'll bet some of these cops know more than they are telling."

"Cops always know more than they are telling."

"Yeah, well, you oughta know."

I said nothing. It was the first time I had ever heard her refer to me in such a way. I had to remember to ask Ferrier if Forensics found that Turner had been beaten or mistreated some other way before being shot.

I studied Nicole for a moment. "The police tell me Dewayne Turner was a drug dealer."

"Even if he was, he stopped," she said.

"You know that for sure?"

"Yes."

"When was the last time you saw him?"

"That night when he was arrested."

"You ever do drugs yourself, Nicole?"

"What?"

"I said, you ever do drugs?"

"No."

"Drinking?"

She rolled her eyes. "Really Dad, hello. Like, welcome to the world. What do you think?"

"Tell me about Regan Quinn."

"What about her?"

"*She* ever do drugs?"

"No. She better not."

"The place she's working's kind of known for it," I said.

"That doesn't mean she's doing it."

"Did Regan know Dewayne?"

"What is this, the Inquisition? Why don't you go ask *her*?" She scraped her chair on the floor and turned to look at the wall.

We sat in uncomfortable silence. Then she faced me again. Her voice softened. "I almost forgot. I was going to ask you, how's my baby Armistead doing?"

"She's just fine."

"You didn't bring her with you, did you?"

"I did, in fact. We're staying out at Jake's."

"That's great. I mean . . ." For a moment she had almost looked hopeful.

"What, honey?"

She stared at the floor. "Nothing. Never mind."

"There's something I want to show you." I reached in my pocket and pulled out the silver chain and cross. The rosewood carving was crude but beautiful. "Have you ever seen this before?"

Her eyes grew wide. "Where'd you find it?"

"It was in Dewayne's hand when he died."

"Oh."

"You know whose it is?"

"I'm not sure," she said.

"But you've seen it before?"

She nodded.

"Where?"

She shifted in her chair, looked at the door, then at the ceiling. "I think they give them out at his church or something."

"You've been—to the church, I mean?"

"A couple times."

"And Dewayne was no longer dealing drugs?"

"I told you he wasn't."

I stood and looked at the bars, steel restrictions I had put others behind many times. "Well one thing's for sure, Nicky."

"What's that?"

72

"If you're telling the truth, whoever put that coke under your car's got a lot of money invested in you being locked up. Either that, or they're going to be a tad upset when they find out their cash crop is gone."

9

The dirt driveway to Jake Toronto's farm was pitted with puddles. The beams from my headlights bobbed up and down, and I scraped my mirrors on sumac as I splashed around a curve and came up the hill to the meadow at the edge of the woods where his trailer perched on a concrete slab. Naturally, he'd heard us coming, and stood in the glow from his porch light, mug in hand, with his retriever, Hercules, on the makeshift deck.

The years had been kinder to Toronto than to me. He still was fit enough to do two hundred sit-ups and push-ups every morning and remained as physically intimidating as ever. The dog bounded from its spot and began barking and leaping happily at the truck.

"I think Herk remembers you guys." He grinned as he stepped from the deck himself and clasped my hand. "Considering the stop you had to make, you're not as late as I'd thought you'd be."

"Some stop."

"Let's get a look at this girl of yours." He made a beeline for the box in back.

I opened the door for him. He had already slipped on his falconer's glove, and reached in. Armistead, still hooded and half-asleep, stepped up easily to his hand.

"There she is . . . She looks great, Frank. Nice job. How's her weight?"

"Forty-one ounces this afternoon when I checked."

"Perfect. She all set for some real hunting this week?"

"I think she's ready."

"Good. I've got one of the mews ready for her out back. Jersey's been pretty quiet today. Maybe tomorrow you and I can take the two of them out and run them through their paces."

"Absolutely."

"But first, I want to hear what's going on with Nicky."

We gathered up Armistead's supplies and I followed him around the trailer to the back. There was a barn there Toronto had built himself, with a metal roof, an open foyer, and three separate rooms for raptors. A hand-carved wooden sign over the entrance read *Maher-Shalal-Hash-Baz*, a gift from one of Toronto's old Jewish friends in New York; the Hebrew name meant a great many things, one of which was "easy prey."

Inside one of the rooms Jersey sat quietly. Even hooded in the darkness, she was an impressive bird. Slightly larger than Armistead, almost uniformly slate gray with a black crown, as opposed to the red-tail's dark brown and white blending to chestnut red. The goshawk flew deftly through the forest canopy and could drop like lightning on her target, either on the ground or another bird in flight.

After we settled Armistead into her own mews, Jake led me around front again to the trailer. We passed through a screen door into his living room, a narrow rectangle carpeted in nondescript berber, a sofa, small TV, and a pair of director's chairs the only furniture. One end of the space consisted of a double window with plastic blinds down but open; the other led into a compact kitchen housing a stove, a sink, and a microwave. A round oak table with three side chairs took up almost the entire room. We both sat.

"Gonna be warm the next couple days. Leaves have started to turn, but this won't help them drop," he said, handing me one of the two beers he'd plucked from the fridge. It tasted just right.

"Indian summer."

"Uh-huh. You guys over on the leeward side of the mountains are used to the warmer weather. But give me a frosty morning with trees stripped bare and a bird in the hand anytime."

I nodded.

"So Nicky's in jail?"

"That's right."

He shook his head. "Jeez, after finding that body on Friday, now this. You doin' okay?"

I snickered. "Well as can be expected I guess."

"You meet the sheriff?"

"Yup. How long's he been in office?"

"Couple of years."

"What happened to the old sheriff, what was his name?"

"Daveys. Retired to Myrtle Beach."

"Well this new one was all over me. Doesn't seem amenable to a peeper sticking his nose into official business."

Jake laughed. "Yeah, right. Like you or I would have been . . ." He sipped his beer.

"The problem is, I'm in a bit of a vice."

"Yeah? How's that?"

I decided to outline the entire story for him from the beginning: the discovery of Dewayne Turner's body and the evidence I'd lifted; my conversations with Ferrier and Nicole, and Ferrier's ultimatum; right through to the most recent party at the Affalachia County jail.

Toronto listened carefully. When I finished he gave a low whistle.

"Any suggestions?" I asked.

"You want another beer?"

"No thanks."

We both stared at the wall.

"Well, for one thing," he said, "I'd be careful who else you talk to. If Nicole really has somehow got herself mixed up in murder, the last thing she needs is her father making the case."

"I see your point. But Nicky swears she's innocent. I promised her I'd help."

He nodded. But then he added: "Thirteen years is a long time to be out of the drug and murder business, *compadre.*"

You could say that again. My homicide investigation skills were more than a little rusty, not to mention my personal involvement in the case, which didn't exactly inspire objective analysis. To be brutally honest, I'd become more a businessman than sleuth, surveillance and documentation my stock-in-trade.

Blame it on the '90s. Blame it on whatever you want. I was a chamber-of-commerce shamus in a town full of lawyers and academics, and now, faced with a daughter possibly mixed up in drugs and killing, I felt like a guest who'd arrived after the party was over. Worse, I wasn't even sure where to start.

"What're you packing?" Toronto asked. I knew he still kept his old .44 locked in a kitchen drawer where he could find it if needed.

I showed him the new Magnum.

"That's all right, but you watch yourself. Whoever wasted that drug dealer might be from around here, and while they would maybe think twice about shooting a cop, they ain't gonna worry—no offense—about doing some piss-ass private eye. I don't wanna be out flying Jersey and find *your* dead body somewhere."

"Your confidence is overwhelming me."

Toronto said nothing more, but I could almost read his thoughts—fear of shooting a cop hadn't helped Singer. My old partner had never second-guessed me, never wavered in his loyalty. We both knew what we saw that night, but I was the senior man, the one who was supposed to have been sure before we fired.

I stood and poured the dregs of beer into the sink. "I guess I better hit the sack. I've got a feeling tomorrow may not be much of an improvement on today. Oh, hey, I almost forgot, I need to check my office machine first—

make sure nothing urgent came in over the weekend. Mind if I use your phone?"

"No. Go right ahead." He handed me the portable handset from the recharger on the table, and I went through the routine.

"That's funny," I said after I finished. "Got a message from Rashid Fuad. He says he's going to be attending some conference at the University in Charlottesville, starting Tuesday, and he'd like to get together for a drink. Says he's got some more news on that imaging software thing."

"What, his computer figure out how the Balazar kid's gun vanished into thin air? Maybe they're making psychic software now."

"Right. But I wouldn't mind talking to Fuad anyway. Be nice to see him again after all these years. You want to go?"

He shrugged.

"Maybe Cat'll want to come too . . . of course, he never knew Fuad."

"Seems to me like you got enough on your plate here already, amigo."

"Yeah. I'll sleep on it. Maybe try calling Fuad tomorrow."

"Whatever . . . and Frank?"

I looked back before turning down the hall toward his tiny guest room. He was pouring himself a cup of high-test coffee from a pot on the stove—I never knew how he could drink so much of the stuff. "Yeah?"

He stared across his kitchen as if surveying some great distance. "You need anything to help Nicky, anything at all, I'm here."

10

Early Monday morning I tried calling my ex-wife. Camille and I had established a sort of truce of late, predi-
cated on lack of communication. The rich widow now,
she lived on two hundred acres, with a long drive leading
to an antebellum home. Jake had already left to pick up
some supplies in town.

A male voice answered the phone. His name was
Kevin Weems, Camille's latest live-in beau. I didn't
know that much about him except that Nicky had nick-
named him "the sponge," figuring he was more attracted
to Mama's dollars than to her sexy figure. He was a good
fifteen years younger than Camille, closer to Nicky's age
in fact. I was trying to keep an open mind.

"What do you want?" he said after I identified myself.

Okay, rudeness off the bat, but maybe he was only
trying to protect his dearly beloved. "I was hoping to
talk with Camille."

"She's asleep. We don't take calls before eight."

"But you picked up the phone."

He said nothing.

"Does she know what's going on with Nicky?"

"She knows." He sounded bored.

"Well if you could tell her I'm here in the area. I met
with Nicky at the jail last night. I'd like to come by later
today and talk with her about it."

He said nothing.

"This affect of yours, it take a lot of practice?"

"What?" He hung up.

Nice talking with you too, Kev.

Cahill's Restaurant took on a completely different character in the AM light. Gone were most of the cars from the parking lot. The beer neons were dark. The bar and the two pool tables were empty, but a few construction workers were eating breakfast.

I nodded to a waitress and slipped into an empty booth, figuring Cat would find me soon enough. Someone had left a fresh copy of the weekly *Leonardston Standard* in my booth and I picked it up. The front-page headline read: LOCAL TEEN FOUND DEAD IN MADISON COUNTY (QUESTIONS RAISED ABOUT SHERIFF'S ARREST). The article gave a brief bio of Dewayne Turner—high school basketball and football star—and didn't mention anything about drugs. But it did mention that the dead young man had last been seen in Sheriff's custody. A smiling Dewayne in a white shirt and tie stared at me from the page.

The waitress came over, and I ordered a bowl of oatmeal, some orange juice, and a banana. Not what I might have asked for ten years earlier, but physiques do change.

As if on cue, a huge man wearing a clean white apron lumbered forth from the kitchen with his back to me, carrying a big spoon. Cat. He scanned the restaurant as if honing in on my signal, surveying all his customers. Exaggerating his stop in mid-stride when he saw me, his face broke into a grin.

"Well I'll be damned." He voice dropped as he made a beeline to my booth. "About time you showed up." He enveloped my good-sized hand with his own.

"Good to see you, Cat."

"I heard about Nicky." Small town.

I nodded.

"How you takin' the news?" Since retiring South, Cat

had slipped right back into his old accent, only traces of which had been visible in New Rochelle.

"I've been better," I said.

He frowned. "I'll bet. Well, you came to the right place for a good breakfast, anyway."

Before I could answer he was yelling over his shoulder toward the kitchen: "Hey Kerstin! Kerstin, come on out! Frank's here!" The rest of his patrons glanced at us for a curious second, then turned back to their food.

Cat's wife, a stout woman with curly blond hair came through the kitchen door. She moved in the unhurried manner with which some people her size seemed born. Cat ushered her over. "I told you he'd be showin' up, didn't I? Just as soon as I heard about Nicky, I knew he'd be on his way over in that truck of his."

"Hello, Frank," she said. "Nice to see you."

"Nice to see you too, Kerstin."

"They told us you came by the other night. I'm sorry we missed you."

"That's all right. It was sort of an impromptu visit."

"Cat and I were up at the cabin."

"She makes me get away," Cat said.

"To hear Cat talk, Frank, I thought you might come riding in here on a white horse."

"I hope you didn't believe him. You know you gotta watch out for this guy."

"Now, now," Cat said. "Man comes in here and in twenty seconds he's already spreading doubts between husband and wife. . . ."

She laughed, and when she did, her eyes laughed too, steady and unblinking.

"Honey, could you check with Veronica, see what's holding up Frank's meal?" Cat asked.

"Sure, Shug." She lowered her voice. "I'm sorry about Nicole, Frank. If there's anything we can do to help, don't be a stranger now, you hear?" She turned back toward the kitchen.

"And ask her to bring me out a Coke too, will you, darlin'?"

She waved her hand affirmatively as she headed through the door. "Diet," she added.

"See what I got to put up with? . . . Ain't she a peach?"

"How are the grandkids?" I said.

"Just great. We had 'em over vistin' last weekend."

"Come on." I gestured. "Pictures."

He produced them from his wallet with a practiced hand and slid them across the table.

"Boys, huh? You must be proud. This one already looks like a linebacker."

Cat didn't answer. He looked thoughtful. "I was awful sorry to hear about Nicky, Frank. I was even going to try to go by there later today and visit her. That is, . . . I mean . . . it's not like you—"

The waitress burst through the kitchen door with my breakfast. "Sorry to keep you waiting, sir."

"No problem," I said.

She set the dishes in front of me and gave Cat his diet soda. "Anything else I can get you two?"

"Thanks, Veronica," Cat said. "Everything looks just fine."

"I'm okay," I said.

She spun off to another table.

Cat gave my breakfast a long look. "What kind of sissy food you eating there, hoss? That what living in a university town done for you? Weakened your stomach? Before you leave town, I'm going to have to fix you a real dinner." Which meant sweet Virginia ham, biscuits with honey, collard greens, fried ocra, and summer squash. Maybe finished off with warm cherry cobbler and vanilla ice cream, all washed down by some sweetened iced tea.

"You were saying?" I said, digging into my suddenly less appetizing oatmeal.

"I was about to say it was good of you to drive all the way down here to try and help out your little girl."

I waited until I finished my bite. "Problem is, she isn't a little girl anymore."

"Ain't it the truth."

"I found her here the other night and she says she was on her way over here yesterday when she was arrested."

He shrugged. "I wouldn't doubt it. We've been seein' a lot of her over here lately."

"Not drinking, I hope?"

He held out his hands. "You know me better than that, Frank. The girl's still underage."

"She usually come in by herself?"

"Usually. But sometimes she comes in with a couple pals," he said. "We talk."

"Un-huh. She told me she shoots pool too. Wonder who would have taught her?"

He feigned surprise. "She told you that? I had no idea."

I nodded, smiling. "You know any of her friends?"

"Not particularly. Why?"

I spun the paper around and pointed to the picture of Dewayne Turner. "How about this guy? Ever see her with him?"

He stared at me blankly for a second. Then he shrugged. "Couple of times. Hey, you aren't thinkin' what I think you are, are you?"

"The kid's been murdered. White girl with a black man. Wouldn't that raise some eyebrows around here?"

"Maybe once upon a time. Not anymore. Most folks just as soon mind their own business, if you know what I mean."

"But some might not take a liking to it."

"I suppose."

"And if they didn't, you'd know about it, right?"

"Uh-huh."

"And you'd let me know about it."

He gripped the corners of the table with his condor-like arms and pouted. "Frank, now I'm feeling hurt. What you tryin' to say?"

"I'm sorry. I'm not here to give you the third degree."

"I know you ain't," he said. "You want to help Nicky is all."

I said nothing.

"Hey, and you still a private eye."

"You make it sound like Hollywood."

"Well why not? From one ex-blue to another, it beats the sugar out of slinging hash."

"Not when it's the finest hash between Winchester and West Virginia," I said.

"And don't you ever forget it." He poked his meaty finger toward me in the air. "You figurin' this Turner murder got something to do with Nicky and her bein' arrested?"

"Don't know yet."

He shook his head. "I heard she was totin' dope. That kid there," he said, pointing to Turner's picture, "what I understand, he used to be into it pretty big himself."

"That's what the sheriff and the state police say."

"State police are in on this deal too, huh?"

"A couple of investigators out of Richmond. Sheriff up in Madison County had his hands full so they picked up on the case."

"My old uncle was pretty shook up about the whole thing."

I wanted to say he wasn't the only one, but instead I asked: "Speaking of sheriffs, what do you think of your new man?"

"Cowan? I think Buford Pusser never looked so good."

We both laughed. The door to the kitchen opened again. A young man stepped out carrying a gray tub. He was tall and black, maybe six-four or -five. He was also efficient. He began busing a row of empty tables to our left.

"So talk to me some more about Nicky," I said. "I've

already been by to see her and I'm heading out to talk to her mother later too."

"You talk to Camille?"

"Not yet. Just got her boyfriend on the phone. Sounds like a toad."

"Yeah. And he looks like a hired wrestler. I'd check out his background if I was you. Guy shows up out of nowhere a year ago. Next thing you know, he's moved in with Camille."

"Nicky doesn't seem to be too much of a fan."

He snickered. "She's got good reason. He put the moves on her too."

"She tell you that?"

"Didn't have to tell me, at least not in so many words. Young girl . . . it messes with your head, you catch my drift?"

"You think Camille knows?"

"Camille knows what Camille wants to know." He sighed. "That is, when she's not stoned."

"More than booze?"

He shrugged.

"Why would Nicky be carrying cocaine? You think she's strung out too?"

"No, sir. Not that little girl of yours. She's too tough for that."

"She says she knew nothing about it."

He thought for a moment. "Maybe . . . maybe not."

"So you're saying you think Nicky's capable of getting involved in a deal to move product."

The big man's face turned sad. "Under the right circumstances, she gets into a situation over her head . . . who isn't?"

"But what for? She wouldn't need the money."

He said nothing.

"You think it might have something to do with Weems?"

"Hey, you the detective, partner. I is just a poor patrolee." He struggled to extricate himself from the booth. "Listen, I got to get back to work. Why don't you and Jake come on by for lunch tomorrow? We got a private room in back and we can talk some more."

"Sure."

"Save your appetite. I'm pickin' the menu . . . how's the oatmeal?"

I made a thumbs-up gesture. "First-rate."

"Hard to mess up porridge." He stood staring at me for a moment. "By the way, you still miss it?"

"Miss what?"

"Bein' a cop."

"I don't know. I don't think about it too much anymore."

"That makes me feel good, cause I do."

"That reminds me, there was a message on my machine last night from Rashid Fuad."

"Fuad?"

"You know, the ballistics guy Jake and I used to work with. From New York. The one who sent you the letter."

"Oh yeah, yeah."

"He said he's going to be in Charlottesville for a conference this week. He's got some new information. Maybe to do with that software of his or something."

"Them machines is black magic, ain't they?"

"Jake and I are thinking of going over to have a drink with him. Want to ride along?"

"Nah. I got a restaurant to run. Besides . . ."

"What?"

"Old wounds, buddy. What's gone is gone . . . Old wounds."

I nodded then swept the air with my spoon. " ' 'Tis but the fate of place, and the rough brake that virtue must go through.' "

He shook his head as he lumbered back toward his kitchen. "Gotta ask Kerstin what she put in that oatmeal today," he said.

11

The bright sunshine on the sidewalk outside the jail almost blinded me. A skinny man riding a lawn mower and chewing a cigar cut the public grass, and the smell of it made my nostrils twitch. A rare autumn haze draped the town. Jake was correct: it was going to be a warm one all right.

I didn't notice the young woman barreling down the walkway toward me until it was too late.

"Oh." She stumbled to an abrupt halt. "I'm sorry, I didn't see you."

"No, it was my fault."

She was dark-skinned with a willowy figure and cocoa eyes. Perspiration dotted her forehead, though she looked anything but disheveled—in fact, she smelled faintly of perfume. Her straight hair was pulled into a headband with a few strands falling to either side. A navy-colored suit clung to her as if it were tailor-made, and a big pile of manila folders with one of those lawyerly briefcases occupied her arms.

"You look like you could use a hand."

"No. No thank you. I'm late for an appointment."

"Okay."

She stared at me for a moment. "You're not Nicole Pavlicek's father, are you?"

"I am."

"She told me you would be coming." She reached out a hand from beneath the pile of folders. It felt cool despite the heat. "I'm Priscilla Thomasen, Commonwealth's attorney."

That a black woman her age had been elected to such a position from Affalachia County spoke volumes, not only about changes in the county, but about the kind of person who had just shaken my hand.

"She mentioned you, Miss Thomasen. You sure I can't help you with some of those?"

"I'm sure . . . but thanks." She turned back toward the building.

"Wait. I mean, can you give me some idea about your case against Nicole?"

She stared at me. Then she asked: "How long have you and her mother been divorced?"

"Quite some time."

"Do you see Nicole often?"

"I try to . . ." Her look forced my hand. "From time to time."

"I understand from Sheriff Cowan and state police that you're also involved in another problem," she said. "Having to do with Dewayne Turner's body being found?"

Seemed like Cowan's suspicions were making the rounds. I wondered why the sheriff hadn't mentioned anything about the Commowealth's attorney. Were they at odds?

"Right," I said. "I'm the one who found it. Not on purpose, you understand. I was out hunting, working with my bird."

"So I was told. You're a private investigator, aren't you?"

"That's right."

"Were you just in talking with Nicole?"

"No. I was on my way to see the sheriff about listening to the tape of the tipster who turned her in. Then I was hoping to see Nicky again too."

"I'll be questioning your daughter myself, along with her attorney, in a little while."

"Any chance I might sit in?"

"I know your background, Mr. Pavlicek." Oh, boy. Who didn't? "Since you used to be a police detective, I may allow it. As long as your daughter or her attorney don't object."

"Thank you." From what I knew of Nicole's attorney, I couldn't imagine him objecting to anything but a price increase in white lightning.

"Good. Right now I really must—"

"Listen, Ms. Thomasen." I reached out and touched her arm. "Just one more thing . . . I understand there may be suspicions about Dewayne Turner's disappearance, allegations that the police may have somehow been involved."

She hesitated. "You understand correctly, but I'm not at liberty to discuss it at the moment."

"Okay, maybe later. But do you, by any chance, know any of Turner's family?"

"Of course. Good people. I know them well."

"I would really appreciate it if you would be willing to arrange a meeting for me with them," I said. "Maybe you could even go along. I know they must be grieving right now, but—"

"Let me get this straight. Your daughter's in jail, maybe mixed up in drug trafficking. And you want me to set up a meeting for you with a murdered man's family and then accompany you? To what, help overcome the black/white thing?"

"Well no. I didn't mean—"

"Look, Pavlicek, as far as I'm concerned, you're on your own if you want to go around bothering Carla Turner. The sheriff needs to talk with her and I've told him so—that's what would really help clear the air around here about Dewayne's disappearance. Right now I'm late and—"

"Do you have any idea if he was still selling drugs?"

She looked at me with suspicion. "From what I understand, no. He'd turned his back on all that."

"Maybe someone from the crowd he used to run with took exception and murdered him."

"Maybe it wouldn't be so shocking, either, if your daughter turned out to be involved with his death."

Wow. Her subtlety was killing me.

"After all," she said, "the apple doesn't fall . . ." She stopped in mid-sentence.

"Too far from the tree?"

"I'm sorry," she said. "I have to go."

The deep voice on the sheriff's department recording was hollow and indistinct. The call had been traced to a pay phone at a gas station on the outskirts of town so it could have come from almost anyone. The voice was very clear, however, about one thing: he specified Nicole by name and he described her car.

"Not much to go on." Cowan pushed the button to rewind the tape. "Guy's probably a doper himself. Probably settling a score. Be lucky if whoever owns that coke don't find him before we do."

"Maybe." But I was thinking the sheriff might be right.

"Who's side you on in all this anyway, Pavlicek? Just 'cause that daughter of yours tells you she's innocent, don't mean she wasn't mixed up in something no good."

"I'm interested in finding out what really happened."

"No bias? No prejudice at all? You know we're big on that down here now, eliminating prejudice, I mean." He smiled and leaned back in his chair, placing his feet on the desk, and clasped his hands across his stomach, twiddling his thumbs.

I said nothing.

"So, have y'all had any great revelations since our get-together last night?" he asked.

"I found out Camille's new boyfriend is about as talkative as a Sphinx, which concerns me."

He grunted in disgust. "Really? Well maybe we'll just have to check that boy out."

"I also bumped into the prosecutor just now out on the sidewalk. She told me you were going to be taking a statement from Nicole later and she gave the okay for me to sit in."

"S'that a fact?"

He stared at me. Then he lifted his big feet down from the desk. "She's the boss. But just remember when it comes to most other things around here, I am."

"Look, sheriff. I'm not the enemy, okay? You say you and your men had nothing to do with Dewayne Turner's murder and I say I believe my daughter when she says she knew nothing about the drugs found on her car. Let's just take each other at face value for the moment."

"All right. But that won't stop you nosing around to see if there's any evidence of Turner being beaten 'fore he was killed, will it?"

I shook my head.

"And don't expect me to stop putting the microscope on who you are and where you come from, Mr. Pavlicek. And that includes your buddies Toronto and Cahill. I know what you boys testified about that night up in New York. I also know the trial went nowhere and a lot of cops still believe you and think you and your partner didn't get a square deal.

"But I'm here to tell you, I ain't one of them. You and your partner fucked up, that's all. Fucked up good. Far as I'm concerned, you both got what's coming to you. Just thought you ought to know that."

I guess the thing about genuine prejudice is, it cuts all ways.

"By the way, your friend Special Agent Ferrier called me again this morning. Seems they found some residue on Dewayne Turner's clothing. Traces of coke in both pockets. Ferrier wants a sample of the powder we took off of your daughter to test for a match. . . ."

Could this get any worse?

"You think I'm riding a loser here, don't you?"

A painful look crossed his face. "If you're really asking, yeah, I do. Ferrier also says he's waiting for you to call him. Said you'd know the number."

"Okay."

"You going to?"

"Call him? Yeah, I will. They figure out what kind of gun was used on Turner?"

He smiled. "You don't give up, do you? It was a nine-millimeter. Which fits my theory," he said.

"Which is?"

"Like I said before. Killed by his own kind. Gang-related."

"You see the paper this morning?"

He nodded and looked toward the ceiling then back at me. "They don't do me no favors," he said. "This department's got three black deputies now. You'd think that'd be enough to satisfy somebody. . . ."

He paused as if he were weighing his words. "We got a few minutes until your daughter's statement. Let me ask you something. I probably shouldn't, but I'm goin' to anyway. The name Boog Morelli mean anythin' to you?"

I sat up in my chair. Fuad said there was an old link to Morelli. But how could Cowan know anything about that?

"I doubt there's a cop in New York doesn't know that name," I said. "He's one of the biggest drug kingpins around, or at least he was, last I heard. Why?"

"His name has come up in relation to Dewayne Turner."

"Ferrier know about it?"

"I haven't discussed it with him yet."

I suddenly remembered the man in the rental car with Maryland plates in the parking lot outside Cahill's the other night. "Listen to me, sheriff. I know you may not think much of me, but if Boog Morelli or any of his people are involved, you should watch very carefully where you step."

For a moment Cowan and I shared something in common. I saw it in his eyes. I remembered seeing it in

Toronto's eyes the night we'd faced the shooters in the dark.

But it passed too flippantly from the sheriff. "Always do . . . You want my advice, Mr. PI?"

"Not particularly, but I'll listen."

"Pack on up and head back to Charlottesville. Nicole's your daughter, I understand, but it's not like you raised the girl or nothin'. Why you want to go make it harder on yourself? A drug dealer's dead and we arrested her carrying coke. Who knows? Maybe the Turner kid had something over her. Maybe she was muling for him. But she's young, the family's got money, and she's . . ." He looked down at his desk.

"White?"

"You said it. I didn't."

"Boog Morelli's white too," I said.

We took turns staring out his office window.

"Ferrier said he and his partner will be down here day after tomorrow," he said. "You'd best come clean with us, Pavlicek. I've told him, either way, I want you out of my hair by then."

12

Nicole's wrists were cuffed again. She was seated, elbows propped on the table, chin resting on her thumbs and chewing on one fingernail, when they brought me into the room. Sheriff Cowan stood off to one side, leaning on the wall with his arms crossed. Shelton Radley sat next to Nicole and Priscilla Thomasen was across the table; both had pens and pads in front of them.

Radley was a wisp of a man in a blue suit with graying temples to match what was left of his graying hair. He looked fairly sober this morning. Nonetheless, I thought I caught a trace of Scotch in the air.

The Commonwealth's attorney's hand was poised over her tape recorder. "Now you understand, Ms. Pavlicek, this is not a trial. But anything you say from here on out may be admissible as evidence and used against you."

"Yes." Nicole looked at me, fear in her eyes. "Are you going to get me out of here, Daddy?"

"We're a ways from that right now, hon," I said. "Just tell them what happened."

I looked at Radley. Little beads of perspiration had already collected on his forehead. I hoped he was up to the task.

"Okay, Ms. Pavlicek, shall we begin?" Priscilla Thomasen nodded perfunctorily at me, which I took as a hopeful sign, before pushing the button on her machine. "Ms. Pavlicek, could you please state your full legal name for the record."

"Nicole Mae Pavlicek."

Mae. My mother's name. I hadn't heard it used in years. Nicole's voice shook as she spoke.

"Let the record show that Nicole Mae Pavlicek is in the room with Priscilla Thomasen, Affalachia County Commonwealth's attorney, Peter Cowan, Affalachia County sheriff, her father, Frank Pavlicek, and Shelton Radley, attorney in private practice representing Ms. Pavlicek.

"We're here to ask you some questions regarding your arrest, Ms. Pavlicek, but before we begin I must ask an important one. Did the arresting officers read you your rights at the time you were taken into custody?"

Nicole looked warily around the room. She nodded.

"Is that a 'yes'?"

"Yes."

"Please speak your answers aloud . . . Do you understand those rights that the officers read to you?"

"Uh-huh."

"All right then, let's begin." The prosecutor consulted her notes. "Do you have any voluntary statements to make, regarding your apprehension on Sunday the twenty-ninth of September, at which time you were found to be transporting approximately two kilos of powder cocaine in your car?"

"She doesn't have to make any statements or submit to any questions," Shelton Radley said, his voice barely above a whisper. He turned to his client. "You understand that too, don't you?"

"Yes," Nicole said.

"We'd also like to question you about your relationship with one Dewayne Turner, a young man whose body was discovered by your father last week up in Madison County," the prosecutor said. "Is there any statement you would like to make about that?"

The prisoner shook her head. "No," she said.

"Since this is all being recorded, I wish the record to be more specific to state that the cocaine was found under the wheel well of my client's vehicle, as opposed to actually inside the car," the older attorney said. Well, touché, Rad.

"Without objection," Priscilla Thomasen said. "Ms. Pavlicek, is it still your contention that you had no prior knowledge of the cocaine that was discovered on your vehicle two days ago?"

"Yes."

"If you had no knowledge of the cocaine then why did you try to evade the police?"

Nicky glanced at the sheriff. "I was afraid they were going to ticket me for speeding. I was afraid I might lose my license."

"Because you'd already accumulated points on your license?"

"Yes."

The prosecutor shuffled through some papers in front of her. "Running's no way to keep from adding more. You've also stated that you were on your way from your mother's house to Cahill's Restaurant, is that correct?"

"Yes."

"Were you going to meet someone at the restaurant?"

Nicole's eyes fixed on me again. "I don't remember," she said.

"You don't remember? It was only yesterday."

"This has been a traumatic experience for my client, counselor, as you might imagine," Shelton Radley said, this time sounding for all the world as if he were whining. "She doesn't have to answer."

"Un-huh." Priscilla fiddled with the volume control on the tape recorder.

Nicole remained mute.

Priscilla sighed and pursed his lips. "Okay, let's talk about another subject. You and Dewayne Turner. How well did you know him?"

A look of panic seemed to sweep through Nicole's eyes. She glanced at me then back to the prosecutor. "Not very well."

"But you were with him the night he was arrested

almost a month ago. The sheriff says you two were arguing, that you even threatened to kill him."

Whoa—this was news to me. What else had the sheriff failed to tell me? What else had *Nicole* failed to tell me? I understood where this might be heading now. They were probing to see if they could build an even bigger case against my daughter.

But Nicole only shrugged.

"Were you arguing with him that night?"

"I suppose."

"What about?"

"Look," she said, rolling her eyes. "Dewayne was a good guy, but he could be kind of scary sometimes."

"Scary?"

"It was just hard to believe that someone could . . . you know . . . change that much overnight," she said.

"Change. You're talking about his conversion to Christianity?"

"Yes."

Priscilla wrote something down on her legal pad. Then she looked straight at Nicky again. "Did Dewayne ever sell you drugs?"

"A leading question," Radley mumbled. "She doesn't have to answer."

But Nicole looked at the two attorneys as if Priscilla's query were the dumbest anyone had ever asked. "I don't use drugs," she said flatly.

"Dewayne used to sell drugs though, and you knew that, didn't you?"

"Yes," she said.

"Yet you were still friends with him."

"Not really friends, like I told you . . . I . . . he . . ." She looked around the room for a moment. "He asked me out."

Priscilla showed no reaction to this revelation. "Did you? Ever go out with him, that is?"

"No. That was before."

"Before . . . you mean before he became a Christian, when he was still selling drugs?"

"Yes."

"So if you didn't go out with him before when he was selling drugs and he wasn't really a friend, what could you two possibly be arguing about?"

Nicole looked at her lawyer. Radley cleared his throat and said: "Does the sheriff's department have any hard evidence, other than the cocaine, which could have easily been planted, to accuse my client of anything?"

No one said anything.

"She has no motive," the old attorney said.

Sheriff Cowan finally spoke, still leaning against the wall. "How do we know she has no motive when she tried to get away after seeing the deputy's lights and she won't even answer all the questions?"

Priscilla turned to the sheriff. "You used the warrant you obtained to search the rest of her car and her room out at Sweetwood?"

The sheriff nodded.

"Find anything else?"

"Sent some latents off to the lab," Cowan said. "That's it so far."

The Commonwealth's attorney looked at me. "How about you, Mr. Pavlicek, you have anything to add to this discussion?"

Nicole stared straight ahead, didn't even glance at me.

"No," I said.

The CA turned back to the prisoner. "Okay, Ms. Pavlicek, no more questions for now. But you should be aware that our office looks favorably on any defendant who cooperates with an investigation. Are you sure you can't tell us anything else about the cocaine that was found under the wheel well of your car, about who you were going to meet that day, why you tried to evade arrest, or about why you were arguing with Dewayne Turner on the day he was arrested?"

Nicole gave no answer.

"Then that will end this statement. The time is ten forty-three A.M., Monday, October first." She switched off the tape recorder. "Sheriff, let's get someone to take her back to her cell. We'll arraign her tomorrow morning on the drug charge."

"What about bail?" I asked.

"That'll be up to the judge, but I wouldn't get my hopes up. We may have probable cause for murder here too."

"She's not a flight risk. You can release her into her mother's or my custody."

"Tell it to the judge. Mr. Radley, I would like to meet with you and the sheriff in his office, if you don't mind. Mr. Pavlicek, I'm sorry, but you'll have to sit this one out."

Cowan went and opened the door. A female deputy came in. Nicole stood, her head bowed, as the woman took her by the arm to lead her from the room. I tried to read my daughter's face as they left, but there was little to decipher. The eyes of a ragged doll appeared instead of hers, where an expression should have been. I thought of pink horses and playthings. In the chalk of the walls, or maybe the dullness of too many years, those images were all I had left of my little girl.

13

Atop a summit in a grove of hundred-year-old oaks, the Rhodes mansion presided over acres of open land. Quarterhorses grazed behind board fence. Brass signage, affixed to a stone wall at the entrance, proclaimed it SWEETWOOD FARM. Nicole's home for over ten years was federal brick with large doric columns, a circular drive, blue-green lawn that extended around back to a swimming pool, and a clay tennis court. Camille must have had the pool area redone since my last visit. A new guest house ran along a sculpted hillside with a little waterfall and large flat stones arranged in such a way that gave them the effect of tumbling into the water beneath.

I braked the truck to a halt in front. As I opened the door a whiff of honeysuckle drifted across my nostrils. The site commanded a view worth a whistle: a forested valley stretching toward a shimmering reservoir in the distance. From somewhere came the sound of a weed trimmer, probably the gardener. I climbed the steps to the massive front door and rang the bell. No response. I rang it again.

After a minute Camille herself, looking a little disoriented, opened the door.

She stifled a yawn. "Well, well, w-ell. If it isn't my old hubby."

"Hello, Camille."

"Lucita's off today. I'm not used to answering the front door."

Hard work. She had come a long way since the night

I had first seen her cheerleading on a Westchester high school football field. Back then she cared little for appearances; it was one of the things I had loved about her. But eventually, it seemed, she came to care for little else. All through the early years of our marriage, before Nicky came, while I was working my way up the detective ranks, she had toiled at the Manhattan headquarters of a large commercial bank, earning enough money to allow her to dress well and for us to dine out, often above our means.

Now, standing in the vestibule of her castle, she wore a peach princess dress beneath French-twisted hair, blonde when it used to be brunette. Her green eyes were red-rimmed, but the rest of her face appeared softly put together—just the right amount of blush and liner and fuchsia lip gloss. She seemed more pale than I remembered, and though she had always been slender, she was exceptionally so now. Some might even call it borderline anorexic.

"If I'd known you were dropping by, detective, I'd have sexied myself up. I've been meaning to ask you, do they still call you that—detective, I mean? Is it a permanent title, like royalty or something?"

"I'm here about Nicky, Camille."

"I know." She let the door swing wide. "Come on in."

I stepped through the foyer and onto a tile floor. In front of us a stairway swept in a wide semicircle toward the second floor. Down the steps came a young brute, about six-two with sandy hair, wearing khaki shorts and a golf shirt with a V-neck cardigan to go with his sardonic smile.

"Frank, I don't believe you've met Kevin Weems. Kevin, this is Frank, Nicole's father."

We shook hands firmly.

"I've heard a lot about you from your daughter." His eyes took my measure. Charming now. Not the same Kevin I had spoken with earlier.

"I hope all to the good," I said.

"Of course."

Camille switched gears into charming too. "I don't think you've been in here since we redecorated, have you, Frank?" She was right. The walls were painted a new yellow and white. A crystal chandelier hung overhead. "It may seem a bit grandiose at first, but I'm pleased with it. Can we offer you something to drink? We have iced tea, or something stronger if you'd like."

"Tea will be fine, thank you."

"Kev, why don't you show Frank into the den while I fix the drinks."

She disappeared toward the kitchen. I followed Kev down a long hall past the dining room and into the den. It was a richly appointed man's room—bookshelves, mahogany, a trophy elk, and several plaques—all George's, not the boyfriend's of course—lining the walls. The floor was carpeted in green pile.

We sat in leather club chairs in front of a well-stocked bar. Framed pictures of Nicole, Camille, and George filled a round corner table like an altar. Unlike on the stairwell, the new man of the house looked uncomfortable with the surroundings.

"Been with Camille long?" I asked.

He drummed his fingers on the leather. "Eleven months."

On the way in I had noticed a green Porsche in front of the barn, Georgia plates. "Where you from originally?"

"Atlanta." His accent sounded more like Mississippi.

"Saw your car out back."

He said nothing.

"How'd you and Camille meet?"

He was looking out the window now. "We met at a horse auction over in Lexington."

"Ah-h-h." I waited for him to elaborate, but he didn't. "If you don't mind my asking, what'd you used to do for a living down in Atlanta?"

"Sales."

"And now you work for Camille."

He finally turned to look at me. "George's old company, actually. Vice president, Marketing."

The marketing must have been going pretty well for him to be padding downstairs at eleven A.M. My own abbreviated career in sales had taught me that those who were truly successful worked most of the time. Others spent as much time playing golf or hitting the bars. And then there were the hangers-on, those who drifted from situation to situation, camouflaging their lethargy. Maybe Kev was one of those. Of course when you were sleeping with the owner, all bets were off.

"Kevin gave me the message that you called this morning," Camille said, whirling into the room. She carried a tray with three tall glasses and set it down on a table next to us. She passed out the glasses, then nervously smoothed her dress as she took a seat on the couch and crossed her legs. "Anyway, I know you'll want to get right down to business. Have you been by to see Nicole?"

"Yes, and the new sheriff and the prosecutor and her lawyer as well."

"Shelton? Oh, I do hope that man does a decent job for her. Are you working with the police?" Her eyes never left me as she sipped her iced tea.

"Not really. I'm here of my own accord. What I'm trying to understand is exactly how our daughter could have gotten herself into such a situation."

"*Our* daughter now, is it? Well there's a switch."

I let the dig pass. "She says she didn't know anything about the cocaine. Anyone could have put that stuff under her car."

"Anyone could have, but did they?" she said. The look told me she thought she already knew the answer. "I think I know her a little bit better than you, Frank. Nicole's always had this rebellious side to her."

"I've never seen it when she's been with me."

"Well I might as well tell you because I know you'll

find out sooner or later anyway. A couple of years ago she was caught with a few friends out behind the school. They were smoking marijuana."

More revelations. Just great. At this rate, pretty soon the little ragdoll girl would mutate into a teenaged hatchet murderer.

I looked at Kevin who was staring out the window again. "Why wasn't I told anything about it at the time?"

"It was when George was still alive. We went down to the sheriff's office and he dealt with it. They agreed to let her off with a warning. As punishment, we didn't allow her to drive her car for a week."

Whoopee. Big hardship there.

"But getting caught with a bunch of kids smoking grass, Camille, is hardly the same as—"

"Maybe being in prison for a few days will cure her of it."

I stared at my ex-wife. There was a new detachment to her voice I didn't like. "The county jail's not prison, Camille. Prison is a lot worse."

She waved the point away as if it were meaningless.

"What does Radley have to say about the situation?" I asked.

"I spoke with him last evening down at the sheriff's office. He says they really don't have that much evidence just yet. He's looking into things."

That was the approach then. Spend some money to hire an attorney. Try to go back to your life and forget about your daughter in jail. For Shelton Radley, "looking into things" meant he was probably planted in his office with a bottle close by, waiting for the sheriff to call. Had things between mother and daughter grown so bad it had come down to this?

"I'm sorry, but don't you think Nicky would be better off with a lawyer who has a little more criminal experience?" I said.

"Don't you think you're a little late to be offering advice?"

Camille. Always one up. We stared at one another. The tea needed sweetening. Kevin looked as if it were all he could do to sit there, let alone pay attention to the conversation.

"Okay," I said. "Let's try to get along. We both want what's best for Nicole. You're her mother and she's grown up with you, so I'll bend to your judgment, for now. But I'm here to tell you I think she didn't know about the coke on the car, until I'm proven wrong."

"You mean Daddy's little girl couldn't have been involved in such a thing?"

"I mean a beautiful young woman with our daughter's honesty and potential wouldn't. She may be caught up in an unfortunate situation right now. But don't underestimate her, Camille."

"Oh I'd never do that. But don't overestimate your daughter either."

I wasn't sure what she meant by that so I waited. She fluffed the pillows on the couch next to her. I set my glass on a coaster in the middle of a reading table next to my chair.

"There's another reason why I drove down here this morning," I said. "Has the sheriff or anyone spoken with either of you today?"

"No. I haven't talked to anyone since I was down there last night." She looked at Weems. "Kev?"

He shook his head. "Un-uh."

"You don't know about the body then?"

"Body? What body?"

I told them about finding Dewayne Turner. They both claimed they had never heard of him before. Maybe they were lying. Maybe when you're busy remodeling or playing tennis, you don't have time to read the papers or listen to news. At some point, Kevin's eyes glazed over, but Camille listened intently.

"So what does this have to do with Nicole?" she said.

"The police and the prosecutor may be trying to link her to Turner's disappearance and murder."

"I need something stronger to drink. Kev, would you mind fixing me something, darling?"

Kevin came to attention, stood, and made for the bar.

"You, Frank?" he asked.

I shook my head.

I waited to see if she would have him go fetch a little chewy toy or something too, but it didn't happen.

"God," Camille said. "Now you've got me, Frank. I can't believe Nicole would do such a thing. How would she have even known this—this person?"

"She says from school."

"Well maybe, but that doesn't . . . look, Frank, why don't I just hire you to prove that she had nothing to do with this boy's death? Wouldn't that just help solve everything?"

My ex as a client. No thank you. "I didn't come down here to be paid, Camille."

"Oh don't get insulted. It's what you do for a living, isn't it? Investigate things?" Kevin came over and handed her a Bloody Mary, then retreated to his chair.

"All I want right now is some answers. Have you and Nicole not been getting along?"

"Did she tell you that? . . . I don't know how she could say such a thing. Why, she's not even here most of the time. She's either at school or out with her friends." She took a long sip of her drink.

"But you support her financially, pay for her car and clothes and all that?"

"Of course."

"Ever get the idea she feels trapped?"

She laughed. "You're really reaching. I shouldn't think a young woman with her opportunities would ever feel such a thing."

I made a point of looking around the room. "How about George?"

Kevin finally chimed in, dropping the charm: "What's he got to do with anything?"

"How was his relationship with Nicole?"

"Fine," Camille said. "It was just fine."

"She talk about him much anymore? I mean . . . I'm sorry, now that he's gone?"

"Not much."

"How about *your* relationship with George?"

"Listen, pal, you got no right to be asking these questions." Kevin must have experienced a sudden testosterone rush. He fixed me with a threatening glare.

"It's okay, Kev. Frank's just doing what he does best." She pursed her lips and turned partly away, wiping her cheek beneath one eye. "I loved George, of course. You, of all people, ought to know that. Do we need to get into this? His death was . . . his death was . . . almost impossibly hard."

What did it take to be possibly hard? Maybe a few million dollars would do it.

"He leave everything to you?"

Kevin was close to the boiling point now. Camille took another sip of her drink. "I don't think that's any of your business, Frank, but since you're trying to help Nicole I'll tell you that he left the bulk of his estate to me. As you know, there's a sizable trust for our child."

"He have any other children from previous marriages?"

"No."

"Okay." I fumbled for the chain in my pocket. "I have something to show both of you." I held up the necklace with the wooden cross.

She stared blankly at it for a moment. Weems looked at it as well.

"Ever seen this before?"

"No," Camille said. "Why? Is it Nicole's?"

"No. Just something I found . . . How about you?" I held it closer for Weems to examine. He shook his head.

"All right then, is there anything else either of you

can tell me? Anything that might tie Dewayne Turner with Nicole and the cocaine?"

Neither spoke. Then, almost as an afterthought she said: "The only thing might be her friends. . . . One in particular . . . she's a year or two older."

"Regan Quinn."

"Yes," she said. "How did you know?"

"Sheriff Cowan mentioned her," I said. "Everybody seems to be reading from the same playbook."

"Yes, I suppose she has a reputation. Did he tell you where she works?"

"White Spade," I said.

She nodded. Then she snickered. "George used to go down there once in awhile, you know. He knew I wasn't too happy about it."

"I'm surprised you would put up with that," I said.

"Oh, I never expected him to be a saint, Frank . . . like you. Just that he'd always come back to my bed . . . He always did." She glanced at Weems and seemed to smile to herself before taking another drink. Could you taste a Faustian bargain?

"Okay," I said. "One more thing. Has the sheriff's office been out here with a search warrant yet?"

"Yes they have. It was embarrassing. They came last night and searched Nicole's room."

"Mind if I have a peek myself?"

"No . . . I suppose not. Was there something in particular you were looking for?"

"Just want to check things out," I said.

"Well they already spent a couple hours pawing through everything, so I guess it's okay," she said.

We all rose. Kevin, still seething, had apparently seen enough to satisfy whatever anxiety or curiosity he bore. "I've got to get down to the office, Camille."

"Sure, darling." She bent toward him, he encircled her in his arms, and they briefly kissed. "I'll be by later," she said. "We'll do lunch."

Weems disappeared. Camille, still carrying her drink,

led me through a spacious kitchen and up a narrow rear staircase to the second floor. I heard the Porsche roar to life and peel away down the drive.

"Nicky moved into this back bedroom when she was in high school," she said. "She likes the privacy."

The room wasn't large—it had probably been meant to quarter servants—but there was a door with panes of glass leading to a private balcony, a canopy with pink ruffles over the double bed and oversized pillows scattered across an inviting window seat. An iMac computer sat in the middle of her desk connected to a printer. A phone with her own answering machine took up most of one bedside table—there were no new messages according to the display. Fashion magazines and a few popular novels were strewn about.

I took in all of this at once, a glimpse into Nicole's life to which I had never been privy before.

"As you can see, it's nothing spectacular," Camille said. She leaned against the door frame, seemed embarrassed at my being there.

"Mind if I search the dresser?"

She swirled the remaining ice cubes in her glass. "Be my guest."

I started with the bottom drawer and worked my way to the top. Skirts, blouses, T-shirts, shorts, socks, bras, and panties were neatly arranged. The top drawer contained jewelry and cosmetics, some travel brochures, and scraps of paper. And folded there, exactly as Nicole had told me, were the Oakley sunglasses.

I breathed a sigh of relief.

"Find anything?"

"Nothing," I said.

Camille gave me a curious look. As we turned to leave I glanced at the mirror over the dresser. There was a Polaroid photo tucked in the corner of its frame that I recognized immediately because I was the one who'd snapped the picture: a full-body color shot of Nicole. She was wearing my falconer's glove, standing beside my truck smiling, with Armistead perched on her arm. The sun shone brightly that day and in the background Old Rag was visible, outlined against the clear blue sky.

"Nice picture," I said.

Camille shrugged.

"Mind if I take it? Maybe Nicky'll want to keep it in her cell."

"Whatever," she said. "Not a very good photograph of her if you ask me."

We made our way, in silence, back down the stairs and through the house until we reached the front door again.

"That's all I have for right now, Camille. But whatever I find out, please give some second thought to hiring Nicole a decent lawyer. I think she feels like you've abandoned her down there."

"You're suddenly the expert on what my daughter is feeling?"

"Believe it or not, I only want what's best for her too," I said.

"Oh, of course, of course. Whatever's best for little Nicky. You just do your little job and I'll do mine," she said.

I wondered what kind of bitterness could have built up in her over the years, why I had ever been attracted to her in the first place. Marcia, for all her imperfections and hurts, seemed to possess no such hate. I suddenly missed her, more than I had thought possible.

"Just what do you think our jobs are, Camille?"

"Our jobs?" She chuckled before pulling open the heavy door again, suddenly a little unsteady on her feet. "Why, I'm the mommy. And you . . . you're the daddy by default, I guess," she said, smiling as she showed me out, back into the sun.

14

It was mid-afternoon—just a few hours before Ferrier's deadline—by the time I parked in front of the White Spade. The sky looked more alabaster than blue. The sun had built the day's heat to its zenith and what remained felt even hotter, like coals left after a fire.

Cosmetically, the Spade resembled a giant bread box. Save for the kaleidoscopic sign in front blaring GIRLS GIRLS GIRLS—as if the first word weren't enough—the building was about as nondescript as they come: pale clapboard siding, a new-looking roof, no windows facing the road, one door. Four or five pickups, a van with a moonroof, and a couple of cars had already begun to fill the dirt lot—men on their way home early who had stopped by to drink and ogle bodies their wives or girlfriends could never own—the daily beer and leer.

Inside I headed for the bar. Heavy metal thumped from a phalanx of sub-woofers. The room was dark except for one brightened stage, cool, but not so cold as to chill the dancers. Only one was performing at the moment, a long-legged brunette wearing a G-string, spiked heels, and nothing else. She spun around a pole, eyes frozen in the blinding light, her mouth bent to a sensual curl. Eyes were frozen around the room too, anesthetized clumps of men, some smoking, not talking, or if they were, joking and jostling with one another. They glanced at me when I came abreast of them, but if any recognized my face they didn't show it.

"What'll it be, my friend?"

The bartender was a wormy, middle-aged white man with a sunken face scarred by acne. His hair looked as if it had been plastered to the top of his head with a grease gun.

"Looking for an employee. Regan Quinn?" I slid a business card across the bar at him.

He scratched his chin, eyeing the card and me suspiciously. "Regan's not on until later. Don't want any trouble. We run a clean place here."

"I can see that," I said, glancing at the stage. "No trouble. Just wanted to ask her a couple questions."

"I'll see if she has time." He turned and disappeared through a door at the side.

A couple minutes later he was back. He held out his hands in a gesture of resignation. "Sorry, but the boss says he sent her home. Turns out she wasn't feeling well today. Thinks maybe it was the flu."

"Flu," I said.

He stared at me and nodded.

"Know where she lives?"

"I'm supposed to keep track?" He peered nervously across the room. "Boss'd kill me if I started giving dancers' addresses out." He turned toward one of his patrons who was trying to get his attention for more beer. I watched him fill a couple tall ones then turn and hand them to the guy in exchange for a five.

Then I said: "Well I guess the boss wouldn't mind then if the sheriff conducts a little inspection tour, you know, to make sure all the rules are being followed." It was a threat I couldn't back up, of course, but the barkeep had no way of knowing that.

He glared at me for a second. Then he picked up a rag and started wiping some glasses, and as he did, he nodded toward a typewritten list of names laminated in purple plastic attached to the wall around a corner. I put a five of my own on the counter without making too much of a show, leaned over, and found her address.

Back outside I squinted at the glare. None of the vehicles in front had moved, but a cloud of dust drifted across a cornfield next door. Far down the highway, before it disappeared around a curve, I caught a glimpse of a speeding, small blue car. Maybe the flu that winter was going to be worse than everyone thought.

I called Jake from a pay phone in town to tell him I wouldn't be back out to the farm until later.

"You had a message from Priscilla Thomasen," he said. "She called to talk and when I mentioned you were staying out here she asked me to tell you to call her." He gave me the number.

"Sounds like you know the Commonwealth's attorney."

"She's a friend."

"Sure. How are our two hunters doing?"

"Fine. I took them both for walks earlier. Flew Armistead to her lure."

"I may have to take a rain check for today. How about we take them both out first thing in the morning?"

"You got it. What's the latest with Nicky?"

He grew quiet when I told him about the happenings of the day so far, especially the part about Boog Morelli and the man I'd seen in the rental car outside Cahill's.

"I was afraid of this," he said finally.

"What do you mean?"

There was a long pause. "Morelli's people were supplying Dewayne Turner back when he was doing business."

"How do you know that?"

"Don't ask me how I know."

Toronto and I went way back. He was only a few years out of the academy when he'd made detective and been assigned to me. But there was always a part of him he seemed unwilling to share. He'd run with a gang himself for awhile growing up. I'd learned over the years when to push and when not to.

"I think we should go over to C'ville and have that drink with Rashid Fuad tomorrow," I said.

"Okay. What about that trooper snooper who's breathing down your neck?"

"I'm going to have to try keeping him at bay. Maybe the Commonwealth's attorney can help. . . . You two are pals, huh? Are we talking carnal knowledge here?"

"Native Americans never speak about their sex lives. Makes for bad spirit."

"That sounds like something you're making up and besides, you're not a full-blooded Native American."

"Who is full-blooded anything? Priscilla's one of the good guys, I'll tell you that. You can trust her."

"That's good enough for me," I said.

She answered her phone herself on the second ring.

"Ms. Thomasen, this is Frank Pavlicek again. I got your message."

"Oh, Pavlicek. Hold on a second."

I waited for half a minute before she came back on.

"You still there? Listen, I spoke with Carla Turner, Dewayne's mother? She's willing to talk with you."

"I must have grown on someone. It was my pretty face, right?"

"Don't flatter yourself. Jake Toronto says you are all right."

I wanted to ask how she had forgiven Toronto, and not me, for our past, but figured I better not push that subject just yet.

"I thought I would let Mrs. Turner decide for herself about your request," she said. "I should tell you I still advised her not to speak with you."

How nice.

"Do you still want to talk with her?" she asked.

"Absolutely. Where and when?"

"You can come by my office in about an hour." She gave me the address. "After we talk, we can leave from here."

"We? You mean you're coming too?"

"That's correct."

I couldn't resist. "To help with the cop/lawyer thing or the black/white thing?"

An uncomfortable silence followed. She had pushed and I had pushed back and now we were at a standstill, except for Toronto.

"All right," I said. "I'll be there."

15

I found her office nestled in a crumbling brownstone a few blocks away from the jail. Apparently the prosecutor's budget wasn't as substantial as the sheriff's. The buildings on the cross street were a mixture of commercial and private dwellings with peeling paint and dark-stained shingles. Mostly concrete in front, but here and there a postage stamp–size lawn.

I mounted the stone front steps, cratered with discernible indentations at their centers. Her door, with the official name and state seal stenciled on the glass in front of a venetian blind, was unlocked. I opened it and went in.

The lights in the reception area were all off. Evening sunlight angled through the windows, casting long shadows across the floor. A window air conditioner moaned at the far end of the room next to a bulletin board overflowing with thumbtacked posters and various legal notices.

"Anyone home?"

Nothing.

Two openings led down hallways toward the back of the building. Down one I could see a partially open door, the pale cast of a dim light.

"Anyone home?" I repeated, a little louder. Someone coughed from behind the door. I knocked softly and pushed it in.

Priscilla Thomasen sat back in her chair, her stocking feet minus shoes, propped on top of her desk. She twirled a pencil in one hand, bouncing its eraser on her thigh, which, along with the rest of her legs were not unpleasant to look at. A phone receiver clung to her ear, her neck craned to one side.

She motioned for me to come in. "You suggest I do what?" She rolled her eyes. The legs came down off the desk. "Plead him down to assault when the man has clearly committed the crime?"

She bounced the pencil harder, this time against the blotter, listening. Then she said, "Yes . . . I know the story. But the guy's got seven priors, what do you want me to do? . . ."

I surveyed her office. Family pictures of a mother and father, brothers and sisters. Priscilla with her father and brothers in a powerboat on a big body of water, maybe the Chesapeake Bay. Diplomas, a B.A. in history from Wesleyan, J.D. from Syracuse. Athletic awards, track.

She wrinkled her nose. "Okay, okay, I'll see what we can work out. But we may be restricted by mandatory sentencing . . . yes . . . yes . . . you know it. I'll see you at the house." She cradled the receiver into the console on her desk.

"Jerk!" she said. Then by way of explanation she added, "Ex-boyfriend."

"Hard if you have to be one too."

"I suppose . . . So, sit down, Mr. Pavlicek. As you can see, staff around here all leave promptly at five." She turned to her computer and started typing something. When she finished she turned back to me.

"I don't imagine Jake Toronto knows about this ex-boyfriend," I said.

She sighed. "You're nosy, you know that?"

"Comes with the many talents required to do my job."

"Well for your information Jake does know about him. He's encouraged me to get back together with the guy in fact."

"Jake would do that."

She flipped open her appointment book and made a

note. "Anyway, we're not here to talk about my love life, are we?"

"Not unless you want to."

"You want to know about your daughter's case."

"That would be nice."

"Well her legal prognosis is, in a word, murky. The truth is I can't see that we have a real solid case just yet, unless we come up with other evidence or can somehow prove your daughter knew about the cocaine hidden under her wheel well. It wasn't even inside the car. Anybody could have put it there. If she hadn't tried to avoid arrest, we might even have had to release her by now. That, plus the extenuating circumstances."

"Extenuating circumstances?"

"Right. You, for one, finding Dewayne Turner's body. I've already gone over the state police reports—"

"Yes, in fact I was hoping—"

"And then there's . . . the other matter . . ."

"Other matter?"

"The whole racial issue could be a powder keg. Especially for me. Anyone can see that."

"You sound like you don't want this case, counselor."

"Yeah, well part of me does and part of me doesn't, because ever since Turner disappeared, the African-American community around here's been kicking up a fuss—not that I blame them—and Cowan, maybe to cover his own butt, has been telling me he's suspicious of your little girl. You did know she was with Turner and about the threat she made this last time when he was arrested, didn't you?"

My nod was a lie. Why hadn't Nicole told me? That's what I needed to find out.

"But Cowan ran the Turner kid in and let Nicole go free."

"That's right. They arrested him for little cause as far as I can tell," she said. "And no one's seen him since . . . that is, until you found him."

"Police misconduct, prosecutor?"

She stared at me for a long moment. Then she leaned forward and folded her arms. "You know, Jake and I have talked some about what happened to you two up there in New York."

"You mean we three. Don't forget, Cat was there too."

"Yes, but he didn't pull the trigger. He didn't have to live with the—"

"Doubt."

"Yes. The doubt."

I examined my fingernails. One needed cleaning. "So what do you think, counselor? Were we closet racists? Tinderboxes, just waiting to ignite?"

"Jake wasn't. I'm convinced of that," she said.

"But someone else might have been?"

"I didn't say that." She bounced her pencil against the blotter once more. "I don't know you well enough yet to form an opinion."

At another time, with another woman, I might have suggested that could be arranged. Not now. Not with Priscilla Thomasen, attractive as she was.

"Fair enough," I said. "But I'm not sure I like the sound of all this."

"I'm not sure I would either, sitting in your chair."

"Exactly when were Nicole and Dewayne Turner picked up?"

"Two or three weeks ago. You can go over and check the arrest log, if you'd like."

"No wonder Cowan is so concerned about the appearance of racism."

"Appearance is one thing," she said. "Proof is another."

"So you want me to help you prove it, if it's true."

"I didn't say that."

"Was Turner still dealing?"

She sighed and looked down at her desk. "There's the tricky part. I don't think he was. You'll see what I mean when you meet his family, especially Carla, his mother.

Their story is that Dewayne found Jesus and turned his life around. Not only had he stopped selling, but they say he was trying to save some of those addicts he used to supply."

"Maybe one of them took major exception to his preaching," I said.

"Maybe. But that doesn't explain how his body ended up where you found it."

Nor a lot of other things, I thought. "So where's that leave Nicole?"

The Commonwealth's attorney chewed on her lip. "I've been honest with you about her case, but I think it's better, until we figure things out, that she remain where she is for now, even if it is in Cowan's jail."

"You sure she's safe there?"

"More sure than if she were on the street."

"Her lawyer may not stand for it."

"Radley?" She rolled her eyes. "I could charge her for jaywalking and get it past him."

"Extenuating circumstances?"

She smiled. "Uh-huh. Especially when she was toting enough coke to light up half the state."

"You've told me a lot. Awful generous to a potential racist."

"Maybe we'll find out for sure if that's what you are . . . That's a big word, you know—*racist*. You don't grow up black in this country without hearing it almost every day. I guess I've come to believe a racist's ultimate victim is himself. He hates what he is so badly he has to turn that hate on somebody else."

"But now *you* wield the power."

"I don't look at it that way. The law is the law. Black or white, racist or no . . ."

"All right, counselor. You've got my vote. But as long as we're sharing problems and the law, I've got one for you. Suppose you know this particular private investigator, who, say for example, may have tampered with evidence in a criminal case."

"I'm all ears."

"His motives were good, mind you. He was only trying to find out the truth and protect someone he loves."

"Uh-huh."

"What would you say might happen to him?"

"I'd say that, on the surface, this individual has a serious problem. But as a prosecutor I might be willing to consider—"

"Extenuating circumstances?"

"Yes."

"But what if the police don't see it the same way?"

She straightened some papers on her desk. "I'm both cautious and respectful when dealing with the police."

"As well you should be. Can you keep them off me?"

She stared at me for a long hard second. "I honestly don't know."

I nodded. "Not to take advantage of your kindness, counselor, but what can you tell me about Kevin Weems?"

"Weems? Isn't he Nicole's mother's boyfriend?"

"You got it. Know anything about his background?"

"Not really. Why?"

"I need to check him out."

"Well I can't officially . . . you suspect him of something?"

"I suspect him of a lot of things, just like everybody else."

"I'll see what I can do."

"Thank you."

"Do you still get along with Camille Rhodes?"

"Reasonably. It works best when we minimize contact."

"I see," she said. "It's a shame, though, isn't it? I mean, your Nicole is a beautiful girl."

I said nothing.

"We better get going to the Turners' . . . Have you eaten?"

"I picked up a burger at one of the fast-food joints down the street."

"Blah." She grimaced. "Rather starve. I can stop and get something on the way. We'll go out through the front, the way you came in. Just give me a minute to close up shop here and check the back."

I made my out to the waiting room again. The shadows had lengthened. The air conditioner still moaned. I picked up a copy of *Smithsonian* and was flipping through the pictures when I heard her panicked voice: "Pavlicek!"

I dropped the magazine and bounded toward her office again. My hand was on my gun.

"Down here at the end of the hall!"

In a dim back room with a kitchen table and coffeemaker she stood trembling next to a half-open door that led to a parking lot.

"There was somebody in here," she said.

"Maybe someone from the staff just forgot—"

"No." She pointed. The door handle was broken and there were deep gouges in the wood.

"Did you get a look at them?"

"No, I heard footsteps and—"

But I wasn't waiting to hear the rest of her answer. I drew my weapon and stepped out the door.

The heat hit me like an ocean wave. The small lot in back was empty, save for a yellow Saab, which I took to be the Commonwealth attorney's; everything was enveloped in shadows cast by the building next door.

The driveway was made of crushed stone. I waited and listened. At first, there was nothing but some distant traffic noise mixed with the sounds made by a flock of starlings that had settled in some trees a block or so away. Then I heard them: two quick steps crunching on the gravel in front.

I moved as fast as I could around the side of the brownstone, keeping my back to the wall. I was in darkness now, hopefully concealed from whomever I was pursuing. When I made it to the front, however, no one was there. My truck was parked against the curb just as I had left it. The street appeared empty except for a couple cars that had been behind it when I pulled in. Some instinct or voice inside said to move toward the bed of the pickup and crouch low, which undoubtedly saved my life.

A single shot from a high-velocity rifle whizzed just above my shoulder and thudded into a bed of roses on an embankment. No other sound—the shooter must have been using a silencer. Dropping, I returned one quick round in the direction from which the bullet had come, and scrambled to safety behind the truck.

Several seconds passed. Then over on the next block, an engine roared to life and tires squealed. I stood and sprinted toward the sound; ran into a high fence and had to detour; bounded a hedge, knocked over a bicycle, and almost tripped over a garden hose. Reaching the next street, I was too late to get a make and model, let alone a plate number or glimpse of the driver. The car was already rounding the corner at the end of the block.

I walked back to the office. "It must have just happened. The staff all go in and out this way. They only left about an hour ago and they certainly would have noticed something like this." The prosecutor had her hands on her hips as she examined the broken lock.

"Which means whoever it was must have come in while you were on the phone or while you and I were talking."

"Damn that noisy old air conditioner. I've already called 911. You sure you're okay?"

"Fine." Not that there was anything fine about someone shooting at me again after all these years, but it seemed like the thing to say. "Anything obvious missing?"

"Nothing that I can see."

"You think our voices down the hall could have been heard from this room?"

"With my office door open, definitely."

Sirens died and cars screeched to a halt out front. Two deputies followed by none other than Sheriff Cowan came down the hall with weapons drawn.

"It's all right, sheriff," Priscilla said. "The bad guys are long gone."

Cowan glared at me as he holstered his gun. "What the hell's the idea of discharging a firearm in the village, Pavlicek?"

The CA stepped in. "I take full responsibility for Mr. Pavlicek's actions, sheriff. I think if your forensic team digs around in that rose bed next door, you'll find a rifle bullet."

"They used a silencer, Cowan," I said. "This was no amateur."

"Uh-huh." He looked at the jimmied door. "What happened here?"

"Mr. Pavlicek had an appointment to see me to ask some questions about his daughter's case. When we finished, I came back here to check the lock before leaving, I found that an intruder had just exited the building. Mr. Pavlicek gave chase. He was fired upon and returned fire in self-defense."

"That your story, Pavlicek?"

"It's what happened."

"Either of you get a look at this, uh, intruder?"

We both shook our heads.

He nodded. "We'll check for the bullet. In the meantime, counselor, I'm not too inspired by the idea of Mr. Trigger-happy here floating around my town loaded for bear."

Priscilla thought about it for a moment. "It's a legal handgun, isn't it, Mr. Pavlicek?"

"Yes."

"I see no problem then with him continuing to carry it, sheriff. That is, uh, unless you have reasonable grounds for accusing him of using the weapon in the course of committing a crime."

Cowan gave a wry smile. "Well, I don't know. We may have to send it off to the lab in Richmond or something to cross-check with the slug we pull out of those bushes."

"I see no need of that. Again, I'll take responsiblity."

He smirked and shook his head and went about the business of securing the scene with his men.

16

Priscilla Thomasen handled the Saab deftly, like she was used to working the manual transmission, as I followed her down Main Street past the sheriff's department and a row of stores. She stopped at a new delicatessen I remembered had once been a hardware store, a neo-Masonic Temple with a row of tall dormers upstairs and two huge plate glass windows on the main level facing the street. Now, instead of nuts and bolts, the tiled displays served up fresh meat and seafood, huge wheels of yellow and white cheeses, and buckets of pasta salad. She spoke, laughing, with a fat man behind the counter. When she came out a couple minutes later, she carried a white paper bag and drink.

We followed Main Street to the edge of town where the pavement forked. To the right the road turned into state asphalt. Down a hill to the left it ran into Moony's Hollow Road, a stretch of bottom land dotted with old elms. The river reshaped the topography here every few years. During the years before civil rights, Moony's Hollow had been where most of the black population lived in Leonardston. Not much had changed since then, except that more had filtered into the middle- and upper-class sections of town.

Kids playing jump rope eyed us with mild curiosity as we passed. We pulled up to a trim bungalow, porch in front, dark green shutters, deck in the rear. Six or seven cars were parked in the driveway.

"A welcoming committee?" I said as we both stepped out.

"Relatives. Funeral's tomorrow."

"By the way, thanks for what you did back there with the sheriff."

"You earned it. And besides, he's an idiot."

We clambered up the front steps, crossed the porch, and I waited while she knocked on the flimsy screen door. The heavier door behind it opened slowly inward, but no one appeared to be pulling on the handle. Through the mesh we could see a hallway and a dining room and several people milling about, talking. Some drank from paper cups. A few saw us and looked up and smiled as we entered, but most simply went on with their talk. I looked behind the front door to see who had opened it and there stood a boy of maybe eight or nine, dressed in a dark three-piece suit, white shirt, and tie. He smiled.

"And what might be your name, young man?"

"Virgil," he said.

"Great job on the door, Virg."

He nodded proudly. "Mama say we gotta be hos-pita-ble. Cause even though Dewayne, he been messin' wid drugs and got hisself kilt, she says that was only his choice, and even though it was a bad one, we still a family."

"Sounds like your mama knows what she's talking about."

"Yes, sir."

Priscilla was across the room already speaking with a tall, bald man wearing a sport coat. She motioned for me to join her.

"Frank, this is Graham, Dewayne's older brother," she said. I shook his hand.

"Pleasure, Mr. Pavlicek," he said.

"The pleasure's mine, Mr. Turner. I'm sorry about your brother."

He thanked me for my condolences.

"Graham's an actuary for an insurance company down in Greensboro," Priscilla said.

"How's your mother holding up?" I asked.

"Best as can be expected, considering. It wasn't even a year ago, you know, we buried Daddy."

"Mr. Turner died of cancer," Priscilla explained.

"I'm sorry," I said.

Another man approached. He was shorter than Graham and had a full head of hair, but he had the same build and strong chin and long fingers. He wore a brown suit with a maroon rep tie.

"Graham, you know who this guy is?" The new arrival casually tried to slip an arm over Priscilla's shoulder. It didn't take a brain surgeon to figure out he meant me. His demeanor made it apparent that he knew me, and, unfortunately, I remembered him too. Warren Turner was a local newspaper reporter who had decided there was a scoop somewhere in Jake's and my move to Leonardston. He had never found anything to publish, but that hadn't stopped him from trying. I wondered what he thought now that Cat was back in town. Maybe since I had moved away, he had given up his digging. Priscilla looked uncomfortable and gently pushed his arm away.

Graham said: "Mr. Pavlicek, this is my brother Warren."

"I know Warren," I said. I stuck out my hand but the newspaper man ignored it.

"The past is still the past, Pavlicek. Don't think any of us have forgotten," he said.

Priscilla looked embarrassed.

"Look, Warren, that was a different time, a different place. Besides, this isn't about any of that," Graham said.

"The hell it ain't." He practiced his best glare on me. I tried to look neutral.

"Yes, sir," Warren said. "Maybe I need to line up an interview with Mr. Pavlicek here, do a little expose on why he's back in town. Seems to me we have all sorts of possibilities and connections."

"Don't you think maybe some other time?" Graham said.

Priscilla grabbed my arm and started to turn us away. "Come on," she said, "Mrs. Turner is waiting to talk with us."

Warren tried his glare on Priscilla too, but to no effect. Next, I supposed, he would try it out on Virgil. Maybe the youngster was performing door duty incorrectly.

The CA led me around a corner into a narrow pantry that led into the kitchen.

"Pleasant chap," I said.

"He means well. Just gets carried away sometimes." She surveyed the room ahead looking for the mother.

"He seemed to know you pretty well too."

She nodded. "The jerk, ex-boyfriend, remember?"

"Oh. No conflicts of interest, counselor?"

She ignored me and continued scanning the room ahead. Her voice dropped to a whisper. "Here's Mrs. Turner. Shhh . . ."

At a table surrounded by a dozen others, a rotund woman sat, her eyes closed, her cheeks full and radiant. The people in the room had formed a semicircle around her and were holding hands. A dark man with blue spectacles and a mustache, dressed in a dark suit like Virgil's, was just beginning to lead them in prayer.

We hung back, outside the room. It was an awkward position to be in, standing apart yet intimate with someone else's entreaty to the Almighty. Priscilla rocked back on her heels, and we watched the man praying.

He prayed for Carla Turner. He prayed for her living children too, even Warren. He was specific in his requests, but he didn't just tick off a wish-list for God, as if the big guy were Santa Claus on-call, the way some preachers do on television. What surprised me was a prayer he offered in thanksgiving for Dewayne Turner's life. From what I knew of the dead dealer, I couldn't see a whole lot for which to be thankful.

When he finished the folks around the table all hugged the woman I took to be Mrs. Turner. The little crowd began to disperse. Priscilla took my arm and pulled me forward into the room.

The large woman beamed when she saw us. "Priscilla, so thoughtful of you to come." She was maybe sixty and exuded an aura that seemed to envelope everyone around her.

"Carla, this is Frank Pavlicek. The private investigator I was telling you about."

"Oh I know who Mr. Pavlicek is, honey. You forget, he used to live around here. And I never forget a face." She reached out and took my hand.

I said, "I'm sorry for the occasion."

For a millisecond a raging form of sadness seemed to sweep across her face, but it passed just as quickly as it had appeared. Whatever demons had conquered her Dewayne, they appeared to have been all but banished from her presence now. There was mourning in her eyes—it made them oddly beautiful—but there was also resolve that could have only sprung from enduring unbearable sadness.

"If this is not a good time . . ." I heard myself saying.

"Oh no, no. Come and sit down here, young man. Rest your bones. Have you met our Reverend Lori?"

The man with the blue eyeglasses had been speaking in low tones with someone else. He quickly excused himself and stepped forward, as if his spiritual antenna had already picked up the thread of our conversation.

"Sister Turner," he said.

"Reverend Lori, this is Mr. Frank Pavlicek, you know, Camille Rhodes's first husband, who now lives . . . where is it, Mr. Pavlicek?"

"Charlottesville."

"Oh yes, over in Charlottesville."

We shook hands. His gaze bore into me, not with accusation, but with question. I hoped mine gave the correct reply.

"Miss Thomasen tells us you may be looking into Dewayne's murder," the pastor said.

"Not officially." I glanced at Priscilla. "I'm, uh, assisting the police."

He nodded. "Uh-huh. How much official time do you think the investigation is going to get?" Clearly the Reverend had not spent all of his time behind a pulpit.

"I guess that'll be up to the sheriff."

"Did you know that Dewayne had returned to the church?" he said.

"That's what I've been led to understand."

"Came forward at an altar call. Turned around a hundred and eighty degrees. Was even beginning to try to reach out to addicts, you know. It was becoming his ministry."

A ministry? I had seen jailhouse conversions before, some genuine but most not. Kids in trouble trying to beat a rap.

Lori seemed to read my mind. "Oh I can assure you, he changed, Mr. Pavlicek. The Bible says we become a new creature in Christ. It's something that won't be showing up on his autopsy. But that young man has a new, perfect body now. I guarantee it."

"Amen," someone intoned from across the room.

A perfect body. The remains of Dewayne Turner transforming into something beautiful. It was a radical thought, all right.

I turned to Carla Turner. Her eyes were moist.

"I know this must be difficult for you right now, ma'am, but do you feel up to answering a few questions?"

Someone produced a tissue and handed it to her. She nodded and dabbed at her cheeks.

I looked at Priscilla again, who nodded.

"Did anyone you know have a big enough problem with your son to want him dead?" I asked.

Her lip trembled. "Dewayne did a lot of bad in his past, Mr. Pavlicek. Stealin'. Sellin' drugs. I suppose it could have been a whole bunch of different people."

"Forgiven," the pastor said. "He was forgiven."

She reached out and the minister patted her shoulder and held her hand.

"What about past friends or acquaintances? He still hang out with any of his old crowd?"

She shook her head. "Not that I know of."

"A young woman named Regan Quinn?"

Her eyes stayed blank.

"Was he working?"

"Yes," she said. "For the church."

I looked at the pastor. "Like I told you," he said. "The young man was developing a ministry."

"He receive a salary?"

"A small one. Our church is not very well-to-do. You're welcome to take a look at our finances if you'd like."

I nodded.

I took out a business card and wrote Jake's number on the back before handing it to Carla Turner. "If you think of anything, anything at all that might be significant, feel free to give me a call at this number. You can also talk to Ms. Thomasen here, of course, or Jake Toronto."

"What about the sheriff's office?" she asked.

I looked at Priscilla. "We'd prefer you contact me directly for now," the Commonwealth's attorney said.

"All right," Carla said. "What will you do when you find whoever did this?"

"That will be up to the police and the courts."

"Neither of which have ever been too friendly to the black man." It was the glaring Warren again, entering the room. But even his demeanor softened in the presence of his mother. "You okay, Mama?"

"Of course, honey. Of course." She didn't turn to look at him.

"Well for now, if anybody else knows something that might help, you know where to find me," I said. "Mrs. Turner, I hope you won't mind if I attend Dewayne's funeral tomorrow."

"You'd be most welcome," she said.

"One other thing, Miss Thomasen may not have told you this, but I was the one who found your son's body."

Suddenly you could hear a pin drop in the room. Warren started to say something but his mother held up her hand. Carla Turner looked at me and nodded, her smile a mixture of confusion and the dark wave I'd seen pass over her earlier. I took the chain with the cross from my pocket and held it out for her. "I found this in his hand," I said. "Do you recognize it?"

"Yes . . ." She choked back a sob. "They give them out at our church, to the young people."

"Then I've found the right place for it." I placed the fragile symbol in her hand. It was illegal to give it to her. Priscilla must have known that too, but she said nothing. Carla Turner's brown eyes glowed.

The prosecutor followed me back out to my truck. "I didn't tell Mrs. Turner, or anyone else yet, about your suspicions concerning your daughter," she said.

"Thanks. But I wanted to let her know something."

"This is about more than just your daughter though, isn't it?" she said.

"It is now."

"You know he may act like a jerk at times, but Warren might be able to help us. He wrote a series of articles a couple years ago on the gang Dewayne was running with at the time—never used his brother's or anybody else's real name, of course."

"You want me to talk with him? We aren't exactly pals."

She shrugged. "Up to you."

"You trust me now then?"

She said nothing.

"Because of Jake?"

She shook her head. "I had to meet you for myself . . . you're pretty sure whoever broke into my office earlier was there to eavesdrop on us, aren't you?"

"Uh-huh."

"And it was probably the same person or persons that killed Dewayne."

I nodded. "What do you think, counselor?"

"I think Carla and the Reverend Lori like you." She stared at me for a moment.

"What's there not to like?" I said.

She watched me back the truck into the street. Then she turned and went into the house again. The same kids were now playing ball in the street down the block. They stood aside to let me pass as if I were nothing but a minor interruption in their game.

As I made my way back toward Main Street, I picked up a pair of headlights tailing me. I purposefully made a wrong turn and drove around a block just to see if they followed and they did. When we reached the main thoroughfare I did the same thing and it happened once more. Only this time I pulled to the curb right in front of a large van, cut my lights, and waited. After a few seconds the car came creeping past and when I spotted it I waved; though the driver tried to act as if he hadn't seen me and quickly hit the gas.

Curiouser and curiouser—talk about standing out like a sore thumb. It was Kevin Weems in his Porsche.

That night I called Special Agent William Ferrier at home. He answered it himself.

"I was about to give up on you. Decided you were taking advantage of my generosity." A ball game blared in the background. The TV volume lowered.

"Sorry for not getting back to you sooner."

"You're in Leonardston, right?"

"In the area, yes."

"So, you ready to tell me what you got?"

There was a long pause. "I don't really have anything more than you do."

He cleared his throat. "That's bullshit and you know it. I want to know what you were doing mucking around my crime scene."

The truth was if I gave him the dollar bill now, I wasn't really giving him much. The sunglasses hadn't amounted to anything. Nicole had been straight with me: Dewayne must've had a pair just like hers. Still, I wasn't ready to add more fuel to my daughter's case, at least not yet.

"I was naturally curious," I said. "I got a look at the kid's wallet before I took your people back out to the site. And when I saw he was from Leonardston, I was even more curious."

"S'that right."

"I should've told you sooner."

"Uh-huh. I hear your daughter's in some trouble over there."

"Yes. Did you also hear someone tried to waste me today with a rifle and a silencer?"

He sighed. "I heard. Let's quit the games, Pavlicek. You know we know your daughter was involved with Turner. You in the picture only makes it harder on you and her."

"What do you want me to do then?"

"Lay off, before you get yourself killed. Give us everything you got and let us do our job."

"You got any kids, Ferrier?"

"Yeah, why?"

"Then you know I can't do that."

He didn't speak for a moment. "Could mean other trouble for you," he said matter-of-factly.

"I know."

"The sheriff down there's not exactly a big fan of you and your buddies."

"Yeah, well Cowan has got his own problems. Can I ask you something?"

He said nothing so I forged ahead: "Your medical examiner find any evidence that Dewayne Turner had been beaten before he was murdered?"

He blew out a sigh. "No. Why?"

"The Commonwealth's attorney down here is looking into allegations of police misconduct."

"Just great. What are you, a magnet for this kind of stuff, Pavlicek?"

I said nothing.

"This is not looking good."

"What are you planning to do?" I asked.

"We'll be down there day after tomorrow. I'm especially looking forward to meeting your old pals. Meantime, I'll be in touch with Sheriff Cowan. I'm recommending he bring you in for questioning, and, if necessary, take you into custody for your own protection and on suspicion of obstructing justice."

"Oh, is that all?"

"You're making your own bed, Pavlicek. I've got six other cases just like the Turner kid's waiting for me at the office tomorrow. I got enough problems without having to worry about you."

"But you can't expect me to just sit around here with my daughter in jail, Ferrier."

"How do I know you, your pals, and this daughter of yours, didn't waste this druggie, and now aren't trying to pull a scam?"

"You don't."

"Damn right I don't . . . the ninth inning's about to start." The TV volume grew louder again. "Anything else?"

"Yes . . . I'd say from where I sit you're a pretty fair cop."

"Yeah, right. *Semper fi.*"

17

Birds, by almost any measure, live precarious lives. Watch them flit about, ever mindful of danger, or scatter in panic along the beach. Diseases and hunger haunt them. Predators—everything from crocodiles to the family cat—snuff them out. That millions roam the earth at any given time speaks more to their tenacity and powers of procreation than to their brawn. Of all other creatures, only man, in his mechanistic and artificial way, is able to approximate their natural power of flight, but birds pay a heavy price for their freedom. Maybe such vulnerability explains why raptors are viewed as such symbols of courage. In their own way they are just as vulnerable as their feathered brethren, but they fight back with a single-minded determination to thrive.

I doubt Toronto considered any such thoughts as Jersey, backed by the brilliant morning sun, alighted on his outstretched glove. She was a striking specimen, a gray ghost indeed, as Jake had called her, with a large round head, dark streaks across her breast, and piercing red eyes. It was a perfect autumn morning, blue sky with no breeze. The trees, their leaves turned shades of red and gold, hung heavy with dew. Soon the valley Jake and Jersey called home would feel its first frost of the season. Already steam curled like smoke from our mouths.

"There's my beauty." Jake deftly slipped Jersey's hood over her head and tightened it with his teeth as he secured her jesses. "A decent workout this morning.

Won't be long now, girl." He fed her from his glove. "She's ready, Frank. She is ready."

We always flew the red-tail separate from the goshawk. They favored different terrain in which to hunt, for one thing: Armistead preferred the open clearing whereas Jersey bound to game more readily in the deep forest. There was also the risk that the buteos might see in each other an enemy or an opportunity for a potential meal. The gos was slightly smaller but had the more ferocious reputation. I would have put even money on such a fight.

I shook my head. "You know it's a pleasure to watch you work with her. Sometimes I feel like I'm overreaching with Armistead, maybe trying too hard."

"Remember what they tell hoop players, even the pros," he said. "You gotta let the game come to you."

I understood what he meant. Part of learning to be a falconer meant learning to work in harmony with the bird. Not necessarily control, but partnership was the goal.

Armistead preened, happily back in her mews, having already enjoyed her outing and morning meal. We climbed a gentle slope through the woods, Jersey riding on Toronto's arm, Hercules bounding ahead of us, the retriever's nose to the ground. Our boots crashed through the old, dead leaves, making noise far out of proportion to our size. We were beaters here, not hunters, clumsy oafs compared to the hawk.

"So you caught someone in Priscilla's office and they tried to take you off the table," Toronto said.

"That's right."

"Figure it was one of Morelli's people?"

"My top guess. The question is, why? And what were they after in the CA's office?"

"What about the sheriff?" Cowan had called at the crack of dawn to say he wanted me to come into his office for questioning. It was not a request, he said. I had managed to stall him by telling him the truth: I might be headed back to Charlottesville. And by letting him believe a lie: I might be backing off a little.

"I'm not sure I trust him either."

"There's also this Weems character hanging with your ex and trying to follow you. You find out any more about him?"

"Not yet, but I'm about to."

"You know I've been thinking about lunch at Cat's later," Toronto said. "What did you say he told you about going to meet with Fuad?"

"Old wounds."

"Right. Old wounds . . . Maybe there's more to this situation with Nicky than what we're seeing."

"What do you mean?"

"Like I told you, Morelli's people up in New York were supplying Dewayne Turner."

"Right."

"If they killed Turner, framed Nicole, and are now after you too, maybe this thing with Fuad is just like a diversion or something. Something to screw with our minds."

"So Morelli's people are in Fuad's computer program?"

"No. No, it's just . . ."

"Hey, but aren't you still curious about what happened that night back in New York?"

"Yeah."

"I think the current buzzword is closure."

"You mean like maybe show for sure that the kid with the fancy footwear was the one who did Singer. I never liked shoes as evidence. You walk down the street in Manhattan sometime. There must be millions of shoes."

"Exactly."

We broke into an unmowed meadow, long gone to seed, above Jake's farm. From up here you could see for miles. A ring of small hills encompassed his little valley and beyond them, taller mountains to the western horizon.

"So if we nail down the ballistics thing," he said, "that's going to make our shooting Balazar, what, more justified?"

"Maybe . . . Plus, I told Cowan I was leaving this afternoon and Marsh will be back home in C'ville later today. Going over there gives me an excuse to take her out to dinner too."

"Okay, Jedi, count me in."

We had reached the back of the mews. Jake raised small quail to feed to Jersey when she wasn't hunting. There was a small wire enclosure beneath a giant maple to one side of the lawn. Maybe a hundred of the immature birds bustled about in the shade. I waited until Jake had finished getting Jersey set up inside her own room.

"Speaking of which, Priscilla Thomasen seems like quite a woman."

"*Fine* ain't the word for it."

"You talk to her often?"

He paused. "We don't, so much, talk, I guess."

"Right," I said. "And how often does this occur?"

He shrugged. "I don't know, every couple of weeks. Sometimes more."

"I guess you don't have to worry about things like politics."

"No-o-o."

"You aren't . . . worried about her personally, though? I mean, in her position and all."

He laughed. "I'd be more worried if I was that person who broke into her office yesterday."

We circled around to the front of the trailer. Hercules had already mounted the deck, his tail switching like mad, and was lustily drinking from his bowl. I could still smell the remnant of Jake's morning coffee aging in the brewer.

"I'm going to head back into town," I said, "and try to avoid the sheriff while I tie up a few loose ends."

"You going to Dewayne Turner's funeral?"

"That too."

Toronto himself avoided funerals like the plague. He turned and was checking a weather station he had rigged on the deck between an Outer Banks hammock and an old charcoal kettle grill. "That's good. You got 'em all off balance, I can tell."

Nicole's arraignment later that morning was nothing short of a disaster. I never even had a chance to make my case.

Lawyer Radley showed up at the last minute, his eyes looking bloodshot and nervous. The judge was an ex-military type, who still had the crewcut to prove it, and it was obvious he had no affection, let alone respect for my daughter's attorney. He took a hard line on drug cases too, apparently, and when Priscilla Thomasen introduced the additional evidence regarding Dewayne Turner's murder—Nicole's threat and the potential match of the cocaine samples—he ordered the prisoner held without bail for the time being, and scheduled a hearing for later in the week, at which time further evidence would be considered.

The only bright spot was a brief chat I had with Priscilla. When I told her about Weems following me from the Turners' house the night before, she went to her briefcase and came back with the kind of info a private investigator can seek his teeth into.

18

I sat at a terminal in Leonardston's public library, grateful to the local taxpayers.

A computer and a phone line have become a ticket to the world. Make a few calls, find out a Social Security number. Or, as in my case, acquire it, along with a few other tidbits, courtesy of a friendly prosecutor. Then plug in and suddenly you're able to discover things most people would never want known.

Take Kevin Weems, for example. I learned that he had, quite legally, changed his name. His original one had been Kevin Pauling and he had, just as he said, been born in a suburb of Atlanta, gone to Emory for a couple years before dropping out to go to work as a stockbroker. Maybe the name change had something to do with his marriage, subsequent bankruptcy, and messy divorce. Not to mention overdue child support payments. Georgia had just begun posting its most grievous offenders' mugs on-line and there he was, in living color, along with a few hundred other upstanding citizens of the peach state.

None of which made him a murderer. Most serious crooks don't bother legally changing their names; it's far too easy to set up and use an alias. Besides, for all his hulking demeanor, I somehow couldn't see Weems as a killer, nor imagine him skillfully and silently popping the Commonwealth's attorney's locked back door. But as long as I was tying up loose ends, it certainly couldn't hurt to flesh out his true intentions.

I went through the same computer process with Sheriff Peter Cowan, Camille Rhodes, Regan Quinn, even Warren Turner. Those searches took a lot less time. Except for Camille's divorce from me, in the world of electronic records, court filings, and credit reports, the lawman, the stripper, the reporter, and my ex-wife were all squeaky clean.

A few doors down from the library, the *Leonardston Standard* had an office on Main Street. I had once known the editor, but the paper had changed hands at least a couple of times since then. It was like a lot of small-town weeklies, I suppose, surviving more on the loyalty of its readership than on consistent profitability.

The building was made of flesh-colored brick in need of cleaning. A large picture window faced the street. The paper's moniker dominated the door, stenciled in palace script across the glass, though the blinds were closed tight at the moment to keep out the morning sun.

Warren Turner probably wouldn't be working today. After all, it was the day of his younger brother's funeral. But a sign on the door said OPEN, COME IN. I did.

A cute gal wearing a microphone and headset sat talking behind a reception desk. She had long black hair and red fingernails and wore a thin halter top that revealed much of her curvaceous upper body. I waited until she was through.

"Yes?" Her eyes flashed brightly in my direction when she hung up, as if she'd only just noticed my presence.

"I was hoping to speak with Warren Turner, if he's in. My name is Frank Pavlicek."

"Pavlicek. Are you related to Nicole?"

"Yes."

"An uncle?" she asked. Born newshound, I guess.

"Her father," I said.

"But I thought her father was . . . Oh . . ." She looked at me suspiciously. "Wait just one minute."

She pushed a button on her console, which seemed to

have about three or four lines glowing at the moment. When someone picked up she said: "Mr. Solomon? A Mr. Pavlicek is here to see Warren . . . Yes . . . I'll ask him to wait."

She put the receiver down. I gave her a hopeful look.

"Mr. Turner is in a meeting with the editor right now, but they're almost through," she said. "He asked if you could wait."

"Absolutely."

"There are magazines on the table." She smiled and pointed to an empty row of padded chairs hugging the windowsill next to a stained coffeetable stacked with popular newsmagazines.

I picked up a periodical, sat down, and started reading. Anyone who tried to digest the mounds of newspeak that flooded the country these days was either a sadist or a maniac. Most of it had become garrulous to me, bland psycho-babble, contributing to, rather than ameliorating, the culture's woes.

About five minutes later I heard someone coming down a hallway that opened into the reception area. It was Warren Turner. He crossed his arms when he came into view.

"So what can I do for you, Pavlicek? Dewayne's funeral is this afternoon in case you forgot."

"I didn't forget," I said. "Just wanted to ask you more about what you think might have happened to him."

He eyed me with curiosity for a moment or two. "How long will it take?"

"Couple of minutes."

He thought about it. "Okay."

Warren, it turned out, didn't have an office. No one at the paper did, except the editor. The rest of the staff, all half dozen of them or so, worked with aging computers in a large room in the back, their separate spaces defined by five-foot-tall cubicles. Warren's was in the middle. He borrowed a chair from an absent neighbor for me to use.

"Suppose you look at this as doing penance," he said.

"Come again?"

"Your investigation. Helping out Priscilla. No one is going to look very hard into the killing of another black teenager who'd been involved in drugs, whether he was still dealing or not. So it's penance, isn't it, for what you did back up in New York?"

"Are we on the record?"

"Not unless you want to be."

"I didn't come down here as penance for anything. What happened to Toronto and me thirteen years ago happened because we were doing our job."

"Maybe there was a problem with the job then." He leaned back in his chair and glared again.

"Look, I didn't come here to debate the merits of police service with you."

"Oh, I get it. You've had a change of heart and now you're only going to do work for public defenders and ACLU types."

I smiled. "Is that what you're hoping?"

"Maybe I *should* put you on the record."

"We both know there are a thousand ways to put something into an article without using a direct quote."

His turn to smile. "Okay. We're probably not going to end up liking each other. So what do you want from me?"

"For starters, just what is it that makes you so suspicious of Sheriff Cowan? Other than his being an integral cog in the patriarchal white male power structure, that is."

"You forget," he said. "Priscilla's part of the patriarchy now too."

"Sort of eased her way in there, didn't she?"

He pursed his lips. "First thing is, Cowan, from what I can tell, had no grounds to arrest Dewayne except pure harassment. I'm certain Dewayne hadn't done anything illegal for some time."

"But he had in the past."

"Right."

"This church thing . . . his conversion was genuine then?"

"As genuine as they come."

"I take it you're not a believer."

"I know Dewayne was."

"Priscilla told me you wrote a series about Dewayne's old gang. You still know any of those kids?"

He nodded. "But don't expect me to compromise any of my sources."

"All right. Maybe you can tell me, though, how they felt about Dewayne quitting the life?"

"Maybe. But I think you'd better ask them that question yourself."

"I thought you said you wouldn't compromise them."

"Oh, I won't. Compromise is one thing. Communication is another."

"They trust you?" I said.

"Some."

"You think you could arrange this . . . communication?"

"Maybe."

"Would it make sense to you if they were involved in Dewayne's killing?"

Someone turned on a copier across the room. "It makes sense, but that doesn't necessarily make it true." He wasn't going to be led where he didn't want to go.

"This a neighborhood gang, Moony's Hollow?"

"Not as far as I can tell. Guys are from all over."

"They deal in drugs?"

"What do you think?" he said. "For them it's the only way to buy all the junk they see pitched at them on TV."

"Can't be that big a dope market around here though, is there? I mean, it's not like we're near a major city."

"No. But these guys move around. They've got connections in D.C., Baltimore, New York, you name it," he said.

"New York, huh? I understand Dewayne had a northern supplier. Man named Morelli."

He shrugged. "I don't know anything about names from up there."

"So what's this gang like, a rural chapter or something?"

"These dudes are their own chapter. You'll see." He drummed his fingers on the desk.

"Let's get back to Dewayne. When he joined the church again, what'd he do, just up and quit the gang?"

He leaned back again and stretched. "Far as I know, that's about the gist of it."

"Did he have a girlfriend?"

"Dewayne? Not really. No one special."

"Did you know he asked my daughter for a date?"

"So?"

"There was something going on between the two of them. The sheriff claims she threatened to kill him and she's not talking."

He snickered. "I suppose that explains why he let her go that night then, and kept Dewayne locked up."

"Doesn't seem logical, does it?"

"Lot of things having to do with black folks and cops don't seem logical."

"I try not to dwell on it. How about Regan Quinn?"

"What about her?"

"You know who she is?"

"I know who she is," he said.

"Dewayne ever mention her?"

"Couple of times."

"He ever date her?"

"Hey, girls like her don't get taken out. Besides, I wasn't Dewayne's baby-sitter. You know what I mean?"

I nodded. "You loved him though?"

The question seemed to startle him. Maybe it was an unfair one to ask on the day of his brother's funeral. He turned his face away to keep me from seeing his eyes.

I gave him a few seconds. Then I said: "I'm sorry."

He still said nothing.

"You got anything else on the sheriff's department, anything solid?"

He looked at me again for a long moment. Finally he said: "I'm working on something."

"Priscilla working on it with you?"

"She told you about us, huh? I mean, before . . ."

"She mentioned it."

He bit his lower lip. "Now let me ask *you* a question or two, Pavlicek. How do I know you're not just trying to protect yourself or your daughter? Maybe the sheriff's department too? How do I know this whole thing isn't anything but another set-up?"

"I guess you don't," I said. "But if it helps you sleep any better, I didn't even know who the new sheriff was down here until my daughter called to tell me she'd been arrested. Besides, if they wanted a poster boy for a cover-up, it sure wouldn't be me."

He thought it over. "You were a cop though. Cops protect each other."

"Kind of like a gang."

He nodded.

I stood to leave. "Thanks for your time, Warren. I know it's a hard day. I'll see you at the church."

He held his hand up. "Hold on a minute . . ."

I waited.

"I heard what happened over at the CA's office . . . Okay, I'll try to set up a meeting for you with the 'bangers. But I want Priscilla in on it too."

Now we were getting somewhere. "That's gotta be up to her."

"Right. If she says it's okay, I'll try and set it up for tomorrow night. Soon enough?"

I nodded.

"You carry a gun?"

"Yes."

"You can't bring it with you if we go. These brothers don't play around."

We'll see about that, I thought, but I said nothing.

He was staring into the dust on his darkened computer screen. "What about other police agencies? Any involved besides the sheriff?"

"There's a state police investigator and his partner on the case. They'll be down here tomorrow."

"Good."

"You gonna do another story on this for the paper?"

He thought about it for a moment. "Not right now. Too many conflicts of interest."

"You and I both," I said.

19

Regan Quinn's house faced the steepest street in town, a narrow climb up a hillside where the trees and any other type of vegetation had mostly eroded away. Structures occupied only one side of the road, and even there precariously. Tall three-families with peeling paint and cantilevered foundations, craning into the electric blue. I could only imagine what the slope looked like after a rainstorm.

I parked behind a big UPS truck and a Toyota that looked like the car I had seen fleeing from a distance the day before. A few window air conditioners made noise from the building. Her apartment was on the second floor and I made a lot of noise myself on the stairs hoping that she would think I was the driver with a package. The bell sounded like a set of wind chimes from inside.

I heard fumbling and footsteps through the walls.

"Just a minute!" Her voice was high-pitched but muted.

There was no peephole. She turned the lock, undid the chain, and pulled open the door.

"Regan Quinn?"

Squinting. Her face dull from sleep. Long blond hair. Narrow waist with hips poured into blue jeans. Confused. "Mr. Pavlicek? I thought you were the delivery driver."

"No, ma'am." I showed her my license. "Just have a few questions I'd like to ask you."

The corners of her mouth twisted toward a frown. "I don't think I should, I mean . . . talk with anyone," she said. She closed the door an inch or two as if to protect herself.

I put my foot over the threshold. "I'm just trying to help Nicky. . . ."

"I know you are," she said with a sigh. "I guess you won't give up . . . might as well come in." She pulled back the door.

I stepped directly into her living room. Huge overstuffed couch. Deep pile carpet. Big screen TV. No whips or chains or strange costumes anywhere that I could see. A collection of Beanie Babies warranted its own special shelf.

"Nicky send you?" she said, but before I could answer she went on: "I'm gonna get some coffee, decaf. You want some?"

"Sure."

She was gone for less than a minute and came back with two mugs. "Cream and sugar?"

"Black's okay."

She handed me mine. "Machine brews it on a timer. Hazelnut. Hope you like it."

There was a big oak rocker next to the couch. She folded herself in among the pillows on the couch with her coffee and bid me sit down.

I like rocking chairs. They remind me of long-ago summers on porches and moments when there is time to just sit and contemplate things.

"I heard about Nicky," she said. "Dewayne too."

"Seems like you knew both of them pretty well."

"We all went to school together, 'til I dropped out."

"You seem intelligent enough. Curriculum bore you?"

"That, and I have an old man who likes to beat the hell out of my mother. Nothing I could do about it since she wouldn't do anything about it, so I got out."

"They still live around here?"

"No, thank God. Moved to Louisiana . . . She's still with him. Go figure."

We sipped the hazelnut.

"Nicky's in a lot of trouble," I said.

"I know." Her eyes suddenly brimmed with tears. She turned her head away. "I know."

"She's been doing okay in school. Why would she want to get involved with drugs?"

"She's not, Mr. Pavlicek. I swear."

"What about the stuff they found on her car?"

"Someone must have put it there. Nicky wouldn't have had anything to do with that kind of thing."

"You and Nicky are real close, huh?"

She snickered. "She always calls me her dark side."

"Dark side." I checked her bare arms. They looked clean. "You ever snort?"

"I've tried it a couple times. But I couldn't see the point, you know? Seems like a big waste of money to me."

I looked again at the tasteful furnishings around the room. "You're a dancer."

"Yes . . . exotic." She added the more descriptive word as if it were necessary, as if we were comparing dinner recipes.

"Why'd you run out on me yesterday at the Spade?"

She bit her lip. "I didn't want to . . . I was afraid you were going to try to pin Nicky's rap on me."

"Why would I want to do that?"

"That's what her mother would try to do."

"Should I have?"

"Should you have what?"

"Tried to pin Nicky's rap on you," I said.

"No. I've got nothing to do with it."

"You see her much lately, I mean, since you've been working at the Spade?"

"Not as much I used to . . . every couple of weeks or so."

"But you're certain she didn't know about the coke."

She nodded.

"Seems inconsistent."

"I don't have to see Nicky all the time to know she wouldn't have had anything to do with that garbage. She's just against all that kind of stuff, okay? Told me if she ever found out I'd been using, she'd turn me in."

"You've got to admit, the habit fits with your profession."

"Hey lookit, not all of us are on the spike. I make a decent living."

"Okay." I finished my coffee. "Let's talk about Dewayne."

She turned her head again and wiped her cheek with the back of her hand. "Nicky told me that you . . . you were the one who found him . . ." Her voice trailed off.

"Yes. Nicky says he asked her out."

"Yeah, right. I wouldn't doubt it."

"What was he like?"

She averted her gaze, seemed to struggle for words. "He was good-looking, kind of muscular. He had kind eyes."

"Kind eyes. Doesn't sound like your typical gang-banger."

"Oh he wasn't . . . I mean, he wasn't part of any gang . . . not anymore," she said.

"You two friends?"

". . . sort of."

"Any idea why he would have been arguing with Nicky the last time he was arrested? Cops said she threatened to kill him."

She put her hand to her mouth. After a few seconds she said: "Dewayne was always a little scary, I mean, you know, he had a reputation."

"Like you, maybe."

She shrugged.

I stood and walked across the room. On the opposite wall there was a bookshelf next to the TV and VCR. A few books were lined up neatly—popular novels—and some exercise videos. The tape cases leaned haphazardly against one another so I could see most of their covers. They all featured women in leotards and tights, but one caught my eye. On this particular cover the women's torsos looked slightly comical in leotards, their faces flushed with special health, their knees bent, their bellies distended. I read the title.

Regan was still trying to keep from crying.

"Is the baby Dewayne's?" I tried to ask softly.

Her eyes flew open, but she didn't say anything. She lowered her head and stared into the carpet. The tears began. Finally she nodded.

"Maybe that's what Nicole was arguing with him about," I said.

She reached across to a side table where her purse lay and took out a tissue. She blew her nose. "He said I should have an abortion. Nicky went to talk with him. I asked her to. They ended up . . . I mean . . . you know the rest. . . ."

"Is that everything?"

"No," she said. "Later, after Dewayne disappeared and all, Nicky came and told me she was sure he was going to change his mind. He was really broken up about it, she said. He was even going to talk to his pastor about it . . . she said she was sure."

A clock on her mantel struck the hour. It was a formal Westminster chime.

"Anything I can do?"

She shook her head.

"When are you due?"

"Five months."

"Have to stop dancing soon. You've got savings, somewhere to go with the baby when the time comes?"

"Yes." She'd stopped crying now. "But one thing. Nicky's got to be there for me. She promised."

I nodded. This was a whole new dimension to my daughter's life, one I had never even imagined, let alone considered. Loyal friend. Fighting to preserve a life, two lives really, the baby's and Regan's.

Guys like to fantasize, watching Rambo or Dirty Harry or Jean-Claude Van Damme. We think bravery has to do with violent upheaval, with extraordinary acts of valor far outside the scope of our daily lives. What we too often miss is the bravery that happens every day, right before our eyes, deeper, more enduring.

I thanked Regan Quinn and left her nursing her mug of coffee, legs tucked beneath her on the couch.

20

The more I knew, the less likely a murder suspect my daughter became.

Rhodes Real Estate and Development Corporation occupied a picturesque Victorian, which served as its headquarters, on another dead-end street in town. Kevin Weems's Porsche was in a slot with his name on a little sign next to it in the lot. Inside the front door another man talked on the phone, seated behind a rose-colored desk. He had a blond ponytail, but was conservatively attired: blue sport coat, white shirt with a tie, chinos.

I waited until he was through.

"You must be Mr. Arnold," he said after hanging up the phone.

"No."

"I'm sorry. We were expecting someone else."

"My name is Pavlicek. I was hoping to have a chat with Mr. Weems."

"Well, Mr. Weems is pretty tied up at the moment. Does he know you?"

"He knows me. I'm Camille Rhodes's first husband."

"Right. Okay. Let me tell him you're here."

He disappeared down a carpeted corridor to the left and I heard him knock softly on one of the doors before going in. A few seconds later the door opened again and Weems' voice rang out: "Come on back."

I followed the voice. The walls were made of dark wood, punctuated by brass wall fittings with brightly-lit bulbs. Mr. Ponytail passed by me without a word on my way through the door. Weems was at his desk, a huge, antique executive model, dressed very much like his office mate. The room had a nice view of the quiet street.

"What can I do for you, Pavlicek? I'm busy." He gestured for me to sit opposite him in a high-backed chair and I did. We didn't shake hands.

"You don't say?"

"Yeah, as a matter of fact, I do. Now what do ya want?"

"You seem to have this remarkable ability to blow hot and cold, almost schizophrenic I think."

"Yeah? So what's it to ya?" He rolled his neck as if he were flexing his muscles.

"I actually came by to ask you something."

"Okay . . . then ask already."

"Who is Kevin Pauling?"

That got his attention.

He crossed his arms and rolled his neck again, this time in a little circle, staring at me blankly. "Never heard of him."

"Uh-huh."

"Should I have?"

"Unless you've developed amnesia. You used to be him. . . . Easy enough to find out."

His arms trembled almost imperceptibly, and his eyes took on a more menacing glow. "You trying to threaten me or something, Pavlicek? Who you working for anyway?"

"Nobody in Atlanta."

"Hey, listen. I got as many rights as the next person."

"Sure. And I'm not a cop anymore either. Otherwise, your name and whereabouts would have already been sent to the Georgia authorities, who in turn would have contacted the sheriff's department here."

He glared at me. "What do you want?"

"Why were you following me last night?"

He said nothing.

"It's a simple question. What were you doing tailing me last night after I left the Turners'?"

"I don't know what you're talking about."

"Are you working for Morelli?"

"Who?"

I stood.

He stood too and came around the desk. For a moment he must have thought he could try the business routine. "Come on, Pavlicek. We must have some common interest in all this. We can get together. We all just gotta do what we gotta do."

But then something animalistic seemed to well up from inside him. His eyes grew small, his knees flexed, and he bull-charged me low. I sidestepped the punch, used a wrist-grab and his own momentum to bend him over. With the same motion I brought my knee up into his chin. He made a sound like a whoopee cushion exhaling as he crumpled to the carpet.

He didn't try to get up. "Fuck, man. I think you broke my jaw."

"I'm still waiting for an answer to my question."

Blood was trickling from his nose and mouth. He pulled out a handkerchief and stumbled back to his chair.

I waited some more.

"It was Cowan, man." His words were slurred.

"The sheriff?"

"You know any other Cowans around?"

"Why'd he ask you to follow me?"

"I don't know, man. He just told me to keep an eye on you, see what you were up to and let him know. He brought up the Pauling thing too. Said if I didn't cooperate he'd run me in . . . Christ, I need to see a doctor."

"That it?"

"Yeah, that's it, man." He made eye contact with me for just a moment.

"I'm disappointed in you, Kev."

"What do ya mean?"

"You're not a very convincing liar."

His face turned hard again. He tried to stand up, but the pain stopped him. "You don't get it. I tell you what you want and I'm a dead man."

"Maybe you'll find dealing with me is worse . . ."

He thought about it. Then he pressed his bloody lips together and shook his head.

I turned to leave.

"Wait a minute," he said. "I wanted to talk to you without Camille around . . . Here, have a seat."

He moaned a little and I sat down again.

"I really think you oughta reconsider her offer . . . to hire you, that is. She's been talking to the lawyer, and, well, this thing with Nicole's got her all tied up in knots."

I shook my head.

"Why not, bud? Pride? Shit, forget all that. Camy's loaded, you know that."

Camy. It was amazing how quickly a guy with motivation could familiarize himself with any situation. He reminded me of some politicians I had met, only less polished. I didn't say anything.

"Well do me a favor and think it over, will ya? I got enough stuff around here to worry about without your ex calling me every hour." Now he'd wised up and was holding pressure on the side of his mouth.

"Did you murder Dewayne Turner, then try to frame Nicole?"

"What? You mean the kid whose body you found, the one from the newspaper? No. way, man. I never done nothing like that."

I wanted not to believe him, but somehow this time his words had the ring of truth.

But I had to be sure. "Maybe something to do with Nicky. Maybe something to do with Camille's money. Maybe you've been dealing a little dope on the side."

He shook his head again. "No, man, no."

"What kind of juice is Camille on?"

"Look," he said. "You need to talk more with her. I ain't saying nothing more."

"What about Nicky?"

"What about her?"

"You made a pass at her too, didn't you?"

He sighed, glared at me from behind the handkerchief. "It ain't like that either," he said.

"Really? Tell me what it's like."

My last view of Kevin Weems was as he bled into his hand, staring blankly at the wall.

Jake's battered Jeep was already parked in Cahill's lot next to Cat's Range Rover. The noonday sun shone at an angle across Main Street, making the storefronts appear frozen in time. But the air felt dry and had kept a pleasant chill. My knee throbbed a little from its encounter with Weems's head, but that was nothing compared to how the rest of me ached knowing Nicky was still in jail.

Cat already had Jake in stitches at the bar.

"Hey, there he is," the big man said. "The guest of honor. We're only eatin' real food, this afternoon, Frank. Remember?"

There were only a few other people in the restaurant at the moment. Cat ignored them and ushered Jake and me through several doors into a small private room next to his office in back. The office door was propped open and inside I could see a computer and several boxes and papers. The only light came from a window that faced the alley. Three chairs were set up around a table with iced tea, a huge bowl of cocktail sauce, and a steaming pile of broiled shrimp.

"It's a start," Jake said.

Cat beamed. "Hey, don't you worry. I got a waitress gonna be doin' nothin' this lunch but bringin' us food."

We talked and ate, and ate and talked some more. The dishes kept coming. Pork barbecue, coleslaw, French fries, onion rings. We talked mostly about superficial things: the weather, a little bit about family and old happenings from our time in New York, the annual upcoming football game between UVA and Virginia Tech. Kerstin even poked her head in from the kitchen at one point to say hello and chuckle with amazement at the amount we were eating, especially Jake and Cat. Invariably, at some point, the talk turned to hunting and falconry, with Jake and I doing most of it. The proprietor was a hunter too, but the firearm kind; he said he didn't have the patience to care for a raptor. No one mentioned anything about Nicky or why I was in town, or Rashid Fuad and our past until we were almost through.

"Cat, Jake and I were talking earlier and we decided we're going over to have a drink with Rashid Fuad in C'ville this evening," I said.

"Okay." He gave a disinterested look.

"You sure you don't want to come along?"

"Nah. Why should I? I never knew the guy like you two. You tell Rashi . . . whatever his name is, that I said thank you for his letter and I've sent my two crackerjack investigators to check it out."

"But you said something yesterday about 'old wounds'."

"Sure, sure." He took a big swig of beer and wiped his mouth on his sleeve. "But mine've healed, fellas. I was talkin' about yours."

"Someone with a rifle took a potshot at me yesterday."

Cat took a sip of his drink. "What I heard, it was more than just a potshot. Hey, listen . . ." He paused.

"What?"

"Ah, I was just gonna say somethin' stupid, like, you ain't gonna be able to help Nicky much if you're pushin' up daisies."

Suddenly Kerstin was at the door again, an uncharacteristic worried expression on her face.

"Cat," she said. "Honey, there's someone here to see y'all."

She stepped aside to reveal Sheriff Cowan, in uniform, his hat in hand, standing behind her in the doorway.

"Why, Sheriff," Cat said. "How are ya this afternoon? C'mon in and join the party."

I stiffened. Cowan looked uncomfortable, which was nothing compared to how I felt. "Hope I'm not interruptin' anything," he said.

" 'Course not. You had lunch?"

"No time right now. Gotta stop by the Turner funeral, then catch a flight out of Roanoke."

"Goin' somewheres?" Cat said. "Vacation I hope."

Right. Like super sheriff ever took a real vacation.

"No, business up in New York. Just for tonight. Be back first thing in the morning. Part of an investigation." He gave me an icy glance. "I thought you was headed out of town, Pavlicek?"

"After the funeral, sheriff. Just like you."

"Uh-huh. Then I can expect to see you tomorrow morning with your friend Ferrier down at my jail, that right?"

I sat up straight and saluted. "Yes, sir."

"I don't like your attitude, Pavlicek."

"C'mon now, fellas," Cat said before things got too ugly. "We're all on the same team here, ain't that right, sheriff? All of us cops. What can I do you out of then?"

Cowan continued to glare at me for a few seconds then turned to Cat. "Had a couple things I wanted to ask you about."

"You've saved us, actually," I said, forcing a smile. "Jake and I were just about to leave anyway. If we don't get out of here before dessert, someone may have to perform CPR."

Toronto took my cue and we both pushed away from the table.

"Thanks for the lunch, Cat."

"Anytime, fellas, anytime. You know we gotta do this

more often. Soon as the sheriff here gets Nicky's situation straightened out, we'll have to invite her too and we can have some supper or something together."

Cowan said nothing.

"Sounds good to me," I said.

Outside on the sidewalk Jake spoke first. "What do you make of that?"

"Probably wants to talk to him about Nicky."

He nodded.

"He's headed up to New York, which means he must be after something to do with Morelli."

Toronto gave me narrow eyes. "This thing is getting serious."

"Every time I turn around."

"What if he's in bed with Morelli? Wouldn't be the first cop the guy's turned."

"The thought has crossed my mind." I could almost picture the sheriff's image of perfection fronting for a sinister reality—racist beatings, murder, a bad cop on the take. Almost, but not quite.

"He didn't seem to want to ask Cat any questions with the two of us there."

"Doesn't trust us."

"You think the guy knows what he's doing?"

"Maybe. Maybe not."

"I don't like this. Being out of the loop."

"You get used to it," I said.

I parked in a line of cars outside the Turners' church. It was called Free Will Baptist Church, a building of modest design but newer than most of the surrounding structures in Moony's Hollow. The only thing stirring the sodden air inside was a quartet of wobbly ceiling fans. I found a seat in a pew near the back.

Up front Carla Turner sat among her children and grandchildren. Pastor Lori bustled about giving directions to an assistant and a couple of ushers. The closed casket, gunmetal gray with a metallic finish, lay on a draped stand surrounded by colorful flowers. Priscilla Thomasen slipped in from a side door and found a place just behind the family, followed a minute later by Sheriff Cowan who came in and stood with his hat in his hand in the back. There were a few murmurs when Cowan entered, but they were soon drowned out by the organ, and the ceremony began.

The service opened with a spiritual about crossing over a river. The green-robed choir, led by a bull-chested man with dreadlocks, swung into the music; the assembled mourners followed; the words were all about suffering, redemption, and faith. It seemed as if we would all be carried away on that river together, a river of peace beyond our present understanding.

The preacher spoke. People stood up. Some walked to the front and said nice things they remembered about Dewayne; Priscilla and Warren were among them. In the end the choir swept us all away again on the strength of their voices, a power that seemed able to transcend death itself. As they sang the pallbearers carried the casket from the church.

Afterward, I joined a procession of cars with their headlights on led by a deputy in a patrol car—the sheriff was no longer in sight. The long line of vehicles flowed for a mile or so into the countryside to a large cemetery where a stream ran through a grove of beech trees. With the sky absent of any clouds, we might all have been going on a picnic had we not been following the black Cadillac wagon with its curtains drawn. Most of the graves bore simple markers, but the grass and shrubs were well-tended. Pastor Lori led the brief interment rites, quoting scripture and allowing that, all things considered, it was a beautiful day to praise the Almighty for another soul gone to heaven.

When it was over, the crowd dispersed and left the casket to a group of three men wearing coveralls, one of which drove a back hoe. I paid my respects to Carla and Graham, who smiled and thanked me for coming. I didn't see Priscilla after that, but Warren was there and beckoned for me to wait.

"Sad occasion," I said.

"Yup." He glanced back at the burial site where the men already were beginning to fill the grave.

"You doing okay?"

"I'll be all right."

I waited for him to continue.

"The meeting's all set for tomorrow night. You cool with that?"

I nodded. "You talk to Priscilla?"

"She said 'Let's go.'"

"Okay then. By the way," I said, "I haven't seen anybody around here that looks like they belong to a gang."

Warren chuckled. "They don't operate like that. In the cities they control projects, whole neighbors. Around here they're more interested in keeping a low profile."

"The sheriff said something about them being like moonshiners."

"A little, I guess . . ." He chuckled to himself. "We still got them too. Moonshiners, that is."

We started walking back toward the cars. "Something else I wanted to tell you," I said. "You remember me mentioning Regan Quinn?"

"Yeah."

"She's pregnant."

"That right?"

"Dewayne was the father."

He stopped. "You sure?"

"Yes."

"Why didn't he tell me?"

"Guess they were trying to work things out," I said. He said nothing. We started walking again.

"I didn't want to tell your mother directly. Thought that might be best coming from you."

"Thanks for telling me, man," he said.

21

Toronto and I were on I-64 in Waynesboro, my pickup climbing toward the crest of the Blue Ridge. The Temptations crooned "Just My Imagination" off my *Greatest Hits of Motown* CD. Behind us the evening sun dipped over the distant Shenandoahs, turning the mountains magenta, the valley mauve, the sky mandarin fading to rose.

"You wanna know what I think?" Toronto said.

I doused the music. "What?"

"I think Pete Cowan is probably on the right track."

"Really?"

"I mean, what else could it be, unless you figure Cowan is crooked? You said yourself you don't think this Weems character would be up to any killing. Odds are it was either a gangster hit or tied in with Morelli. Maybe both, with the Turner kid's background and everything."

"If you're right, Priscilla and Warren and I may be walking into some trouble tomorrow night."

"Exactly. Which is why I would argue it's time for you guys to back off and let the cops handle it from here."

"Not you too. What, you don't trust Warren Turner?"

He snickered. "Oh, I trust him all right, about as far as I can throw him. But that's not what has me worried."

"Oh?"

"What concerns me is if these 'bangers turn out to have itchy trigger fingers, what are you gonna be able to do about it?"

"I'll cross that bridge when I come to it."

"That ain't gonna fly, bud. You gotta have a plan."

"I do. Like the sheriff was saying, Ferrier and his part-ner are going to show up in the morning. I'll throw them a bone or two and see what they think."

"Yeah, but what if Cowan does turn out to be dirty? You need some decent backup. Maybe let this state de-tective go in as primary, you and Priscilla stay out of the way."

"Only one problem," I said. "I doubt if Warren can get the 'bangers to agree to any meeting with the state police."

"Priscilla's sort of police, isn't she?"

I said nothing.

Jake smiled. "I'm shocked to think of them 'bangers as reverse racists."

At the top of Afton Mountain the fog lights built into the roadway glowed amber against the descending night. It was migration time for wild hawks and other birds of prey. Many would pass right over this ridge line, some-times hundreds a day.

"Don't worry, I don't plan on dragging Priscilla into some kind of fire fight."

"Now you're talking."

Like it or not, Sheriff Cowan, if he did turn out to be legit, was my best hope for getting Nicky off the hook. He wasn't exactly forthcoming about the progress of his investigation, but I wouldn't expect him to be, not with me at least. Now I knew the way a bird must feel, gliding toward the invisible fowler's snare. Something else was out there, I could sense it. It might try to destroy me, but what choice did I have except to fly on?

"You sure Armistead and Jersey will be okay?" I said.

"They'll be fine, as long as we're back sometime to-night to check on them. What time is dinner with Marcia?"

"Not until eight. I figured that would give us some extra time, if we needed, to talk with Rashid." The little man had agreed to meet us in the lounge at the Omni where he was staying on the downtown mall.

"You worried?" he asked.

"About what?"

"About what Fuad might have to say. He confirms the kid we put down couldn't have been the one who shot Singer, then that removes any doubt."

I stared silently at the highway for a moment. "Which doesn't exactly bode well for those of us who've secretly hoped all these years that some evidence would surface to prove that maybe we had been more justified in what we did."

We watched the highway ahead in silence, maybe neither of us wanting to think about something we had agonized over for years.

Then Jake said: "Gotta watch out for those secret hopes."

The Omni Hotel in Charlottesville was an oblong, glass-and-steel monument to fiscal largesse. Having gone bankrupt not long after opening, the city had used public funds to bail out the enterprise, figuring a flagship hotel might spur development on the end of a revitalized Main Street-turned-pedestrian mall. Time, a great economy, and developers who poured buckets of money into the area, had either proved the city council prescient or some of the luckiest politicos to ever manage a town.

Fuad, Toronto, and I sat in deep club chairs next to a glass wall that looked over the thoroughfare to a new indoor skating arena with a copper roof. The firearms expert still had the same nervous tic I remembered from years before, an intermittent tremor of the left side of his face that seemed to have worsened somewhat. Otherwise he looked as though he had hardly aged a day.

"You bettin' on the Knicks this year, Rashi?" Toronto asked.

"Ooh-no," he said. "Not since they got rid of Starks."

"Hey, you never know. New blood, new management."

"I will not hold my breath."

"How are things in New York?"

"Things are . . . some ways better, some ways worse." It was a favorite Fuad saying.

"How long have you been with the department now?" I asked.

"Twenty-seven years."

Jake whistled.

"This seems like a nice town you have chosen, Pavlicek," Fuad said.

"Glad you approve."

"You own horses? There are many big farms here, are there not?"

"There are, but I can't afford horses."

"I see. Oh, that's right. You gentlemen are into birds, aren't you? Falcons or something . . . now who was telling me about that?"

We made chitchat for awhile about the hawks. Fuad asked a lot of questions and seemed impressed with Toronto's knowledge.

After awhile Toronto said: "Hate to have to rush you, Rashi, but Frank and I have a genuine dinner date with a beautiful woman in less than hour. We don't wanna keep her waiting."

"Of course." He clicked open the clasps on his battered briefcase, lifted the cover, and riffled through a pile of documents before extracting a manila envelope. "Here is what I have," he said.

There was a typed report with a lot of official and technical language along with several blow-ups of microscopic bullet views.

"Can you give us the bottom line in English?" I asked.

"Yes. There is absolutely no doubt now that the weapon used to murder Officer Singer is the same one we tested years ago that belonged to the Morelli organization. Any question has been erased since the gun has surfaced."

"Surfaced? What are you talking about?"

"The gun itself was sent to our labs, just a week ago."

"You're kidding. By whom?"

"Boog Morelli himself, through one of his attorneys. I compared test-fired rounds with those retrieved from Singer's body." He held up one of the photos. "You see the scores left by the barrel of this particular Glock? They are identical to the patterns in the bullets taken from Singer." He showed us the second photo for comparison and then a third. "And here are rounds from a control, another Glock, same model, same load. Different type of pattern altogether. So our computer program was accurate."

"Let me get this straight," I said. "Morelli, out of the blue, just up and sends you this gun. Why?"

"Who knows?"

"No one's talked to his lawyer?"

"Probably someone has, but I don't know anything about that."

I looked at Toronto, who threw up his hands and shrugged.

"So what else can you tell us about the history of this gun?" I said.

"Not much yet, I'm afraid. From what I understand, that's where things begin to get a bit murky."

"You know who checked in the weapon?"

He fumbled through his records. "No. But if it's important I can make a call and find out."

Was it important? The gun showing up right now was too big a coincidence to ignore. And what, exactly, was Morelli's relationship with Dewayne Turner? Were we chasing peace of mind or ghosts?

"It's important, Rashi." I gave him my card with my cell phone number. "Can you call me as soon as you have a name?"

"Of course."

"You doing all this on your own?"

The little man shrugged and pushed his glasses higher on his nose.

"No matter how it turns out, we owe you."

Fuad looked embarrassed. "I do what I can. You gentlemen were among the best."

"Rashi," I said. "You still are."

22

After lunch at Cat's a light dinner was all I wanted, but Toronto was hungry again. Marcia said she wouldn't get in the middle of such a debate, so we compromised and ended up eating gourmet pizza at Rococo's just off Hydraulic on Commonwealth Drive. Toronto and I had stopped by my office and apartment earlier so I could pick up my mail and return a few calls. Walter and Patricia were away at the beach, Walter playing golf no doubt. The mail was mostly bills and junk, but a couple of checks would come in handy, one rather sizable from a law firm, which I promptly deposited at the closest bank machine.

We sat at a table by a window in Rococo's upstairs dining room. Marcia looked, in a word, stunning. Her bolero vest over tight blue jeans, hair done up in a bun, complemented by pearls. Perfect for pizza.

"You know that waitress has been giving the three of us long looks ever since we came in here," she said. "I think she has a bet with the bartender downstairs over which one of you is my date."

"Easy to see her difficulty," Toronto said.

Mouth full of pepperoni, defenseless, I took a long swig of Amstel Light and decided to let that one pass.

"Hey, you remember what we were saying earlier in the truck, about Cowan?"

"Yeah?"

"Maybe you oughta call this Agent Ferrier, or whatever his name is, kinda brief him before he has a chance to go face to face with the sheriff."

"Why? You think Cowan might cast some spell over him?"

"No. Just being cautious."

"I thought Toronto and caution were antonyms," Marcia said. "Might this have something to do with a certain Commonwealth's attorney I've been hearing so much about?"

"Ask the lone ranger here," Toronto said. "He's spent more time with her lately than I have."

"Really?" Her eyes flew up in mock wonderment.

"Now hold on there," I said. "There is a big difference between time and quality time."

Toronto smiled. "Which is what we're spending now. At least you two are. I are just a third wheel."

"Funny, I've always thought of you as anything but a third wheel," Marcia said.

"More like a Harley engine," I said.

"Well this engine's gotta motor off to the little boy's room, if you know what I mean. Excuse me while I check on that waitress's wager you were talkin' about." He stood and sauntered away, which for Jake, in his Tony Lama boots and bulging oxford shirt, was akin to whooping and hollering across the room.

"You think he'll ever settle down?" Marcia asked.

I shrugged.

"You know you two bring out the best in each other. I can see why you were such a good partnership."

"Mmmm."

"Did you find out anything interesting from your meeting earlier?" Her eyes bore gently into me now, the patient listener.

"We did, in fact." I didn't want her to worry so I didn't elaborate.

"Was he a friend of yours, the man with whom you talked?"

"I wouldn't say 'friend' exactly. He knows what loyalty is, and hard work, and commitment."

"A good person then."

"He didn't have to do what he did for us, that's for sure."

She sipped her wine, glanced around the room for a second before looking at me again. "I'm worried, Frank, about this talk of you and this reporter and attorney meeting with some gang tomorrow night. It might be dangerous."

"More dangerous than what I usually do?"

She scoffed at me. "I think you can answer that one for yourself."

I said nothing.

"It seems almost eerie to me, you know."

"What?"

"This whole thing. You and Jake meeting with that man tonight about what happened long ago in New York. You and a gang dealing drugs and dead bodies again. It's almost like some unresolved entity is drawing you back in. . . ."

"Well one thing I know for sure is unresolved is Nicky. I just can't see her involvement with any of this."

"You don't think you're wearing a father's blinders?"

I pursed my lips and shook my head.

"Maybe you should be focusing more on that aspect. If you listen, really listen, she might tell you some things she would never tell anyone else."

She had a point. Nicky was clearly hiding something from everybody, even her mother. "But I have listened," I said. "Besides what would she gain by keeping anything from me now?"

"You've never been a teenaged girl."

"No, but I seem to remember kissing a few."

"Oh? I'd like to hear more about that. . . ."

At this point Jake interrupted, having circled the room and come up from the other side. "What's this about Frank and teenaged girls?"

"Never mind," I said. I punched him on the shoulder, which felt like hitting an oak.

"I always miss the good stuff," he said.

"You two having fun over there with your hawks? It'll be gun season soon, won't it?" Marcia asked.

"Few more days," Jake said, reaching his arms above his head and stretching.

"What did your waitress have to say?"

"She had her money on me, of course. Said she thought you looked like the kind of woman who would be attracted to younger men."

Marcia smiled and gave me a wink.

"Ouch," I said.

Marcia said: "I was just talking to Frank about Nicky and you two coming over here to see this man from New York."

"Yeah? He tell you about Boog Morelli too?"

"Boog Morelli? No. Who's he?" Marcia looked at me.

I gave Toronto a look and shrugged. "Just a bad guy from New York whose name has come up in all this. Looks as though the Affalachia County Sheriff's flown up there to check things out."

"A bad guy from New York." Now she looked at Jake. "How bad?"

Jake shrugged too. "He's nowhere near the baddest."

"Oh, *that's* reassuring," she said. "First you guys tell me someone tried to kill Frank yesterday and now we've got big-time criminals from New York."

No one said anything for a few moments. Marcia crossed her arms and looked at her glass on the table.

I waited until she looked up. "I know," I said. "You're with me, maybe you didn't sign on for all this."

She held up her hand. "No .·. . I think I just need to get used to the idea."

Jake was nodding his head.

"Besides, if all you did was spend the rest of your life snooping around divorce and insurance settlements, you might turn into something that neither of us would like."

I was watching her very carefully. She finally picked up the glass and took a final sip of wine, smoothed out her jeans—not that they needed any smoothing—then very deliberately reached across the table and offered me her hand.

"Like I said, 'third wheel'." Jake's eyes were rolling toward the ceiling.

"Shut up, Jake," Marcia said.

I took her hand in mine. She kept it there until we paid the bill and were preparing to leave. On the far side of the room the waitress was whispering something to the hostess. When we reached the door, Marsh just smiled and offered each of us an arm. Jake and I made a show of ushering her out, a rose between two thorns.

"I don't have to tell you, you're going out on a limb here," Ferrier said.

I had interrupted his late supper. No TV game in the background tonight. I was on the car phone, climbing Afton Mountain again, this time from the other side. Jake was already snoring, his head propped between the seat belt and passenger door glass.

"I know," I said.

"I've already talked with Priscilla Thomasen. We need to have some serious discussion about this little get-together you all are planning for tomorrow night. You two are in over your heads."

"She talk to you about Sheriff Cowan?"

"Yeah. You got any hard evidence of his involvement with Morelli, or just conjecture?"

I said nothing.

"Didn't think so. . . ."

"But you've got to admit, it all looks suspicious," I said.

"Maybe. But you forget, the sheriff's got his investigation going too, you know."

"What does he have?"

"I'm not going to get into that with you now, Pavlicek. He hasn't shared much with us yet, anyway. We'll talk more in the morning."

"He talk to you about his trip to New York?"

"Not yet."

I debated whether or not to tell him about Fuad, but decided I better wait. "Morelli's a big name," I said. "If his people are in on something with these local gangsters, could mean a whole different problem."

There was silence on the line.

"You still there?"

"Chad and I will be at the sheriff's department in Leonardston in the morning." Evasive. "We'll talk more then."

"Right. I'll try not to get into too much trouble before then."

"Why am I not reassured?" he said.

Sometime after midnight I was blowing cold air in my face from the vent to stay awake as we passed within a mile of the cutoff to Leonardston. Jake, who had snored most of the trip, had finally stopped, but hardly stirred. I wasn't thinking anymore about Ferrier or what would happen in the morning with the sheriff; I was thinking about Nicky and the things I might say to try to break through her silence.

Suddenly my cell phone bleated. Toronto shifted beneath his seat belt with a moan.

I reached under the seat where I kept the handset and picked it up. "Pavlicek."

"Oh, Frank, thank God I caught you."

"Camille?" Her voice sounded strange, as if she were speaking from very far away.

"He's gone, Frank."

"Who?" I glanced over at Jake who was looking at me inquisitively.

"Kevin. He's gone. I came home tonight from shop-

ping at the mall over in Lexington and he was just . . .
gone. His clothes are all missing. Looks like he took
some of my jewelry and silver, a bunch of cash too."

"You call the sheriff's office?"

"Not yet. I wanted to talk to you first."

"Me. Why?"

"Some things I need to tell you. In person. Not over
the phone."

"Now?" Static filled the line, threatening to end our
conversation. There was no moon tonight and the headlights swept over several deer along the road.

"Yes, now . . . that is, if you can come."

Jake was interpreting my end of the conversation, already beginning to shake his head. I knew I'd be drinking more of his coffee, sooner rather than later.

"Give me half an hour," I said.

23

You could smell honeysuckle outside the Rhodes's mansion, even in the dark. A short Hispanic woman answered the door.

"Yes, sir?" Her accent was thick. She looked to be about fifty.

"Good evening. My name's Pavlicek. Mrs. Rhodes is expecting me."

"Oh yes, Mr. Pavlicek. Come in. She very upset."

But as she turned to let me enter, her boss stepped in behind her. "It's all right, Lucita. I'm up now. Thank you for coming in so late to help clean up," Camille said.

"That's okay, Mrs. Rhodes. Anything more I can do?"

"No. Thank you. I'll take care of this gentleman. You go ahead and run along down to your house. I'll see you in the morning."

"Yes, Mrs. Rhodes," the woman said and walked toward the back door.

"She live on the property?" I asked.

"Yes. We have a little cottage behind the stable with a separate driveway. The men who take care of the farm come in that way too."

Camille's hair was pinned up in back and she wore a satin bathrobe. She opened the door a little wider, leaning on it as she did.

"Thanks for coming over, Frank. I hope you won't mind if I lie on the couch." She led me through the dining room again but this time to a bright, glass-walled atrium with a sofa and several large plants and a large, expensive-looking throw rug covering part of a flagstone floor. She reclined on the couch with her eyes half closed, her head propped against a mound of pillows.

"I'm sorry it's so late. Would you like some coffee or something?"

"Already had some of Jake's."

"Right. I forgot you're staying with him."

"You don't mind if I drink while we talk, do you? It helps calm my nerves." There was a half-full bottle of tequila with some orange juice and a glass on a small portable serving table in front of her.

"It's your home," I said.

"With everything that's gone on lately, I guess I'm still, as you can imagine, in a little bit of a state of shock."

"Understandable, I suppose."

"You talked to him, didn't you?"

"Who?"

"Kevin."

"Weems? Yes. Earlier today . . ." I glanced at a clock on the wall. "Although I guess it was yesterday now."

"That's why he ran then. He knew that you were on to him about his ex-wife. Not that it matters much now."

"You knew who he was then, about the name change and everything?"

"Of course."

"And you just let him keep living with you anyway, in the same house as Nicky."

"Oh, pooh. Nobody cared, until now." She waved her hand to indicate she wasn't interested in pursuing the topic any further. She settled deeper into the pillows. "Come on, Frank," she said, patting the cushions beside her. "Sit down. I won't bite."

"That's okay, Camille. I think I'll stand."

She made an exaggerated pout with her lips over the rim of her glass.

"You said you had some things you wanted to tell me," I said.

"Yes. But first, do tell me, how do you find living in Albemarle County?"

"I'm not really up for socializing in the middle of the night, Camille. Charlottesville's fine. Why?"

"I have some good friends there you know. The Darlingtons? They have a place out in Farmington. Wonderful views. I went riding up there last year," she said.

I nodded, not wanting to encourage her chatter any further.

She said: "I apologize for being so evasive the other day. And I didn't mean to insult you with the offer of money. I should've expected you to come down. I mean you are Nicole's father after all. You've every right to be, now that . . . well, now that George is gone."

"Camille, you and I both know I don't have any rights when it comes to Nicole," I said. "But she's in trouble, and if there's something more that you can tell me that might help matters . . ."

"There is." She sipped her drink. "Ummm . . . there is, and I'm sorry I didn't tell you this sooner."

"Tell me what?"

"Our daughter . . . well . . . Nicole is an addict."

"A what?"

"She uses drugs. She's hooked. That's what you call it, isn't it?"

"I haven't seen any evidence of that," I said.

"She manages to hide it well."

It didn't make sense, did it? Though Nicky being a junkie could explain a lot, maybe even the coke in her car. Dewayne Turner's murder as well?

"What is she using?"

"What kind of drugs, you mean?"

"Yes."

"I don't know. I think they call it speed or something."

"Pills?"

"No, but I found a box and some syringes in her room."

"Show me."

She set her drink down and stood, motioning for me to follow. We went back through the dining room, into the front hall again, and up the main stairs. At the top were a row of original oils in expensive wooden frames: one of George Rhodes, one of Camille, and one of Nicole. I thought the artist had done a good job of capturing Nicky's pretty face, but he had missed something. She looked too serene, too composed.

Halfway down the hall Camille opened a door.

"This is the sitting parlor off the master bedroom. George and I used to spend a lot of time here," she said. "But I don't go in here much now. After I found the box I locked it in the safe in the closet in here. Nicole never said anything, of course. Although she must have realized I had found something."

"When was this?"

"Oh, I don't know. Maybe a month ago."

"A month ago. And you didn't do anything about it?"

"Well what was I supposed to do, Frank. Turn my own daughter in to the police?"

"How about talking to her about it?"

"I tried, without letting her know I had the box. She denied everything, of course."

We entered a small enclosed space that was nearly dark. No windows. At one end a door was partially open and I could make out a large bedpost in the bedroom. She flipped a switch and the walls glowed with soft light from a lamp in the corner. Books and magazines scattered about. Deep pile carpet. A layer of dust. Another couch.

"I don't let Lucita clean much in here anymore," she said, sounding embarrassed.

The closet was built into the bookshelves and inside was the safe, a combination-style with a heavy metal door. She spun the dial, clicked open the latch, and extracted an old cigar box. In the cigar box were several

Band-Aids, four or five needles, a looped rubber tube and a couple vials.

"What is it?" she said.

"Methamphetamine, I think."

Her voice became a little shaky. "What's that?"

"It's bad news."

She put the box back where she had gotten it, closed the safe, and then the closet door. "What are we going to do, Frank?"

"First, I'm going to have a talk with Nicky. And we're going to have to let the sheriff and the state police know."

"You think so? But isn't there some other way? I mean, it will be in the papers and everything."

"Nicky's already in the papers, Camille."

She nodded. Then she reached into a stack of books and pulled out a large binder that looked like a photo album, her hands trembling. She plopped down on the sofa.

"Here," she said, her voice quivering a little. "Come and sit down."

I sat beside her as she began flipping through the pages. She took her time until she found the one she wanted. She held the album open and handed it to me, pointing to a particular photo. It was another Polaroid of a smiling Nicole holding a large fish by one of its gills. She was framed by two men: Jake and myself.

"She's always wanted to be like you. Even with everything I've tried to give her."

Her hands began to tremble again. She closed the photo album and held it beneath her chin with her eyes closed. A tear ran down her cheek. I rested my hand lightly on her arm, just to let her know I was there, to provide some comfort. When she settled down she put the photo album back, we both stood to leave, and she snapped off the light. As I turned in the sudden darkness something brushed up then came hard against me. It was Camille. Suddenly, her robe was peeled back, exposing her breasts. She had her arms wrapped around my back, her head buried in my chest and she was shaking again, her body fragile and desperate. I couldn't believe how emaciated she'd become.

"I'm nothing but a whore, Frank," she said. "An expensive whore."

She kissed my neck, which, even in her present condition started to bring the same old reaction, but I managed to find both her arms and grip them, not hard enough, I hoped, to hurt her, but firmly enough to hold her away from me. We stood motionless, like awkward dancers caught off guard, before she realized what was happening.

"You son of a bitch," she said and kicked and tried to claw at me with her pinned arms. "I've had better men than you. Kevin was better. I've wasted better men than you."

She continued to fight, but I kept my grip. She cursed some more and screamed at me. After maybe a minute she stopped and began to sob again uncontrollably. Then she collapsed against me, her eyes closed, face a pale mask, supported only by my arms, vibrating with minor convulsions.

It was no act. I stood her upright and pulled her robe back up over her shoulders, got her moving while she was still semiconscious, almost carrying her down the hall. I found the master bedroom door, switched on a dim light, and guided her into her bed. Her forehead was hot to the touch. I pulled the sheet up to her chin. After moaning and moving around a bit, she fell asleep.

I went to the bathroom and found a washcloth on the towel rack next to the sink. I soaked it with some cold water and placed it above her eyes. Just then I heard something tumble to the floor downstairs. The maid had already left, but we were not alone in the house.

Had Weems returned? I crept down the hall toward the staircase. My gun was drawn and I kept my back to the wall. I don't care what anyone says, once you've been shot at for real, your attitude changes—you take little for granted. Another sound, from the kitchen, this a screen door slamming. Fleeing?

I made my way as quickly and cautiously as possible downstairs to the kitchen where I did indeed find the back door ajar. No car started in the distance this time, however. No shots were fired. I turned on all the lights and searched the rest of the house thoroughly, but found nothing.

Upstairs Camille still lay unconscious. There was a phone on the nightstand next to the bed. The radio-clock next to the phone said it was now after one A.M. I picked up the receiver and dialed the sheriff's office.

"I'm calling to report a larceny," I said.

24

Rashid Fuad called early the next morning while I was in the shower. Toronto took the message and handed it to me along with a cup of coffee when I showed up in his kitchen.

"Hack Wilson? That who checked the weapon in and talked to the lawyer?"

"No. Some guy from one of the Manhattan precincts. But Rashi says Wilson's talked to the guy. Knows him from police benefit work or something."

Wilson had been a NYPD detective long before I had joined the ranks. He was competent, but shallow. A glad-hander from way back.

I dialed his number and he picked up on the second ring.

"At work early this morning, aren't we, Hacker?"

"Hey, a voice from the past. How ya doin', Pavlicek? Rashi Fuad said you were gonna give me a call. Yeah, I made lieutenant, you believe it? We got the VP coming in here this morning. Boss wants everybody on alert."

"The vice president of the city council?"

"No, you idiot. Of the whole friggin' country. He's on a get-tough-with-crime tour. You know, waving the flag for the masses and everything . . . So how's life in the Himalayas?"

"I'm a long way from the Himalayas, Hacker."

"Yeah? Hey, it might as well be that to me. Rashi said you was wanting to know about this lawyer who turned in the gun."

"Yeah. Seems pretty curious, doesn't it?"

"Curious ain't the word for it. Guy I talked to says it was weirdness all around."

"Weirdness?"

"Yeah. This greaseball who's worked for Boog Morelli for years shows up downtown and presents them with this weapon. Says it needs to be sent to Rashid Fuad's lab, for Fuad to check the serial numbers and he'd know what to do with it."

"That's it? Nothing else?"

"That's it."

"What's the latest on Morelli?"

"Ain't no latest. Guy's been in and out of the joint, you know, for years. Now, word on the street is he's creeped out."

"Creeped out?"

"Yeah, you know. He's gettin' older. Remember Howard Hughes?"

"Still doing business?"

"What do you think?"

I recognized the pale Caprice. It was parked among the dozen or so cars, including Priscilla Thomasen's Saab, in the lot outside the municipal building with the engine still plinking, a little puddle of liquid dribbling from beneath the front bumper. Early morning sunshine had given way to a bank of steel-gray clouds advancing from the west. Ferrier and Spain would be a little saddle-sore if they had driven all the way from Richmond.

The sheriff's department buzzed with activity. People came and went through the glass doors. Two deputies were in the office, one on the phone, the other doing paperwork.

"Pavlicek. Suprised to see you up so early this morning," Cowan said. He was standing in a doorway holding a clipboard against his hip with his other hand resting atop his gun. He was back in his work clothes today. The muscles in his forearms flexed like he was showing for Mr. Universe. "After that little party out at the Rhodes's house last night, I was afraid we might need to issue you a wake-up call."

"I could say the same about you. How was New York?"

"Interestin'," he said. "Real interestin'. Your state police pals are finally here. Just arrived, in fact, but I guess maybe you already knew that."

I nodded. Call me Sherlock Holmes.

I followed him down a corridor that led to a stairway door and a set of concrete steps. We went up half a flight to another door that led down another hallway with yet more doors.

"Will I be able to get in to see my daughter again this morning?" I asked.

He stopped and turned and looked at me before he spoke. "We'll see."

We entered a door with a sign next to it that read: CONFERENCE ROOM B. Agents Ferrier and Spain sat talking with Priscilla Thomasen at a long table. They all stopped speaking when we walked in.

"Look who's come to join us this morning," the sheriff said. "Guess there's no need for introductions."

I nodded at the two investigators and Priscilla. Priscilla was the only one who gave me any sign of recognition.

Cowan and I took chairs across the table.

Cowan said: "Agent Ferrier here was just about to tell us how you said you found the Turner boy's body."

I looked at Ferrier. "I thought we'd been through all that already," I said.

"Yes we have," he said. He gave me a funny look.

"You've got a choice to make, Pavlicek," the sheriff said.

We stared at one another. No one else said anything. Priscilla was looking down at her notes.

At last Ferrier said: "What the sheriff's leading up to, Frank, is—you either back off now or he'll have to take you into custody on suspicion of obstructing justice . . . and for your own protection. These people have already tried to kill you once. We all just need to do our jobs here." There was no change to his expression as he said this.

So that was it. Either Cowan had managed to convince them they needed to watch out for me, or Nicole might be going down, and for obvious reasons they didn't want me to be part of it. I needed to talk to Priscilla alone. But right now that seemed impossible.

"Did you find something out in New York? Is Morelli involved?"

No one volunteered any answers.

"When family's involved, easy for anyone to lose their objectivity," Cowan said. He'd produced a toothpick from somewhere, stuck it between his teeth, and pursed his lips. If I could have, I would have reached across the table and smacked it out of his mouth.

"I tampered with evidence," I said. "I've admitted as much. But every one of you, in my shoes, would've done the same thing."

"It's not just that," Priscilla finally said. Her look seemed to be telling me, *Shut up for your own good.*

I waited. No one else offered anything.

"Okay," I said, placing my hands on the table. "You guys say back off, I back off."

Cowan looked surprised. "Just that simple?"

"Just that simple."

"Look, sheriff," Ferrier said. "Frank here is a pro. Let's cut him some slack."

"I prefer you stick around town though," the sheriff said to me. His tone was the bland one he probably used at county meetings and on speeders.

I looked at Priscilla. "What about the meeting Warren Turner set up for us tonight?"

"I was just getting to that," Cowan said. "My opinion is, and I'll say it again—absolutely no way. I don't want any cowboy civilians killed on my watch. Whole thing

seems like a fiasco, you ask me. But the Commonwealth's attorney here feels strongly otherwise."

"We've agreed to let the meeting proceed, on the condition that the sheriff and his deputies, as well as Chad
and myself, are there to track your every move and to
provide full backup and support," Ferrier said.

That sounded reasonable, under the circumstances.
Except it probably wouldn't work.

"You think Warren's going to sit still for that?" I said,
looking at Priscilla.

"He will if we don't tell him," Cowan said.

Priscilla said nothing.

"Either way," the sheriff added. "Like I said, the
whole thing's most likely goin' to turn out to be a wild-
goose chase. This office's investigation has, um, taken
off on some more productive tangents. . . ." His eyes
tried to outstare mine.

"If you've got something concrete of which you want
to accuse me, Sheriff, I wish you'd quit beating around
the bush."

"Just wonderin' what you were plannin' on doin'
today, that's all."

"After this discussion, not much," I said.

"Good." He tried to stop himself, but a little smile was
beginning to creep across his authoritative demeanor.

"You gave the sheriff's deputies your statement about
your conversation last night with Mrs. . . . Rhodes, is it?
The revelation of your daughter's, um, substance abuse.
Anything else you've found out you need to share with
us?" Ferrier said. His eyes flicked almost imperceptibly
toward Cowan then back to me. I didn't think the sheriff
caught it. He was too busy enjoying himself.

"No."

"Okay. We'll be in touch then."

Priscilla said: "In the meantime, Mr. Pavlicek, anything changes, you be sure and contact us . . . Any questions?" She slid one of her cards across the table to me
as she said this, which seemed unnecessary. I was about

to turn it down, but the odd stare she gave me convinced me otherwise. When I turned the card over I saw she had written in small letters on the back so that only I could read them: *Don't worry. This is all b.s.*

I looked at her for a moment, then said: "What about visiting Nicky?"

"I don't see any problem with that," she said. "You, sheriff?"

Cowan clearly had been thinking about something else. "Um, no. I guess not."

Cowan and I pushed our chairs from the table and stood up. Priscilla returned to her notes. Ferrier and his partner sat stone-faced as before.

"You've stirred up the pot some," Cowan said. "Appreciate that." He was actually grinning now. He stuck his hand across the table for me to shake. Maybe it was just my imagination, but he seemed to squeeze mine extra hard, as if he needed to drive home the point that he was still in command of the situation, that nothing could penetrate that perfect cop persona he had spent so much time developing. I had an eerie feeling the sheriff might genuinely be on to something, but I worried those in the room had yet to truly appreciate how virulent it might become.

25

A deputy led me down the corridor and through the by-now-familiar entrance to the cells.

"I'll give you ten minutes. Can't get away with no more," he said.

"Thank you," I said. "I understand."

Nicole was lying prone on her bunk, flipping through an old *Good Housekeeping*. When the deputy left she looked up at me with a frown. "Don't they have anything good to read in this place? I feel like I'm in an episode of the *Twilight Zone*."

"You know the show?"

"Sure. Mom and I used to watch tapes." She continued flipping.

"I guess you must feel a little like *Twilight Zone* whenever you're around me too, huh?" I said.

"You're not *that* bad." She gave a poor imitation of a smile.

"They treating you okay?"

"You mean besides the fact the food tastes like microwave mush and there's nothing to do? Yeah. But you can tell Mommie Dearest I've learned my lesson." She closed the magazine and tossed it on the floor.

"She hasn't been in to see you?"

"Nope. Not since that first night."

I moved across from her and stood with my back against the wall. "We need to talk about a couple things."

She sat up and crossed her legs, Indian-style. "Great.

You want to play twenty questions again, I've got nothing better going on."

"Not twenty questions . . . First of all, I had a talk with your friend Regan."

She nibbled at one of her fingernails. I don't think she even realized she was doing it. Her eyes were red-rimmed and puffy around the edges. Hard not to cry when you're not even out of your teens and cooped up all day in a place like this.

"I know about her baby," I said.

She shifted uneasily on her bunk for an instant, sat up, then nodded. "Okay."

"Was that what you and Dewayne were arguing about the night you two were arrested?"

She stared at me for several seconds without moving. Then another nod.

"He wanted Regan to have an abortion . . ." I said. "and you didn't. . . ."

She made a funny noise, like she was blowing air out between her teeth, and frowned again. "You got it, Dick Tracy. That's . . . correct."

"I'm sorry."

"What would you know about it?" Her eyes burned defiantly.

"You're right. Not much, I guess."

She said nothing.

"How'd you and Regan get so close?"

"Since grade school . . . we were always chums. Gonna go to college together too. But her parents . . . well . . . I kind of went one way . . . she went the other."

"But you stayed friends anyway."

"Uh-huh."

"And your mother doesn't like it."

"You kidding? She told me she ever caught me down at that place where Regan works, she'd kick me out of the house."

"Hard to stay friends with someone when they go down like that. Sometimes you have to let go," I said.

"But Regan's not going to stay that way, Dad. She's not like the other girls down there. You watch . . . after she has her baby and everything."

"She says she has money, and a place to stay afterward."

"That's right," she said, almost proudly.

I nodded, waiting for her to go on, but she didn't elaborate. "You think Regan's pregnancy might have anything to do with Dewayne's murder?"

"What, you mean like, 'cause she's white and he was black?"

"Yes."

She thought about it and gave a little shrug. "Maybe you oughta be asking the sheriff."

I nodded. She wasn't giving me anything new I could use.

"Something else," I said. "Kevin Weems is gone."

"Gone?"

"Right. Weems isn't his real name, either, or at least it didn't used to be. Turns out he's a child-support fugitive from Georgia. Probably moves from situation to situation. Always trying to stay one step ahead of the authorities."

"Big surprise there," she smirked. "Hey, do you think he put that stuff in my car, I mean, to get back at me because I wouldn't. . . . ?"

"No, I don't think so. I think it may have been someone else altogether. Ever hear of a man from New York named Morelli?"

"No. Why?"

"I'm beginning to think he or someone who works for him is behind Dewayne's murder."

"Over drugs."

"Probably."

"So they put the drugs in my car?"

"Maybe. We'll see."

Well . . . I'm glad Weems the Sponge is out of here," she said. "Mom sick?"

"Yes. How did you know?"

"She always gets sick when something bad happens."

I thought about that. "She drinking a lot?"

"Probably. Who knows?"

"Regan's baby and Weems—that what you and your mother been fighting about?"

"Right." She laughed bitterly. "Now you know all my little secrets."

"Maybe not all ..." I moved toward the bunk. "May I sit down?"

"Sure."

"Let's talk some more about you."

"Okay." She pushed an errant strand of hair from her face.

"All these problems—Weems, Regan and Dewayne, your mother's drinking—how's that affected you?"

"What do you mean?"

I said nothing. I tried to search my daughter's face for some trace of deceit, some sign that she had become what her mother had said she was, but I saw nothing. Was I that blind?

She narrowed her gaze. "What's wrong, Daddy?"

"I think you may already know, or at least suspect."

"Suspect what? What are you talking about?"

I looked at my watch. Only a few more minutes. I reached in my pocket and pulled out a syringe, one I'd taken from the cigar box in Camille's safe. I'd had to clear it with the guard to allow me to bring it in.

"Ever seen one of these before?"

Her top lip was quivering. "It's a needle, isn't it? Like the ones doctors use."

"Yes, but this one didn't come from any doctor. Your mother says she found it along with a lot of other drug paraphernalia in a cigar box in your room."

"What? What are you saying?" she said.

"I think you already know."

"I swear, I don't know what you're talking about, Daddy."

"Honey, you don't have to—"

"I told you before, I don't use drugs. That's the truth."

She shuddered then, a tremor so violent that it seemed to take both of us off guard. Her face dissolved into tears. Maybe because she thought for a moment I didn't believe her, even though the truth was, I did. I took her into my arms and held her head against my shoulder. Her own arms were strong and easily wrapped around me. I could only begin to imagine the pain she felt. The hard part was knowing that some of it was because of me.

After awhile the crying stopped. We were running out of time.

"Okay now?" I asked.

She pulled away and nodded.

"We've only got a couple minutes, babe," I said, standing and looking down at her. "I want you to know—I believe you."

"Yeah, well great." She half choked on a sob. "At least somebody does."

"This is very important. Can you think of any reason why your mother would want to accuse you of using drugs?"

"Mom?" Suddenly, her face turned to stone. "Maybe."

"What is it?"

She folded her arms and looked at the floor. She said nothing.

"Are you scared, Nicky, is that it?"

"Not scared, but . . ."

"But what, honey? You've got to tell me everything you know right now, otherwise I may not be able to help you."

The cell was silent, except for the sound of water running through pipes, coming from the corridor overhead. She considered my words for a long moment, but then she began to slowly shake her head. I was losing her. Whatever torn loyalties she was haunted by, whatever

spell her mother or Weems or Dewayne Turner or whoever else had over her, I wasn't going to break it in just
a couple brief jail cell talks.

"All right, listen," I said. "I want you to do one thing
for me right now. If you feel ready to tell me more, or
if you think of anything else, ask to see me or the prosecutor, Miss Thomasen. Don't talk to anyone else."

"Now you're scaring me," she said.

"No reason to be afraid. But do you understand?"

"Yes."

"One more thing. Was Regan Quinn who you were
going to meet at Cat's the other night when you were
arrested?"

"Uh-huh. She doesn't work on Sundays."

"Did anybody else know you were going to meet
her there?"

She shrugged. "I don't think so. Maybe someone
Regan talked to, maybe Uncle Cat."

"Okay." I reached in my pocket. "Look . . . something
I brought you," I said. I pulled out the Polaroid I had
pulled from her dresser and handed it to her.

"You took it from the mirror in my room," she said.

"Right. Thought you might like it down here."

"Can I ask you something else?" she said.

I glanced at my watch. "Sure, but you better make
it quick."

"What really made you come all the way back down
here to help me?"

I looked at her figure stretched out on the bunk, how
much she had grown. "There was a spring afternoon
about ten years ago," I said, "not long after we moved
down here. Your mother and I were still married, but I
knew not for long. I don't think you realized what was
happening. I took you in the company car I had at the
time and we drove way up on the Blue Ridge Parkway
to do some hiking. You were only five or six then.
You remember?"

"I think I remember . . . a little."

"That afternoon it hit me—not only was the marriage over, but I was probably going to lose you too."

She reached up and placed her hand gently on my arm.

"Anyway, I've always remembered that hike. The Winnie-the-Pooh sneakers and the little T-shirt that you wore. The way you ran all around and giggled and collected sticks. We had to hurry because your mother wanted you back by supper. . . ."

The door to the cell block clanked open, and a second or two later the deputy fiddled with his keys on the other side of the bars.

"I wish I could remember more of it," she said.

26

"So what was all that about? The little maneuver with the card at the end was pretty nifty," I said.

"I used to pass notes in class," Priscilla said.

I held the receiver in one hand while I tried to balance the twin-blade and foam gel in the other. I had headed straight from the jail back to the farm, figuring if I were going to be stonewalled for awhile, I might as well catch up on some of the sleep I had missed the night before. Jake had gone into town to visit the bank and post office. Calling Priscilla at her office was easier after the nap.

"Something's up," I said. "Why else would Cowan want me off the case?"

"C'mon, Frank. You know as well as I do that you're lucky they put up with you this long."

"That doesn't make it any easier to stomach. I was the one who started this whole thing. Remember?"

"Yeah, well I wouldn't keep harping on that, if I were you. It only makes Cowan more suspicious. He's worried that you and Jake are running some kind of scam."

"Right. And we're also working for the CIA."

"Did you talk with your daughter again?"

"Yes."

"How'd it go?"

"Very well, actually."

She paused, just long enough to telegraph that she didn't have time for games. "You confront her about the drug use?"

Andy Straka

"I did, and she swears on a stack of Bibles she's not using and I believe her."

"Which would make your ex-wife a liar."

"Exactly."

"Which doesn't surprise you."

"Not really."

"Why would she falsely accuse her own daughter of being an addict, risk bringing shame and embarrassment on the family?"

I finally wiped off with a towel and made my way with the portable phone from the door of the bathroom to the kitchen and sat down. "I haven't figured that one out yet. Besides, I'm off the case."

"You think this guy Weems was into something? Maybe that's another reason he did the ghost?"

"I wouldn't rule it out. The guy was moling for someone. My gut says he turned tail and ran. Wouldn't be surprised if he turned up dead too before long."

"You're starting to sound more like Jake."

"Batman and Robin. We used to fight crime by night."

"Is he there, by the way? I'd like to talk to him."

"No. He's probably right down the street from you. Went into the bank and the p.o."

"Maybe I should have a talk with Camille Rhodes."

"Might not be a bad idea."

"But I'm sure Cowan or Ferrier will talk to her. They don't exactly appreciate my interference."

"What do you expect? Cops have to stick together."

"Cowan tell you what he found out in New York?"

"No. I don't even think he's told Ferrier and Spain that much. He and Ferrier got into an argument over jurisdiction."

"Great. Just what we need. A glory hound."

The line was silent for a moment. She said: "You know, it just occurred to me. What you said about cops. That might be the reason Dewayne Turner was killed. Maybe because of loyalty to someone, or something."

"Someone in the gang?"

200

"Maybe."

"Interesting theory. The only way we're going to be able to test it, is if we go through with the meeting tonight."

"That's not the only way. Cowan and Ferrier have been arguing all morning about whether or not to drag Warren in here and question him, maybe round up some of the suspected gang members. The sheriff says he already knows who most of them are."

"Sure. That would just convince Warren even more that the sheriff has something to hide. Speaking of which, where are you on that angle?"

"Nowhere. I've talked informally with almost everyone who works here, including the two deputies who were on duty in the office the night Dewayne and your daughter were arrested. Even a cleaning lady who was in the building at the time. They all swear Warren Turner left the building sometime after Nicole did, safe and sound."

"Anyone see where he went?" I looked out the window. A gunmetal sky muted the brilliance of the red and gold leaves.

"Just walked away, they said, down Main Street."

"Dewayne have a car?"

I heard her flipping through some papers. "Yeah. Blue Audi, a leftover from his dealing days. It's still parked in his mother's garage. Looks like the sheriff and his people went over it long ago, after he was first reported missing."

"So we're back to the gang theory," I said.

"Don't forget your daughter. I know you believe her, but Cowan and Ferrier sure aren't necessarily inclined to. And if it were up to the sheriff alone, you'd be cooling your heels down here in his jail along with her."

"But, hopefully, they'll need me to go with you tonight."

"Hopefully."

"Why not send Ferrier or his partner? The gang members might not make them for cops."

"It's been discussed. Ferrier convinced Cowan to let you stay in the picture."

"Is that right? Nice to know I've earned a little bit of trust."

"Yes. But, don't abuse it."

"You talk to Warren about when and where we're supposed to get together?" I said.

"Yes. He wants us to meet him in the newpaper's parking lot at seven-thirty."

"It'll be dark by then. Ferrier and Cowan and their people going to be able to stay with us?"

"I hope so."

"You okay with deceiving the old boyfriend?"

"No, but I guess it comes with the job."

"Sometimes," I said.

After we hung up I fixed myself a quick turkey sandwich with a glass of milk from Jake's refrigerator, then went out to the mews to check on Armistead.

The air was getting colder with what felt like the beginnings of a winter wind. I wore my work boots and zipped my three-quarter jacket around me. Armistead seemed full of energy, fanning her wings and footing her perch.

"I know, girl. You're busting to get out. Don't worry. Jake will be back a little later, and we'll all walk out together. In the meantime, I've got a couple little errands to run myself."

I might have been officially told to bug off the investigation, but that didn't stop me from talking to family, even ex-family for that matter.

Lucita answered the front door at the Rhodes estate again. She understood English perfectly, despite the accent and halting speech, which was helpful because, from the way she described things, Señorita Rhodes still didn't seem to be doing all that well.

"Is she awake?" I asked.

"Oh yes, señor, but like I told you, she is crazy. I think she is ill." She led me into the house.

"Did you call a doctor?"

"No. No, she say no doctors."

"Have other men been out to talk to her yet today? The sheriff?"

"*Sí señor.* A couple hours ago."

We made our way to the same atrium where Camille and I had spoken the night before. The room had taken on a different quality now, much brighter, from all the windows. On the Oriental rug Camille lay shivering under a heavy comforter. Her forehead was bathed in sweat. I helped Lucita get her onto the couch.

"Hello, Frank," she managed to say.

"You need a doctor, Camille."

"Oh hogwash . . . Thank you, Lucita. That'll be all for now. I'll call for you if I need you."

"You sure, Mrs. Rhodes?" The maid hesitated.

"Yes, of course I'm sure. Go ahead. Mr. Pavlicek is here and if something drastic happens, I'm sure he can manage the situation."

Lucita disappeared into another part of the house.

"Come and sit next to me, Frank," Camille said. She gestured toward the end of the couch.

"You remember our visit last night?" I asked.

"Yes. Yes, I'm sorry I fell asleep on you, but as you can see, I haven't been feeling too well. I've been under a great deal of stress lately." There was a box of tissues, a big pitcher of orange juice, and an empty glass on the table in front of her. I smelled the juice. No booze.

"Well, I wasn't really referring to the falling asleep part. I thought you might remember stripping back your dress and grabbing hold of me in the dark."

She lowered her head, crossed one arm under the other, and put a hand to her brow. "I'm sorry, Frank, I . . ."

"Nothing happened. I put you to bed."

"I guess I should thank you for that." Or maybe not, she seemed to be thinking.

"Did the sheriff and the state police come talk with you this morning?"

She nodded. "They asked me a lot of stupid questions."

"About Nicky?"

"Yes."

"I talked with Nicky in her cell again this morning. She says you haven't been in to see her."

"No. I've been busy, and, as you can see, I haven't been feeling up to the trip."

"She claims she's not using any drugs, Camille."

She pulled the comforter up around her more and squeezed it with her fingers. "Well, of course she would, wouldn't she. That's what kids usually do when they've been discovered."

"The needles and stuff you showed me," I said, "the cops confirmed it's methamphetamine. On the street they call it crank."

"It sounds . . . it sounds awful."

I sat down and, before she could react, reached beneath the comforter, took hold of her arm, and twisted it out and up for her to see.

"Ouch!" she said. "What are you doing?"

"Don't try to tell me you've been donating a lot of blood."

She stared at her arm with an almost surprised look. Then she began to smile.

"Well, that—those marks mean nothing. I mean, every once in awhile I—"

"More than every once in awhile, if I don't miss my guess."

"What do you know? You have no right invading my privacy. I . . ." She turned on her side and curled into a fetal position, staring blankly at the sofa.

"There's treatment, Camille. I want to help. Nicole will too, if you would just—"

"Nicole." She laughed hoarsely. "That daughter of

yours is turning out to be more trouble than she's worth."

"You don't need to let this stuff destroy you," I said.

"It's not destroying me, for chrissake. What do you know about it? I'm just a little under the weather. I can quit anytime I like." Her eyes avoided mine.

"I need to know who's supplying you," I said.

"What for? You back to working Narcotics now? I didn't know they let private detectives do that kind of work."

"Is it a gang? Was Dewayne Turner involved?"

She acted as if she had trouble comprehending what I was asking. "I'd like a drink," she said.

"Stick to orange juice." I refilled her glass and she drank some, but didn't seem too happy about it.

Then her demeanor suddenly changed. Her mouth dropped and she sat up and clutched at my arm. "That boy was killed, you know."

"Yes I know, Camille. I was the one who found him. Remember?"

She giggled, shaking her head. "Yes, that's right." She pulled away and lay back on the couch. "Oh Christ, Frank, I've made a mess of things. The money . . . everything . . . I . . ." She began to cry.

I'd seen those tears before, on drunks or on addicts in the tank. Nothing that a pint or a smoke couldn't handle.

"You're willing to let Nicole take a rap and maybe go to prison, to let yourself go to waste? For what?" I said.

"You just don't understand. You don't know what I've been through. You were never here."

"I'm here now though, aren't I?"

Her eyes went cold again. She turned away and spoke into the couch. "Goddamn you for messing up our lives . . ."

She seemed to absorb her own epitaph, her body wracked with sobs, curled on her side deep in pillows. I waited for maybe a minute, before looking up to see Lucita in the doorway again, a question on her face.

I threw the grande dame a tissue as I left.

* * *

"Looks like you and me need to have a little talk."
Sheriff Cowan was just exiting his cruiser, parked behind
my truck in the driveway out front. He leaned against
the vehicle, crossed his arms, and frowned.

"What about?"

"About whether I arrest you now or you turn yourself
in down to the department."

"Come on, Cowan. I told you I'd back off, and I am.
That doesn't mean I can't go visit my ex-wife."

"It doesn't, huh? Just a social call then?"

"Right. A social call."

He stared at me.

"She's lying, you know. You even said it yourself.
She's the one on meth, not Nicky."

"Know that for a fact, do you?"

I held out my hand toward the house. "Why don't
you go ask her for yourself?"

He puffed his cheeks and blew out some air. "I'm not
the bad guy in all this, Pavlicek."

"Never said you were," I lied.

He snickered. "Shoot," he said under his breath. I was
pleased to hear him make reference to rather than attempt to perform the act. "Let's talk about you."

"All right."

"Still hard for me to believe you just so happened to
find the dead Turner kid."

"Sure."

"You being a PI already puts you under suspicion in
my book. Somebody wanted to set something up, you'd
be the kind they'd ask to do it."

"Right. Except I didn't."

He stared at me long and hard. It was the same stare
he'd used in the conference room earlier, only this one
had a trace of fear in it, like he was out there on the
edge of something and knew it. "So you say," he finally said.

"Somebody's going to go down for Dewayne Turner's murder."

He shrugged. "Then I ain't got nothing to worry about. How about you?"

"Does it make any sense, if I did, I'd be hanging around here talking with you?"

"Maybe," he said. "Maybe not."

"We don't even have to take sides, do we?"

"You become a nigger-lover since you went and killed one when you was a cop?"

"No," I said. "Before that."

He chuckled and scuffed his boot against the driveway. "Tell me about your buddies Toronto and Cahill."

"What about them?"

"You three were pals up in New York, right?"

"Not really. That is . . . not until after the shooting. Jake and I were partners, but we didn't know Cahill until that night."

"Ummm," he said.

I waited.

"Your old chief up there says you and Toronto were good cops."

"We pay him to say that."

He didn't see the humor. "Look, Pavlicek. We ain't gotta like each other when it comes to this Turner thing. We just gotta figure out what happened to the boy."

"At least we're in agreement there. What about Ferrier and his partner?"

He shrugged. "I ain't too proud to work with them, but like I told you before, this is my county. This thing's gonna get solved."

"You think you got it figured out?"

He worked his jaw around a little. "May be getting close."

"Care to share any theories with an old detective?"

He shook his head. "Un-uh. Not yet."

"Just feel free to waste my time then."

"You tell me then, Pavlicek, how am I not supposed

to wonder when your daughter's caught haulin' coke and you show up the next morning, all but carrying a dead dealer in your arms?"

The man did have a point.

"Kind of makes things interesting, doesn't it?" I said.

"What's that?"

"The mutual suspicion."

He shook his head and looked toward the house.

"What was so important it made you fly all the way up to New York?"

For a moment he seemed on the verge of telling me, but something stopped him. Fear maybe. Maybe pride. "This thing's turnin' out to be some kind of god-awful mess, I can tell you that."

It was my turn to sigh. "God probably wishes he could sit this one out."

27

Armistead dropped out of sight below the ridge line where a stand of sugar maples shed their last bit of gold against a backdrop of gathering gray. Her bells were no longer audible. We had put a tail transmitter on her so it would be no problem locating her with the telemetry unit, but I was perturbed and a little fearful of losing her, nonetheless.

Jake walked about ten paces behind me, whistling. "Some say you don't truly know falconry until you've lost your first bird."

Mr. Encouragement.

The temperature hovered just above freezing, and the brown landscape was looking more barren by the day. Soon there would be little cover left for prey to conceal themselves from a pursuing hawk.

Priscilla had shown up at the trailer with a bag of fresh donuts and coffee just as we were setting out. She said she would wait, maybe tidy up a little, until we came back, which caused Jake a half-worried, half-hopeful expression that earned him a peck on the cheek. The wind was picking up. Armistead, skillful flyer that she was, seemed to revel in its strength, as if drawing from it her own. She had spotted a groundhog earlier and made a halfhearted swoop at the thing before the sizable critter disappeared with unexpected swiftness down an unseen burrow. To my relief, she popped above the maples again and glided forward to alight near the top of one.

"There's a meadow other side of this hill," Jake said.

"She holds her station, we can get down over there and flush a rabbit or two."

We climbed together to the crest. The meadow on the other side was not large, but the grass was serviceable, the ground soft and ripe for tunneling. Prime rabbit habitat. Beyond the field the forest began again, but there were open spaces there as well. Armistead stayed put, swaying a little when the branch moved with the breeze.

We separated, about twenty yards apart as we entered the meadow, loping downhill. We had only gone about ten paces when they started, a trio of cottontails raised instantly from sleep into a crash of twigs breaking, a panic-stricken dash for their lives. Armistead flashed by us and went after the slowest. She took the prey with ease.

"All right! Attagirl!" I turned to see Jake stepping toward me with a smile on his face.

I let out a war whoop into the cold as Jake and I slapped palms.

"I knew you had her trained, Frank, but, man, she's gonna be a hunting machine."

We let her feed for a short while before calling her off the kill with an even bigger reward: a piece of one of the quail Jake raised. If we let her grow too sated, we risked the loss of her seeing us as the best provider of her next easy meal. The rabbit looked healthy; its pelt could be turned into clothing or decoration and it would make an excellent stew.

Later, after Jersey had enjoyed a successful hunt too, we sat over coffee, hot soup, and donuts in the trailer.

Priscilla was still there. "You guys love this, don't you? This hawking thing," she said.

"Yeah." Jake was tying some new jesses while we ate. "It kind of gets in your blood."

"It's a little savage, you know, for a city-bred girl."

"World can be savage sometimes. Doesn't always make it bad."

"I suppose."

"Even city girls can appreciate the call of the wild," I said. "We're just giving more of the birds a better chance is all."

She looked at Jake. "I've watched him with Jersey. I know what you mean. . . . It's almost enough to make a girl jealous."

Jake simply smiled.

"How are you holding up, Pavlicek? I mean with your daughter still in jail and everything," Priscilla asked.

"I've hardly slept for forty-eight hours, but Jake's coffee's keeping me going. I guess I'm doing all right."

"There's not much more we can do for you at the moment."

"Maybe there is." I told her what I had told Cowan about Camille.

"We'll see. Maybe we'll learn more tonight."

"Nicky's telling the truth."

"Detectives aren't usually known for being optimists," she said.

"Except when it comes to their own daughters."

Jake heard a sound, leaned over, and peeked out his curtain. "Someone's coming up the drive."

We all watched through the window as a small white Hyundai popped into view.

"It's Pastor Lori," Priscilla said. "Looks like he has Carla Turner with him."

The car pulled in front and came to a stop. The minister jumped out and went to open the door for Mrs. Turner. He wore a down vest over a sweater that seemed to add about thirty pounds to his wiry frame. Carla Turner hoisted herself from the car, using the pastor's arm and a metal cane for support.

Jake went to help.

"Hello, Mr. Toronto," Carla said. "Ms. Thomasen. We were hoping to find Mr. Pavlicek still here."

"He's here, all right," I said, stepping from behind them.

"Oh, good, Mr. Pavlicek. May we come in?"

"Come on in and pull up a chair," Jake said. We waited while she made her way into his little kitchen and sat down.

"Would you like something to eat?" Priscilla asked. "We've got soup, donuts, and coffee—it's fresh brewed."

"Oh, no thank you, honey. I'm just fine."

"How about you, Reverend Lori?"

The pastor shook his head.

"What can we do for you then?"

"Mrs. Turner here's the one insisted on coming," the Reverend said. "Said she felt the spirit moving her. And who am I to argue with that?" He smiled, I thought, a little nervously.

We all looked at Carla Turner who leaned toward me and said in a low voice: "There be rumors flying about some things happening tonight, Mr. Pavlicek, and well, like I told Pastor Lori, I just had to come."

"I appreciate the sentiment, Mrs. Turner," I said.

"Lord, ain't no sentiment about it. Your daughter's still in jail, ain't she? You and me, we sharing an agony when it comes to a child."

"Thank you."

"I told the pastor, I just got to go over there and pray for that man."

"Oh, that's okay, Mrs. Turner. I mean, I appreciate it, but—"

"No, no, Mr. Pavlicek. Prayer is what we need. I'm telling you, as sure as I be sitting here. Prayer's the thing."

The pastor nodded.

I hemmed and hawed some more, but to no avail. A minute later she had us all around the table with our heads bowed and holding hands, talking, she said, as naturally as if it were to someone else in the room, to the Lord.

I do not remember the words of her prayer. She might have prayed for resolution, for safety for Nicole, I'm not sure. Maybe my mind was fried from lack of sleep or I was too buzzed on caffeine. What I do remember is Carla Turner's voice, how it seemed to slow down, to modulate, to grow. If there were angels in the room in that moment, they sounded like Dewayne Turner's mother, who through love seemed to gather up and blow away all uncertainty. It was clearly a power beyond herself.

When she finished I thanked her again.

She took my hand in hers. "One thing to remember about prayer, Mr. Pavlicek. God always answers. It may not be what we want or in a way we can know right away, but you can always count on a reply. You understand?"

I nodded. Jake seemed to take her words in stride the way he took everything. Priscilla dabbed at her eyes.

"And you need to know," she said. "Lots of times, when He answers . . . things, they gets a lot darker before they gets light."

28

Light from my headlamps blended with the parking lot illumination to make the pavement sparkle outside the *Leonardston Standard*. The spaces were otherwise empty. The temperature had not dropped significantly enough for it to snow, but the raw cold felt supercharged with moisture. I had pulled on a heavy sweater to wear beneath my slicker—no problemo, since I had no weapon to conceal. Sure hoped Ferrier and whatever forces he had brought with him were keeping us under good watch.

Sheriff Cowan, I would find out later, had told everyone at the last minute that he wasn't coming; he said had a more promising lead he needed to check out. Naturally, Ferrier and Spain were not too keen about proceeding on such a potentially volatile mission minus the sheriff. But they had a number of his deputies, even a few state troopers all set to go. In the end, it was decided that by not moving forward as planned, they might miss their best opportunity to flush out Dewayne's killer and maybe simultaneously put a dent in a major drug ring.

We were not supposed to see any danger. Unbeknownst to Warren, once he had done his thing and we approached whatever meeting place he and the gang had chosen, the plan called for us to cut out and let the calvary surround and move in. Priscilla had the task of informing Warren when the time came. No one was naïve enough to think he would take it well.

The last thing Jake had said to me before I left was:

"Stay tight to the lawyer. Anything happens, I want her protected." He was staring at the concrete floor of Jersey's mews, patiently hosing off the waste, taking care that every little speck was rinsed away so as to avoid any potential source of disease.

"I hear you."

"And don't try to be a hero."

"Yes, boss."

He didn't laugh. Jake can be such a cutup sometimes.

I pulled the truck into an end parking space and cut the engine and lights. Almost as if on cue, another set of headlights appeared and the Commonwealth's attorney's Saab purred in quietly beside me, with Priscilla at the wheel. Warren Turner sat in the passenger seat. We all stepped out.

"I'll be doing the driving," Warren said. He was draped in a Burberry trench coat, looking like some kind of spy.

"Whatever you say," I said.

"No weapons, right?" He made a show of patting me down, the way he'd probably seen them do on TV. Priscilla wore a chartreuse waterproof parka trimmed with some kind of imitation fur. If the 'bangers ever got a look at her we would all be in trouble.

In the car they let me sit in front to stretch my legs while Priscilla climbed in back. Warren reached down to the floor in front of him and came up with a pair of sleeping masks, complete with elastic bands attached.

"Here, you two. Put these on."

"You've got to be kidding," Priscilla said.

"Jeez, Warren. Didn't know you were into kinky," I said.

"It's either wear them or we aren't going."

"I really am kind of partial to my sight."

"Gang has rules. If I don't follow them, I lose their trust."

You're about to lose more than that, I thought. I looked in the mirror at Priscilla. She said nothing more and was already beginning to slip on her own mask. I didn't like it, but we were just going to have to trust the unseen cops to stay with us. I put on the mask.

Warren threw the car into reverse, jerked us to a stop and into first gear. He accelerated across the lot and took a turn onto Main Street, then, quickly, another turn to the right, and another, then a wide sweeping turn to the left. Pretty soon I had no idea in which direction we were headed.

Priscilla finally spoke. "Could you take it a little slower please, Warren. You're going to make me sick to my stomach back here." It was a good ploy, if that's what it was, to make it easier to track us. Warren slowed down.

"How long you been in touch with these characters?" I asked him.

"Four, five years," he said.

"When you began talking with them, Dewayne was still part of the group?"

"That's right."

"What's the leader's name?"

"Don't know his real name. Kids all call him Smoke."

"Cute. You know his story?"

"He's been in jail, I know that. More than once. Red Onion the last time, I think."

I let out a respectful whistle. "Maybe I *should* have brought a gun."

We drove on in silence after that. Warren worked the gears as the car twisted through curves and up and down hills. We were still on wet pavement—you could hear the tires slicing through the sheets of water, the occasional popping noises when the rain mixed with sleet against the windshield. But judging from the lack of noise, no other vehicles passed us going in the opposite direction. In a funny way it reminded me of long car trips when I was young, my eyes closed, half-sleeping in the back, trying to balance the counterweight of acceleration and deceleration, swings to the left and right, the beat of the wipers metronoming against the rain. I drifted into sleep.

Vibration and the sound of stones bouncing against the undercarriage jolted me awake. We were turning onto a side road.

"You snore, man," Warren said.

"Comes with age. We there yet?"

"Almost. Another minute or so." A few more accelerations, a few more sharp turns of the wheel and the vehicle began to slow.

"Warren?" Priscilla said suddenly from the back. Her voice sounded anything but sleepy.

"Yeah, babe?"

"We need to talk."

"Yeah sure, in a minute."

"No really," she said. "Right now. Please stop the car."

"Well I can't just—"

"Please, Warren. Stop the car. Now."

"Okay." The Saab lurched to a halt. "But I don't want to keep these guys waiting."

The wipers kept up their pace and a few big raindrops pelted the roof.

"This has got to be the end of the road," Priscilla said.

"What?"

"I'm taking my mask off." I heard her remove her mask and mine came off too. We were headed uphill in a steady rain on a narrow dirt track through thick woods. It was completely dark, except for our headlights. About fifty yards ahead I could make out the shadowy silhouette of a two-story house.

"What are you talking about, woman?" Warren said. "You want to get us all killed?"

"I'm sorry, Warren. I couldn't tell you any sooner. The police know about the meeting. I gave them permission to follow us."

"You what?" The look on the reporter's face was a mixture of uncertainty, rage, and horror.

But something was wrong. Instead of Ferrier and a group of deputies approaching the car, five or six young black men, dressed similarly, with dark sweatpants and hooded rain jackets, brandishing weapons, their mouths steaming, surrounded the car.

They jerked open all four doors.

"Out, motherfuckers!"

I was pulled to my feet. The cold hit like a fist.

"Keep your hands up."

They spun me away from the others and patted me down.

"Hey, fellas, I'm sorry I didn't come all the way up to the house like you told me," Warren said.

"Shut up." The one doing the talking had a high-pitched voice and was behind and to my right, where Priscilla must have been standing. "What, man, you think we're stupid? Move." I was shoved uphill toward the house by the barrel of a gun. I kept my eyes straight ahead. From the sounds, it was apparent the rest of the group was moving along behind.

"You fucked this thing up royal, Mr. Reporter. We don't want to be bumping titties with no state cops."

"It wasn't me," Warren pleaded. "I didn't know anything. I swear."

"Just shut the fuck up."

We were outside the building now, a grayish-white farmhouse with broken shutters and very little paint that wasn't peeling. We clambered across the porch and through the front door. Inside the air didn't feel much warmer, but at least it was dry. My hair and jacket were almost drenched.

"It's okay," Priscilla said over my shoulder. "We'll be all right."

"Quiet," the high-pitched voice said.

They walked us through an open cellar door down steep steps onto a concrete floor. The basement was alight with halogen lamps, some of which were pointed at our faces. Unfinished, from what I could see, but there was a refrigerator, a couch, a television, and an expensive-looking stereo. In the background I heard the sound of a dehumidifier whirring. Behind the lights six or seven more young men sat or stood in various positions of repose around the room. Most of them wore heavy coats, expensive hiking or basketball shoes. Almost all carried handguns. Priscilla and Warren stood to my right at the bottom of the stairs.

"Okay," a new voice said. Much deeper. It belonged to a bald, muscular mulatto with freckles like pepper dotting his face. He sat on one end of the couch, his thick leg draped over the side, not moving. Instead of sweatpants he was dressed neatly in jeans and a thick leather jacket, a bright red durag wrapped around his head. CEO garb. A nine-millimeter Browning was stuffed carelessly in his coat pocket.

He went on: "Miss Fresh Priscilla Lawyer here and Mr. Newspaper Man done dropped a shit on us."

"Smoke," Warren said. "I'm telling you. I didn't know anything about—"

The leader stood so we could better appreciate the size of him. Warren started to say something else, but kept quiet. The big man was staring at Priscilla.

"Miss Priscilla Thomasen," he said. "Miss Commonwealth's attorney herself. And one fine-looking freak." There were snickers from around the room.

The mulatto turned his gaze toward me. "But you brought the Pollock too, Warren. Nice work."

"Smoke, you know who this dude is?" one of the others said from behind me.

"Shut the fuck up, Banjo," the leader said. "I knows who the man is."

He came closer, examining me, his eyes the color of steel. My hands remained at my sides.

"You told Warren you had information about Dewayne Turner's murder and Nicole Pavlicek's arrest," Priscilla said.

He spun back toward her. "Oh, yes, ma'am," he said

loudly. "We got us some information. But all of a sudden now don't seem like the time we oughta be sharin' it. What with no sheriff's deputies and state patrollers stuck a couple miles down the mountain . . ."

He saw the looks on our faces.

"That's right. Your little escorts, seems like they got themselves a little lost. . . ."

More snickers. Then silence. They all seemed to be examining us like specimens, like creatures of the night that had inadvertently strayed into their headlights. *Should we kill these ones or just let them go?*

"What do you want?" I said.

He tilted his head in my direction again. "What do we want? The man wants to know what we want." He squinted. "Who the fuck you talkin' to, cracker?"

There was a noise and a minor commotion on the stairs. Everyone looked in that direction. A pair of large combat boots clomped casually down the steps, the gang members who were perched there respectfully making way for their owner. I knew almost instantly whose they were. Jake, wearing an Orioles baseball cap, came into view, smiling.

The leader's demeanor suddenly changed. "Mr. Toe-ron-to," he said. "What it be?"

The master falconer walked casually up to the young man and they lightly slapped palms. His .45 was holstered neatly beneath his open jacket. No one tried to take it from him. Priscilla and Warren stared, wide-eyed.

Jake turned to us. "Understand you folks got a little problem here."

"You know these people?" Priscilla said.

"Been around enough to know them."

"But you aren't, uh, associated with them, are you?"

He smiled. "No. Let's just say we've developed a healthy respect for one another."

"Let me get the headline, here, Mr. Toronto," Smoke said. "You cool with these people?"

Jake nodded. The dehumidifier clicked off. You could

hear a pin drop in the room, but the tension suddenly vanished.

"Thas all right then," the leader said. "We chilled out. Ain't got no reason to dis you, Toronto." He and Jake bumped fists this time.

"Seems to me," Jake said, looking around the room, "all anyone really needs here is an exchange of info. The whiskers down the road are going to be tied up awhile. Looks like a couple trees happened to fall across the road in their path."

The gangsters all chuckled. Smoke ambled back to his couch and sat down.

"How about it?" Priscilla said. "You fellas know anything about Dewayne Turner's murder?"

"I know it ain't been one of us who wasted him," Smoke said, looking at his fingernails. Bored.

"He quit your gang, didn't he?"

Smoke shrugged. "Dewayne, he got Jesus. But he wasn't about to do nothin' to us."

"He used to deal for you, didn't he?" I asked.

He looked at me and nodded almost imperceptibly. "We made some bank."

"You know his swing man?"

"Don't know 'im."

"The name Morelli mean anything to you?"

He shook his head.

"Don't you use the same connections as Dewayne?"

"Un-uh. That way Dewayne could be cool just zonin' out."

"Someone might not like losing the business," I said.

He shrugged. "You look for 'em, they be plenty of dudes around."

"What about my daughter, Nicole Pavlicek? She was arrested carrying a load of flake."

"Don't know nothin' about that," the leader said.

"You mean someone could drop that much coke into your neighborhood and you fellas wouldn't care?"

"Didn't say we didn't care, Irish," he said. "All I say

was we don't know nothin' about it . . . you so interested in Dewayne and how he was connected why don't you go and talk wid the sheriff. He the one been talkin' to Dewayne's man."

"How do you know that?"

" 'Cause he busted one of my chicos this mornin', boy who run lookout sometimes. They didn't have nothin' on him so they couldn't hold him. But he say the sheriff braggin' he already know who kilt Dewayne. Somethin' to do wid the swing man."

I glanced at Priscilla who gave me a look that said she knew nothing about it.

"Whoever was supplying Dewayne either killed him or knows who did it?" I said.

"You stupid? Ain't that what I just say?"

From outside, still some distance away, a police siren's faint *whoop-whoop* filtered down to the basement.

"Uh-oh. Reinforcements," Jake said.

"Time we disappeared." Smoke was already moving. Around the room the gang scrambled into motion, unplugging equipment, picking up anything of value. Most were already pounding up the stairs.

"One thing, Mr. Toe-ron-to?" Smoke said.

"Yeah?"

"You find out who did Dewayne, I'll nine 'em for you myself, you want. No charge."

Jake raised his eyebrows at me. "Thanks, Smoke. We'll keep that in mind."

The leader shot us a freckled smile before snatching a stereo speaker and turning to follow his troops up the stairs.

"Are you people insane?" Ferrier said, standing in the middle of the cellar.

He and about twenty cops had surrounded and secured the farmhouse while Jake, Priscilla, Warren, and I remained in the room. It took some convincing for them to realize they had lost their intended targets.

"Who's this character?" He pointed at Toronto, who was now seated with one combat boot draped over an arm on the couch where Smoke had so recently reclined.

"Agent Ferrier," I said. "Meet Jake Toronto, former NYPD detective and my former partner."

"Jesus H. Christ." He swiped his fingers through his remaining hair. "Just what we need."

Toronto nodded, his mouth a perfectly straight line, obviously flattered.

Ferrier turned to the Commonwealth's attorney and the reporter. "Miss Thomasen, Mr. Turner, maybe one of you can tell me what went on here."

Warren, who for the last several minutes had been seated in a straight-back chair in the corner looking a little peaked, was speechless. Priscilla, standing next to me with her back to the wall, said: "The gang surprised us. They're smarter than we thought."

"Anyone hurt?"

"No."

"You get anything on them, counselor?"

She glanced at Jake. "Nothing I can use, except that they didn't kill Dewayne Turner. And they don't know anything about the cocaine confiscated from Ms. Pavlicek either."

"I suppose they just volunteered that information, did they?"

She glanced at Jake. "In fact," she said, "they did."

Ferrier eyes searched mine, then Jake's, then finally Priscilla's. Finally, he shook his head. "Why do I get the strong feeling you people aren't telling me everything?" he said.

Priscilla shrugged. I shrugged. Jake shrugged.

The state police investigator pointed at Jake and me. "I oughta drag both of you into custody right now, is what I oughta do."

He turned to his partner. "Chad, I want this place sealed and a team in here ASAP to go over it for prints and any other evidence. Let's use the sheriff's people if you can. Otherwise, we'll have to bring in our own."

He looked back to us. "And as far as you folks are concerned. I want you down at the sheriff's office by eight tomorrow morning. We're gonna find Cowan, wherever he is, and talk this thing all out. This may be his jurisdiction, but I'll be damned if I'm heading off on another expedition for fool's gold."

"I'll make sure we're all there," Priscilla said.

Only as it turned out, I would be the one meeting Sheriff Cowan. Alone. And a little earlier than any of us planned.

29

The next morning's weather report called for a cold cloudiness and the possibility of more rain. Farther north, into the mountains of West Virginia, they were predicting the season's first snow. The lights were on, but only three vehicles occupied the lot outside Cat's place where I stopped for coffee before sunrise. I hadn't slept much. Jake's phone was temporarily out of order and he'd spent the night over at Priscilla's place.

The door was open, as always, so I went in and sat down, a dog-eared paperback copy of George Garrett's *Do, Lord, Remember Me* in my back pocket. I was in a foul mood. What if Dewayne Turner had been selling crank to Camille? What would have happened when he stopped? What if Nicole knew about it? If you listened to Camille, the whole mess was somehow my fault.

I was only partway through Howie Loomis's opening soliloquy when Cat came out from the kitchen. "Mornin', Eagle."

"Hey, big guy."

"You up early. Didn't get enough to eat the other day, or just after company?"

"I couldn't sleep."

He looked as if he hadn't slept too well himself. "Can't say as I blame you. Coffee?"

"Sure."

He went over to a serving station beside the bar and poured a couple steaming mugs from the pot.

"Where'd you get that slicker? Looks like something even the Salvation Army wouldn't take," he said.

"Keeps me drier and warmer than all that space-age stuff," I said.

He chuckled. "I'll bet . . . how was the trip to Charlottesville?"

"Fine."

"You see that fella from New York?"

"Rashid? Yeah, we saw him."

"Anything new?"

"Yeah. He's got the gun that did Singer. Guess who turned it in?"

"Who?"

"Boog Morelli."

"That a fact."

"Yeah, but if it was a gang gun, it won't be that easy to trace."

Cat shook his head. "Probably no tellin' where the thing's been."

"Umm . . . Let me ask you something. Just speculation. From what you know of Nicky, if she were put in a situation where she knew something about someone that was close to her, something that might get them in trouble, how do you think she'd react?"

"Nicky? No question," he said. "She'd stay loyal to the person. Maybe she'd try to get them to work it out."

I nodded. "That's the way I see it too."

We sipped the hot liquid.

"Oh," I said. "I almost forgot. What did the sheriff want to talk to you about yesterday?"

"Your daughter and that Turner kid."

"You mean about the night they were picked up here?"

"Uh-huh."

"Anything else?"

He hesitated. "Yeah . . . well he was asking about my relationship with you and Toronto."

"He was, huh?"

"Asked what I knew about your PI business, that sort of thing."

"You think he's planning to make a run at me?"

"Don't know, buddy. I guess you'll have to ask him that one yourself. But I'd watch my back, I was you."

I said nothing.

"You talk with Nicky again? How's she doin'?"

"I talked with her. She's okay, for someone in jail."

He grunted, looked toward the door for a moment, then back at me.

"Have you noticed anything . . . well . . . different about her mother the last few months?"

"Camille? Not really. Course, I don't see her that much. Why?"

"No reason."

"Hey, that boyfriend she's running around with—now he's something different," he said.

"Was," I said. "He skipped town."

"Can't say as I'm too surprised."

"Good coffee," I said. "What blend?"

"Just regular old joe." He squinted at me and winked. "Part of your problem, see. You move down from New York, you're okay for awhile, but now you've gone and got civilized again livin' up there in that university burg."

"Oh? What did I get when I lived over here in Leonardston?"

"Education," he said with a smile.

We drank in silence for awhile. He glanced out the windows in front. "Looks like it's comin' on to more rain later."

"Looks like," I said. "I've got a meeting in a couple hours. Maybe I'll take a little drive, see some scenery before then."

My cell phone rang just as I was climbing back into my truck.

It was Jake. "Someone's trying to get ahold of you."

"Yeah? They finally discover my old winning lottery ticket?"

"No. Cowan called. He said he wants to talk to you alone this morning."

"You mean before we all meet with Ferrier?"

"That's what he said."

"Where, his office?"

"Un-uh. Says he goin' fishing."

"Fishing?"

"Right. You know that little reservoir up past Yellow Mountain?"

"Sure."

"Says he'll be there after sunrise. Asked if you could stop by."

"What time did he call?"

"About four-thirty. Woke us both out of sound sleep."

"Odd, don't you think?"

"Yeah. You want some backup?"

"No. Not this time. I'll be all right."

"You sure?"

"Yes."

"Suit yourself."

Though I had learned much about the woods from falconry, fishing was not my forte. On the way to Yellow Mountain I stopped by a combination gas and supply store, where I filled the truck and bought a cheap rod and reel with a spinner, the kind the store normally sold to tourists.

"Guess you don't really plan to catch much of anything." The store clerk was a smart-alecky, freckle-faced youth with red hair.

"It'll be real peaceful then, won't it?" I said, smiling.

The road to the reservoir wound northward from the state highway through an expansive cedar grove planted by the civilian conservation corps when the dam that formed the body of water was built. The reservoir itself occupied a wide canyon that had formed between the back of Yellow Mountain, most of which had long ago been blasted out for mining, and a group of smaller, thickly forested hills. The sun was up but the area around the mountain was now encased by fog.

Reaching the water, I saw no sign of the sheriff or his car. I drove on a rough course along the shore, headed toward the dam a mile or so distant. I passed a few other fisherman out on the water; they waved to me and I waved back.

Pretty soon I came to a high hill where a rockslide angled all the way down from the ridge above into the water. No way a vehicle was going any farther on the track. That became even more obvious when I caught sight of the sheriff's cruiser parked in the turnaround. Cowan was probably down the shore a ways casting.

I stepped from the truck, unpacked my gear, brought out the .357 just in case and strapped it to my belt. If the sheriff were up to something devious, I didn't think he would try something in broad daylight and with a handful of witnesses in easy earshot. Hadn't heard of there being any alligators or man-eating hippos around either, but you never knew.

I locked the truck and, balancing the rod in one hand, began to pick my way across the slide. On the other side I entered a stand of white pine.

I kept moving, expecting to come upon the sheriff at any moment, but there was no sign of him. After a few hundred yards I began to hear the noise from the dam.

I passed a large red sign, clearly visible from anywhere on the water, warning all craft away. Around the next point of land the levee itself became visible; it wasn't a large one, as such structures go, a fairly old embankment dam. There was a walkway across the top with iron railings on either side. The clear, deep water looked fairly placid upstream, though I knew that could be deceptive; as it neared the dam you could see its current begin to narrow and speed up in a powerful flow that crashed through the spillway. Hydraulic doors could broaden the flow, if necessary, and they were wide open now.

Still no sign of Sheriff Cowan. I walked down to the dam. The roar from the spillway became almost deafening. I looked around a bit then carefully crossed the walkway to the far shore. I walked along the water again until I rounded a point, just out of sight of the dam. An owl, perhaps disturbed by my presence, left its sleepy perch in the woods and glided soundlessly through the trees. If I couldn't find Cowan, maybe it was best to let him find me.

My cheap spinner cast clumsily into the water. I put slack in the line and propped the rod with a forked stick anyway, hoping for blind luck. I sat on the bank to wait, but a pack of blue jays caused me to look up with a start. Their jagged cries were approaching from the woods behind me.

Suddenly, a broad pair of dark wings with translucent windows, a burnt orange underbelly and a tail with narrow black-and-white bands, flew from the woods with the jays in pursuit. A red-shoulder hawk, cousin to the red-tail, glided overhead, as if flirting with its tormentors; the jays spun like angry bees in its wake.

At that point I became aware of the figure of a man, seated with his back to me, some distance down the bank. Had to be Cowan. He seemed to be waiting patiently, his line in the water. I undid my rod and started walking toward him. As I drew closer I saw I was right: it was Cowan. He wore blue sweatpants and hiking boots, some kind of thick sweatshirt covered by his brown windbreaker with the words SHERIFF stenciled on the back. His sidearm rode on his waist, and I could even make out his badge gleaming there too.

"Sorry. I didn't see you," I said as I came within earshot.

There was no answer.

"Cowan?"

He didn't move.

A WITNESS ABOVE

I pulled out my weapon and began to step sideways as I came around in front of him. It was not a pretty sight.

Affalachia County's all-American sheriff, Peter Cowan, was dead.

30

The Beechcraft nineteen-hundred bound for La Guardia climbed out of Charlottesville later that morning, its nose pointed at the sun. The rain and clouds had receded beneath us while the rest of the world blended into arctic blue. Toronto sat across the aisle from me scanning a fresh *Wall Street Journal* from behind amber glasses. In his fancy boots again, this time with a heavy sheepskin overcoat, he looked like an eccentric foreign investor or a Hollywood stuntman who had somehow gotten hopelessly lost.

"What time we make the gate, hoss?" he said.

"Eleven-forty-five."

"Still early for Morelli. My bet is, if he's been doin' the nose-brain thing, he'll be sleeping things off."

Boog Morelli was infamous for late-night bar-hopping with his little entourage in tow, usually a couple of bodyguards and a group of thugs and hangers-on who followed him around like puppy dogs, mostly for the coke.

"We'll be his wake-up call then."

"Sure. You got a plan?"

"Nope. But I'll know one when I see it."

Toronto flipped to another page of his newspaper and smiled.

Ferrier and Spain, after visiting the lake, had grilled us individually for a couple hours. We were lucky to be out of jail ourselves. We were not to have any more involvement in the case. The two state agents were locked onto target now, what with a dead county sheriff, dozens of reporters, and their own higher-ups in Richmond with which to deal. Though not considered suspects, for the moment at least, we were not supposed to leave the state either. Luckily, we hadn't run into any SWAT teams barring us from doing just that.

Sheriff Cowan had been shot several times in the face, probably with the same weapon that had murdered Dewayne Turner. If it were one of Morelli's people, we would know soon enough. All Jake and I had had to do was call one of our falconry pals who lived about a half hour away to come care for Armistead and Jersey for a short while, book the flight to LGA and retrace Cowan's footsteps—simple enough in theory, especially since we used to call the Big Apple home. What might not be so simple, Jake noted, was how to keep from getting killed along the way ourselves.

The sky was clear when we reached New York, as clear as it ever gets anyway, and the sun was beginning to try to warm the frigid air. We picked up our rental car in the parking garage across from the terminal.

The swarm of trucks, cars, and buses on the Grand Central headed for Manhattan throbbed like some gargantuan aorta feeding the city. We made one quick stop on the Major Deegan near Yankee Stadium then threaded our way up along the Harlem River and took the Cross Bronx to the Henry Hudson north into Riverdale.

A phone call told us Boog Morelli still lived in the same penthouse we remembered, at the top of a highrise overlooking the Hudson and the Palisades. To many of his wealthy neighbors who didn't know he had done time up in Ossining, he was probably nothing more than a reclusive, odd-looking businessman who seemed in need of a great amount of protection and came and went at unusual hours. Thirteen years might have slowed the Boog down some, just as Hack Wilson had said. Then again, maybe not.

The grim-faced guard on duty in the lobby wore a

kelly green uniform with matching hat, bright gold braid, and epaulet. He gave Jake and me hard eyes when I handed him my card and told him whom we had come to see. Morelli's man.

"Mr. M. doesn't normally accept visitors before two o'clock," he said.

"He'll see us," I said. "We're old pals."

He studied my card and Jake's sheepskin as if they might yield additional information that would tell him what to do. Maybe he was thinking he would just have us stand there until two. I decided to wait him out.

At last he said: "Have a seat. I'll see what they say upstairs."

We plunked down in a pair of black leather chairs facing a matching black sofa and looked at a marble-and-onyx sculpture on a chrome-and-glass table. Sort of an art deco thing, I guess, but the lack of color made it look depressing. The guard spoke with his hand cupped over the receiver to keep us from hearing. Must have been taught that in guard school. He even maintained his surveillance of Jake and me at the same time. Probably graduated near the top.

"Okay, fellas. Your lucky day. Mr. Morelli doesn't like it, but he says he'll see you." He put down the phone and jerked his thumb toward the bank of elevators. Then he went back to the copy of the *Daily News* he must have been studying before we came in.

I looked at Jake and shrugged. We stepped to the elevators and the doors of one on the far end slid open. There was one man aboard who motioned for us to join him.

Cherry-paneled walls and railing with brass fittings. The man was tall, about six-foot-seven, but not too muscular. He had blond hair and wore a blue tracksuit. A deep scar ran across the base of his chin.

"You guys carrying?" he asked. "I'll have to search you anyway, but it might make things simpler." Real polite.

Jake held his arms up and waited while he was patted down. I did the same. Neither of us had brought a handgun, but the stop on the way in from La Guardia had been at a self-storage facility where Jake had disappeared for a few minutes before returning to the rental car carrying an oversized, weathered briefcase. He passed the case to the man now.

The track star whistled when he snapped open the locks. "You guys planning to go to war?"

Inside, in their padded cut-outs, were two Ingram M-11 semiauto pistols and enough clips to do some real damage.

"If necessary," Jake said.

The man laughed but he stopped when he saw the look in Toronto's eyes. We rode in silence the rest of the way to the top.

The doors whisked open again, this time on a dimly lit hall where a fat man about a foot shorter than our guide stood like a cigar store Indian. He too was dressed in a dark running suit, but I could see the bulge from his shoulder holster through the material.

"We had to wake him up," the man said, expressionless. "Almost time anyway."

The tall man led us, carrying the case, to the end of the corridor where a set of heavy double doors were locked with an electronic mechanism. He punched in a code, the handle clicked, and he stood to the side holding the door open. We stepped past him into the suite.

Not much light here either. Heavy drapes hung over the windows, blocking the brilliant sunshine but also spoiling the view. There were several pieces of Ethan Allen furniture and a lot of boxes piled neatly around the walls. Some large water bottles took up one corner and what looked like air tanks. Boog Morelli was nowhere to be seen.

But we could hear a deep, rattling cough coming from the far side of a hospital bed deployed in the middle of the living room. An Asian woman in a short skirt bent over the matress helping her patient drink from a paper cup with a straw. No one else was in the room.

"Mr. Morelli," the tall man said. "Your two guests are here."

"Ah, Christ." The voice was a whispery reed. "Can't even let a man get his friggin' rest. C'mon in. C'mon in."

Boog Morelli used to arm wrestle some of his little misfits and hoods just for fun. In his prime, it was said, no one could beat him, and though the competition might have been somewhat suspect, I guess he had been pretty good. He was a bottom-heavy mass of fat and muscle and deep-set eyes that, along with a distinct curvature of his upper spine, made him resemble, for all the world, a scale model Tyrannosaurus Rex.

But the shrunken man in the bed didn't look much like the old Boog. He weighed maybe a hundred pounds at best, his arms as thin as broomsticks. His skin was pockmarked with blue and black nodules. He had long white hair and his cheekbones looked as if they were about to collapse.

"Old pals, my ass. Pavlicek and Toronto. How ya doin', boys? Been a long time. C'mon in."

We moved around to the front of the bed.

"Hello, Boog," I said. "You don't look well."

He coughed so hard his whole body convulsed, but it ended in a chuckle. "I don't look well. Jesus, you hear that, Marina? I don't look well." He looked at the tall man.

The tall man said: "Mr. Morelli suffers from late-stage malignant melanoma."

Jake was nodding.

"I'm sorry," I said. "That doesn't sound good."

"It ain't," Morelli whispered. "I used to sit over at Jones Beach all day, all day long, you hear? Put baby oil on, that was all. Used to look like a lobster then turn brown as a nigger. Now these shots I'm takin' don't work. I'm dead."

No one said anything. As if to fill the silence the tall

man added: "We've tried Interferon and now we're experimenting with a vaccine."

"Are you an RN or something?" I asked.

"Oncologist, actually, among other things."

"Only the best for old Boog, ain't that right, Pavlicek?" Morelli managed a weak smile. I hesitated to ask what "other things" meant.

"So what is this?" Morelli asked. "A Confederate invasion? First this bumfuck sheriff a couple days ago. Now you two."

"Sheriff Cowan is dead," I said. "Found him this morning with most of his face missing."

"S'that right?" He stared blankly ahead, trying not to show any reaction, apparently, but one of his arms gave a visible shudder.

"You know who did it?"

"You think it was me."

"We were thinking maybe you might have ordered it done."

He coughed again, hard this time. The young woman rushed forward to put a cloth to his mouth. When she took it away there was a visible bit of blood. Morelli shook his head. "Not me, pal. Don't give a shit about no sheriff." He coughed some more.

I waited until he finished. "What about Dewayne Turner?"

"What about him?"

"You care anything about him?"

He snickered, but then he smiled. "He was a good kid."

"You know he's dead then too?"

He nodded. "Your sheriff fella there told me."

"You know what happened to him?"

"If I did, the sons of bitches would be joinin' him in a hurry."

"What was your business with Turner?"

He adjusted his blanket and sheet for a few moments as if he hadn't heard me. "You know Dewayne, that kid comes up here about a month ago. Sits in the chair right over there and tries to tell me we all gotta die sometime." He pointed, then wiped the corner of an eye with the back of his hand. "Like I fuckin' don't know . . . We had the curtains open to watch the sunset and it was beautiful out over the water and the cliffs, you see what I mean?"

I nodded.

"I tried to tell him, there ain't gonna be much hope for an old thug like me, but he wouldn't listen."

"He must have thought there was some."

Boog Morelli stared at the heavy drapes and gave a raspy chuckle. "Maybe so. Maybe so."

The tall man moved to the corner, picked up a clipboard, and began writing notes.

"You two want some breakfast?" Morelli asked. "I was just about to have some myself."

"No thanks."

"That's okay. It ain't exactly steak and eggs. . . ."

The Asian woman disappeared for the moment into the kitchen.

"Turner used to work for you?" I asked.

"Sure, sure. He was a good boy."

"What about Smoke and the rest of his gang?"

Morelli shook his head. "Bunch of punks. None of them's got the brains." Another coughing spasm shook him. "Listen, I ain't got no time to lie here answering no more questions. I suppose you two come about the money."

I glanced at Jake. "Money?"

"Yeah. You bring me my money?"

"I don't know what you're talking about, Boog."

He looked at Jake then back at me and saw that it was true. "Jeez Louise, you mean I gotta send somebody else special down there to collect?"

"Collect? Collect what?"

"The money that's owed me for the kilos, you dipstick, what do you think I'm talkin about?"

"Who owes you for the kilos?"

"Who owes me for the kilos?" He shook his head in wonder. "You guys fly all the way up here to talk to me and you don't know your buddy Cahill owes me fourteen grand?"

Jake's eyes grew wide and mine must have too. "What's Cahill got to do with kilos?" I was suddenly afraid I was already beginning to guess some of the answers.

He laughed. "What are you guys, some kind of joke? I don't hear nothin' from the lot of ya for years and then out of the blue Cahill calls me up all hot under the collar about some fuckin' old weapon. Says one of my boys was supposed to get rid of the thing. Like I'm supposed to fuckin' remember."

"When was all this?"

"I don't know." His whisper sounded tired now. "Maybe a month ago. I don't remember exactly."

"What did you tell him?"

"Hey, what can I say? People screw up. It was still lyin' around."

"Did Cat say what he was going to do about it?"

"No. But I had an idea. That was right after the boy you was talkin' about came to see me. So I started thinking maybe, hey, since the kid ain't doin' business for me no more and I got all these people waitin' down that way, maybe Cat would be looking to supplement the cop pension again. You know, kind of make it up to him for the screwup with the gun."

"Cat used to do business with you?"

"You people must have stepped off another planet. I thought you two was buddies with the guy. Sure we did business. He and—what was his name?—his old partner before he got wasted by those punk kids over in New Rochelle. You guys were there, weren't ya? Wasn't that what got ya kicked off the force?"

"This is really important, Boog. What did you tell Cat about doing business again?"

The girl had returned and Morelli signaled for her to

give him another sip from the straw. We waited while he drank.

"Like I told ya, the kid was just here. So I got ahold of him and had him take the message to Cahill. Told him to tell Cat I could make up for the gun crap with some real business, set him up again and everything."

"Then?"

"Then nothin'. I don't hear nothin' until a week ago and Cahill calls me and says he wants two kilos fast. I figure, okay, he thought about it and he's taking me up on my offer. So I send down the stuff, but he stiffs my guy who, by the way, ain't ever gonna work for me again, and sends a message he won't have the cash for a few days.

"So what do I do? I call up one of my legal whores and have him gift wrap the piece for the NYPD. Why not? What's it to me? Next thing I know this bumfuck sheriff comes by asking questions. And now you two idiots show up, so I figure you must be bringing me the dough."

Jake was biting a fingernail, listening intently.

"We haven't got the money, Boog. And I'm afraid I have bad news for you—the cops have your coke," I said. "I don't think Cat was ever planning to sell it."

"He wasn't? When I'm tryin' to do the guy a favor. What's goin' on?" There was a seed of dark anger in his eyes, but it seemed incapable now of blooming.

He looked at Jake who looked at me and said: "The gun thing."

"Yeah," I said.

"The gun thing?" Morelli said. He started to cough again. Weak and confused.

It was all coming together now.

"Sorry, Boog. Cahill's stolen the money from you, and if I'm right, he murdered Dewayne Turner and Sheriff Cowan. Not to mention his partner, Singer . . . We've got to go."

"Cahill killed Turner?"

"Yeah. Part of covering up his past. I think Cat must have gotten into some kind of dispute with Singer who was his partner all those years ago. Who knows? Maybe Singer got cold feet.

"Those kids didn't shoot Cat's partner. Cat did. We must have stumbled in right after it happened, but we never made the connection. Cat must have somehow switched barrels on the Glocks—he had one and the kids had them too. Maybe he had planned something like that all along. It makes sense. He didn't realize two NYPD detectives were so close, and was going to pin it on one of the kids until we showed up. But he managed to shift the focus to us and cover everything all up. Except that now he knows that the missing weapon can prove he did it."

"Christ," Morelli said, trying to piece it all to together. "So when I sent the Turner kid with the message to give him. . . . he what . . . he offed the kid because he might know about the gun then too?"

I nodded. A large bit of whatever life remained in Boog Morelli seemed to drain from him then. No doubt he had ordered killings and beatings of various kinds himself, done his share and more of heinous crime. But this was something else.

"And I was the only other one who could make the connection. The bastard figured I was already good as dead. . . ."

"You never knew the truth about what happened in New Rochelle?"

His face was a blank. "Maybe I had an inkling. But that was a long time ago. I never figured your buddy Cahill for somethin' like this."

His lower lip began to tremble.

"We need to go, Boog."

"So now you guys are gonna take care of Cahill."

"We're going to try," I said.

A crude but maybe adequate justice. The old murderer slumped down between his pillows. "I need ta rest." His exhaled words were barely audible.

"You didn't have to turn that gun in when Cahill stiffed you, did you, Morelli?"

"You fellas believe in absolution?"

"Maybe there'll be a nice sunset again tonight, Boog."

"I need ta rest."

He dismissed us with a birdlike wave of his fingers. The young woman moved in and pulled the sheet higher around his shoulders for him to close his eyes.

31

Priscilla Thomasen was already waiting on Jake's deck when our headlights swept across the trailer. It was almost eight P.M. Traffic from Riverdale back to La Guardia had moved like sludge, when it moved at all, and the first flight available back to C'ville had been delayed by more than an hour.

"The news is not good," she said as we got out. "I told you we had the hearing, she made bail, and was released into her mother's custody."

"Yeah?" I said.

"I just talked to one of the deputies down at the jail. It turns out Cahill was with Camille when she was bailed out, and the three of them left together."

"Just wonderful." I looked at Jake whose face was cold as stone. "Couldn't they have kept her in jail?"

"Hey, how was I to know? I didn't talk to you guys until long after they'd gone."

"Sorry."

"Yeah, well, it gets worse. The deputy also told me they just took a report a little while ago from a hysterical housekeeper out at Sweetwood Farm. The woman lives on the property. Thought she heard a commotion and went to investigate. She found Camille Rhodes unconscious. Looks like some kind of drug overdose."

"Where's Ferrier?"

"From what I understand, he's been fending off reporters half the day. And they're busy chasing down every suspected gang member in the area."

243

"Figures."

"I went by the restaurant. No sign of either Cat or his Range Rover."

"Was Kerstin there?" I said.

"The wife? Yes. I saw her go in and out of the kitchen a couple times."

"We'll start with her then. She's got to know something."

All the way back we had debated whether or not to inform Ferrier of what we had found. We had settled on bringing in only the Commonwealth's attorney. If it came down to some sort of hostage situation, the one advantage we had was Cat's assumption that Jake and I were still mostly in the dark regarding the truth. A huge posse would only tip him off.

Cat had been good—we had to give him that. Deception, not just once, but over a number of years. Bringing in family. The guy had broken just about every unwritten code there was. And he seemed to be growing more desperate with every killing, every move he made. He had to suspect we were onto something—he just didn't know how far we had come.

Or how far we were willing to go.

Priscilla handed Jake a note she had found taped to the door.

"It's from Hal Stenirude," he said. The falconer friend. "He just left a couple hours ago. The birds are okay."

We had replaced the briefcase where we had picked it up in New York. We couldn't risk trying to check it on the flight. Jake said if we were going to be doing this kind of thing again from time to time, he would have to rent another self-storage space closer to home. We picked up more ammunition for our handguns from the trailer and were all set to go.

"Jake?" Priscilla said. "If you two are planning something that will in any way affect my prosecution, I need to know about it."

Jake paused and took her gently by the arm. She did not resist.

"Priscilla," he said, "I respect who you are and that includes what you do. But this isn't about prosecution anymore."

"But if you have new witnesses, they need to be—"

"I know the drill. But right now Frank and I are more worried about his daughter than the chain of evidence."

"I understand."

Jake nodded slowly. He was checking the load on the .45. "You're coming, aren't you?" he asked.

"You betcha," she said.

Priscilla sat between us in the truck on the way into town. "A couple things I don't get. How did Cahill manage to change the barrels on those guns without Ballistics catching on to him?"

"Glock barrels from the same model are interchangeable," I said. "That's why they have their own serial numbers. It's fairly simple to break the piece down too, if you know what you're doing.

"You remember, don't you, Jake? Cat was the one who went after Balazar when we shot him. You were trying to help Singer while I chased the runner. You and I both know we saw a gun in that kid's hand and we were right. It must have been a Glock, same model as Cahill's. The other kid must have had one too. Cahill admitted he knew the kid we shot. He must have supplied them with the guns, one of which had the barrel from his own Glock in it while his had the barrel from that gun. There might have been four or five different weapons in the mix so Cat could kill Singer and one or both of the kids, then tag Singer's shooting on them."

Jake nodded slowly. "But he didn't count on Frank and I being in the neighborhood and showing up so soon after he called in. When we downed the kid, he must've hit on the idea of not just switching the barrels, but taking that weapon out of play altogether and substituting the pipe. Safer. Or so he thought."

"It *was* safer," I said. "He thought Morelli's people had taken care of the gun for him. But now Fuad writes to say they've got a match on the weapon and the barrel all these years later. If someone's able to tie it to Morelli's organization and starts asking enough questions— you could see how Cat might get concerned.

"He thinks he's okay when he finds out Morelli's about to kick the bucket, but then the Turner kid comes into the picture, and suddenly he knows about the gun too. Cat goes into panic mode."

"Murders Dewayne Turner," Priscilla said. "Then looks for an easy mark to pin that crime on and Nicky Pavlicek just so happens to fit the bill. He had to know you'd be coming over to look into things though."

"Right. Which might have been exactly what he was hoping."

"Feel us out. Find out what we know. Use the opportunity to cast suspicion on all of us, then try to eliminate us somehow too before he's through. Probably no one else would ever be in a position to piece the whole thing together," Jake said.

"How did Cowan find out about Morelli?" Priscilla said.

"My guess would be through Camille. He must have had an idea she was using. He said he knew the family well. Dewayne Turner, at one time, was probably her supplier. When that ended she probably got desperate and went to the gang or someone else on the street. In fact, that's probably where Weems came into the picture. And he somehow got mixed up with Cat too, which is why Cat had him following me. Turner himself might have mentioned Morelli to Camille. Remember, he was trying to evangelize a lot of his former contacts. He might have figured he would have a better chance if he kept tabs on who was still in the supply chain."

"So Cowan goes to New York. Finds out about the drug deal, maybe the gun too. Why not just come back and arrest Cahill?"

"He needed better evidence to tie Cat to more than just the drugs. Plus, he was still suspicious of Jake and me. He might have figured Cat was working for the two of us. He even went so far as to contact Cat in the hope he could use what he had to get more information. My bet is Cat somehow manipulated Cowan into meeting him again out at the lake."

"And now he's got Nicole," I said.

"That's a lot of supposition," she said. "The only way a prosecution can be successful is if the gun in New York can be definitively linked to Cahill along with additional evidence linking him to the current killings."

"We know Cat murdered Singer and set us up. Then he murdered Turner and tried to frame Nicole by planting the coke and putting traces of the same material on Turner's body. He murdered Cowan, now maybe Camille Rhodes as well. If I find out he is holding my daughter against her will, please excuse me if I shoot first and ask questions later."

"If everything you say is true, we've got to consider the possibility that your daughter may be already dead, Frank," Priscilla said.

She was right, but I didn't even want to think about that.

We reached the outskirts of town. Except for a Roanoke TV station van in the municipal lot, Leonardston looked peaceful enough. You would never guess the local sheriff had been murdered the night before and that a killer was still at large.

Jake said. "You think Kerstin's in on this thing too?"

"Hard to say. She may not know anything about it. He fooled us, didn't he?"

We pulled into Cahill's lot just as another car was pulling out, a green Toyota station wagon with a family inside. There were only two other vehicles outside the restaurant, the same as earlier in the day, with one glaring omission. Cat's Range Rover was still missing.

I turned off the engine and cut the lights.

Jake asked: "What now?"

"We go in and see if we can find Kerstin. I'll do the talking."

The three of us entered through the front. The lights were all on but the place was empty, almost eerily quiet. Then Kerstin Cahill came out from the kitchen.

"Frank, Jake, Miss Thomasen" she said. She nodded at the Commonwealth's attorney. "How nice to see you all. You need menus?"

"No, thanks. Actually, we were wondering if you could spare us a few minutes," I said. "Is Cat around?"

"No. He's off hunting. Called me a little while ago from a pay phone."

I glanced at Jake who showed no reaction.

"Would you folks like some coffee? Just put on a fresh pot of decaf."

"Thanks," I said. "That'd be great."

"Just help yourselves to a seat. I'll get us some mugs and be right back," she said.

She disappeared into the back again. We picked out chairs around a table in the middle of the room and all sat down. Kerstin came bustling back from the kitchen carrying a tray with the coffee. She set a full cup of the steaming liquid in front of each of us and put the pot, creamer, and a glass dish filled with sugar packets in the middle of the table. Then she picked out her own chair and sat down.

"So. What can I do for you people this evening?" she said.

"Do you happen to know where he's gone hunting?" I asked.

"Of course. He's gone up to the cabin that we own near Totter Creek. You know the place. . . . Why? Is something wrong?"

"We're not sure yet. He seem okay to you when you last saw him?"

"This morning? I suppose so. He looked tired." The big woman looked at Jake and me with searching eyes and I realized then that she was in the same position we had been: she didn't know.

"If you don't mind my asking, Kerstin, how's business?"

"Business. Well, I . . . I don't know really. We've been busy off and on. But Cat handles anything to do with money. We've never had any problem, if that's what you mean." She twirled a strand of hair through her fingers. Nervous. Maybe she had begun to suspect the truth by then. Maybe our being there was beginning to confirm it.

"Just looking for information," I said. "You said he called from a pay phone. Is there a phone up there at the cabin?"

"No. The place has electricity and running water, but no phone."

"How about Cat's cell phone? Could we contact him on that?"

"Sorry. He never takes it up there. It's outside the coverage area and besides, he says sometimes he just likes to get away from everything."

I tried to smile. "Sure. You don't think he'd mind if we went up there to visit him, do you?"

"I don't see why he would," she said. "But if you can wait until tomorrow, I'm sure he'll be back by lunchtime. We have a new cook starting then."

"That's okay. If it's all the same to you, we really would like to talk to him before then."

"Are you sure everything's all right?"

I would not be the one to tell her of his deception. Not yet at least.

"Let's hope so," I said.

Outside in the parking lot Priscilla was the first to speak.

"You two aren't planning to go up there after him in the dark, are you?"

I thought it over.

"What do you think, Jake?" I said.

"Seems like too much of a risk if he's got Nicky. Assuming he didn't kill her right away, a few more hours won't make any difference. Plus I've got an idea that can get us in there without Cat suspecting a thing."

I nodded. "We'll go at dawn then."

32

The plan was simple enough. The Cahills' cabin balanced on a steep hillside high above the creek that flowed through a gap in the mountains. A dirt road that had been cut along the power line provided the only motorized way in. Toronto and I would approach from above where, a hundred yards into the woods, the slope leveled to a long plateau. It wasn't the best place for a red-tail to hunt, but hopefully Cat wouldn't know that—Armistead would ride on my gloved left hand.

Priscilla would remain concealed on our flank with a handgun for protection. If something went awry, she was to get out and bring help, but if everything went according to schedule she had a more important job. Jake and I would try to get Cat away from the building. Priscilla would move in to look for Nicole and hopefully take her out of the equation, assuming she were there and still alive, before the big guy realized what was going on. I prayed he hadn't killed her yet; he could use her if it came down to bargaining with Jake and me.

My .357 was in its holster concealed beneath my thick, unbuttoned jacket. Jake had his big rig strapped to his boot just above the cuff of his trousers. How he walked without a limp, especially on the hill carrying that thing, I never knew, but somehow he managed.

Much of the forest's color had dropped to the ground by now. A breeze gusted from time to time, spinning the remaining leaves through branches like paper from a ticker tape parade in the gray first light.

I kept Armistead hooded until we got within sight of the cabin. We were counting on her training and discipline to provide a distraction if needed. I suppose we made quite a picture descending through the brush.

As we drew closer, we could make out a small puff of smoke curling from the cabin's chimney. Cat's Range Rover was parked in front. When we came abreast of the vehicle, I called out the way I would if we were greeting him on a chance encounter.

"Yo, Cat! It's Frank and Jake!"

No reply.

"We were up here hunting when we saw your truck!"

The cabin remained silent.

"Anybody here?"

Still no answer.

We circled slowly around the side then back by the car. No sign of movement from the windows. Armistead stirred a little on my fist but I held her in place. The sun was just beginning to poke over the ridge and, blocked by the cabin, caused the front stoop to remain in shadow.

"Yo, Cat! You home?"

With a creaking noise, the front door opened and the big man himself stepped slowly out. He wore a grin on his face, huge camouflage pants and jacket. Over his arm, draped in the carry position, hung a Bernadelli side-by-side, its twin barrels broken away from the stock, loaded. A bit much for squirrels. Enough stopping power for both Jake and me, one trigger for each.

"You fellas caught me napping," he said. "I was just headed out."

That meant he had decided we were alone. All we had to do now was get him away from the cabin. He might have had the same thing in mind.

"Why don't you come on and walk with us awhile?" I said. "You ever see a red-tail in action?"

"Can't say as I have. She's a beaut though, ain't she, Jake?" he said. "What's her name?"

"Armistead. This is her natural habitat," I lied.

"That right?" He seemed to fiddle with the latch on the door. "Give me a second while I lock up." He slipped a padlock with a key out of his pocket, put it though an outside dead bolt mechanism, and clicked it shut. The key went back in his pocket. He turned and took a step forward off the stoop. For a guy who'd been sleeping, his face was bathed in sweat.

"Jeez, Cat, you just get out of the sauna, or what?"

He grinned again, but said nothing. He was only a few paces in front of us now.

"Couldn't ask for a better day, eh,?" Jake said.

Cat was almost beside us when a loud thump, followed by what sounded like a chair scraping on a floor came from the cabin. I gave the owner a curious look. Out of the corner of my eye, I noticed Jake take an instinctual step sideways, setting himself.

"Damned dogs," Cat said. "Never can keep 'em quiet."

But another sound penetrated the cabin walls, this one even more usual. We all heard it. Muffled, a little garbled. Faint at first, then a little louder. Until it could be recognized as a human voice.

"Da-ddy!"

Everything clicked into slow motion. Cat's eyes became obsidian, serpent-like. His huge hands came together as he slammed the barrels of the shotgun to the stock. I reached for my gun. Jake tossed a piece of quail in the air toward Cat as I cast off Armistead. With two powerful strokes the hawk bore down on the bait, her talons extended, causing Cat to turn and raise his arm to shield himself, not realizing the bird would cut away. By the time he recovered, both our guns were pointed at his head.

"Nice trick," the big man sputtered.

We were all breathing hard now. He glared at us. The last time I'd seen such hatred from him was the night his partner died.

"Why, Cat?" I said.

He spat behind him. "Why? Gotta couple years to listen?" He laughed hoarsely. But there were tears forming in his eyes. "Y'all just been in the way from the beginning, that's all."

A shout came from up the hill, a sheriff's deputy with Detective Ferrier, too far away for a decent shot. Priscilla was with them. I guess she had decided we needed insurance.

"Drop the weapon, sir!" Ferrier yelled at Cat. "Do it now! Put your hands where we can see them in the air."

Cat's eyes flicked upward at the many others who must have also been approaching.

"Don't do it, Cahill," Jake muttered beneath his breath. "It's over now. Don't be stupid."

But the big guy grinned again as if he had actually planned it this way all along. He barely paused before he started to lift his gun.

The strange thing was, the actual act of pulling the trigger still felt no different than pumping target rounds at the range. The old training, the instincts returned. The impact of the bullets spun Cat around before the reports had even started to echo from the nearby hills, his bulk twisting down to come to rest against the foundation.

Only the sound was left then, rolling back to us like thunder, interspersed with the red-tail's distant cry.

33

Priscilla Thomasen and I were playing spades against Toronto and Agent Ferrier in a fifth floor visitor's lounge of Roanoke Memorial Hospital, sunlight pouring in through the unshaded windows. The Star City spread out below us, encapsulated in a cobalt sky.

"I don't believe it. The girl's going nil on us," Ferrier said.

Priscilla raised her eyebrows for a second as if to say: You never know.

"Play it out, pardner. Just play it out," Jake said, slapping down another sacrificial trump.

It was Saturday afternoon and a lot of healing would need to be done. Camille Rhodes had been moved from Intensive Care an hour before, looking like a rag doll with sunken cheeks, her prognosis uncertain. There had been some damage to her heart and she faced a long course of drug rehab from which there were no guarantees. Nicole, on the other hand, was being released from the hospital that afternoon. They'd had to do surgery on a wrist broken by Cahill. She'd suffered cuts and bruises and probably some psychological trauma as well during her captivity, but at least she had survived to tell the tale.

I had also been on the phone with Marcia and several others, making arrangements for her to transfer to Charlottesville High School to finish her senior year. In addition to the primary support team—Jake, Priscilla, and myself—Carla Turner, the Reverend Lori, and others from their church had mobilized on behalf of the sick, arriving in waves of comfort bearing food and flowers and cards.

Cat Cahill's funeral was scheduled for Monday. The restaurant had already closed for good, a FOR SALE sign in the window, listed by a Leonardston broker. Kerstin was rumored to be moving back to New York.

Priscilla lost another trick. I attempted to read her expression, but somewhere along the way, the Commonwealth's attorney had developed a decent poker face.

"Hear anything from Warren?" I asked.

"Sure. He wants to interview me for another article he's writing about gangs in the region. I told him no thanks," she said.

"Hey, you two playin' or just jawin'?" Ferrier said.

"We're just bored by the competition, that's all," I said.

"Course. Any guy can hop around the mountains with a bird on his arm the way you two do gotta be wearied by cards."

"I'm not bored," Jake said.

"Nor boring," Priscilla said, throwing him a wink.

"Wait a minute. No fraternization when you're trying to go nil," I said.

"Absolutely." She smiled. "Couldn't agree more."

We were down to the last hand and everyone out of trump. Ferrier led with a six of diamonds. I followed with a jack of clubs. Jake put in a ten of hearts. Then Priscilla threw down a four of diamonds with a flourish.

She and I stood and high-fived across the table.

"Guess your luck is holding," Ferrier said.

Priscilla looked at him and stuck out her tongue.

"You know, Frank," she said turning to me, "that daughter of yours must be thinking about following in Daddy's footsteps. Guess what she asked me this morning? Wanted to know what I thought about a young woman getting a degree and some experience so she could become a private investigator."

"Oooeee, child. Here were go," Ferrier said, chuckling.

"Are Mrs. Turner and the Reverend still around?" I said. "I think I'm gonna need a lot more prayer."

Jake was standing and stretching, smiling at me and shaking his head. Chad Spain entered the room, wheeling a briefcase on top of a rolling overnight bag. Ferrier said they had to get going back up to Richmond. We walked them out to the elevator.

"You keep in touch now," I said to him as we shook hands.

"Count on it. I still want one of you guys to take me out hunting with one of those hawks of yours."

"Anytime."

"Before we go though, I want you to tell me one thing. . . . You knew this character Cahill for what, ten years?"

"More like thirteen."

"You considered him a friend?"

"That's right."

"And all the time you never suspected anything?"

"Maybe I was too busy feeling guilty and sorry for myself."

"Guy lives a double life. On the take. Murders his partner." He shook his head. "What makes a cop turn like that you think?"

I did think about it. "People perish for cold metal," I said.

"Yeah . . . You make that one up?"

"No. Guy named Solzhenitsyn."

"Sure."

"I'm still going to miss the man he was as a friend."

"I know what you mean," Ferrier said. "I tell you one thing—if I knew the answer for a fella like that, I wouldn't be messing with this kind of stuff anymore. I'd have me a shingle hung on Monument Avenue in Richmond, driving a Benz and living out on River Road."

After the two agents left, Jake and I accompanied

Priscilla downstairs. We picked up a wheelchair from a nurse's station and made our way to Nicole's room.

"Hey, sport," I said through the doorway.

The curtains in the room had been pulled open, the place already cleaned. Her belongings were packed neatly in the corner. She lay on the made bed, propping a magazine with her good hand against her cast, the bruises on her face and the swelling around her eyes mitigated somewhat by a touch of makeup.

"About time you guys got here. I was beginning to think I was going to have to call a cab." She had on jeans and a light blouse, but over everything still wore a hospital gown.

"You look hot," Jake said.

She punched him in the arm. "Liar."

"I think you look remarkable, for a young woman who has been through what you've endured," Priscilla said.

"Thank you, Priscilla. Dad, can I hire her as my attorney?"

"I'm afraid it doesn't quite work that way, Nicky."

"Oh, boo."

We gentled her into the wheelchair, then darted around back, making a show of tucking her in.

"This is more embarrassing than having to use a bedpan," she said.

"Don't knock it," I said. "Things could be worse."

"Hey!" She was looking through the doorway at a new arrival. Regan Quinn stood there clutching a teddy bear and a box of chocolates. "What are you doing here?"

"These are for you," Regan said. "And you can't say no to the candy."

The both cried and hugged one another.

"Guess what?" Regan said.

"What?" Nicole was digging into the chocolates and passing the box around.

"I just had an ultrasound downstairs. It's going to be a boy."

"Wow!"

There were more tears and laughter and congratulations all around.

We all wheeled Nicole along the corridor and rode the elevator to the ground floor, eliciting several sidelong stares. I bought both her and Regan balloons from the gift shop, over mock protests, and tied Nicole's to the arm of her chair. She thought it great fun to ride in the chair and challenged Jake to a race across the lobby, but an austere security guard standing at the entrance with his hands behind his back put the kabosh on that plan.

Regan said good-bye with kisses and hugs. Jake and I went to retrieve my truck and Priscilla's Saab from the parking garage. It was much warmer than it had been earlier in the day. When we pulled up behind one another outside the main entrance, Priscilla and Nicole were already by the curb, gabbing like old friends.

"What are you two so chatty about?" I wondered.

"Girl talk, for your information," Priscilla said. "None of your business."

It would be a brave new world having a teenaged daughter live in my house, if only for a year or so before she started college. How bad could it be? Nicole already had everything figured out, even down to finding a group home near C'ville, called Emmaus, where Regan could live while she had her baby.

Jake helped me hoist Nicole, with her balloon, onto the pickup's seat.

"Wheeee," she said. "I could get used to this."

"You going to follow us?" Jake said, closing her door. We needed to swing back by Leonardston to pick up Armistead and the rest of Nicole's things.

"Lead on."

"Oh. You know I almost forgot. Carla Turner asked me to give you something." Priscilla was rummaging through her purse.

Before I could object, she had pulled out a silver chain and pressed it into my hand.

"Dewayne's cross. She didn't need to do that."

"She said it would remind you."

I nodded. She gave me a hug before stepping into the Saab next to Jake.

In the truck I buckled my belt and looked across at Nicky. "You okay?"

"I'm okay. You think Mom is gonna be all right?"

"I hope so, honey. We can come back to visit whenever you want."

The Saab lurched away. I pressed the accelerator to follow. Suddenly, as if it were the most natural act in the world, Nicole's good arm draped across the seat, her hand coming to rest against my shoulder. Surprise, Daddy? Welcome home? Passing from the shade of the hospital portico, I could almost think so.

Nicole rolled her eyes and shook her head when I tuned the radio to an oldies station. The Vogues were in the midst of singing "Special Angel," after all. The clean sky behind branches rushing past reminded us the season was new again, and for the first time I may have caught a glimpse of grace from a higher station, where eyes see earth more clearly and the hunter waits, her quarry known.

Lawrence Block

TANNER ON ICE
19410-1

Once Evan Tanner was known as the thief who couldn't sleep, carrying out his dangerous duties for a super-secret intelligence agency. Then someone put him on ice—for 25 years. Now Tanner has returned and is about to embark on a new assignment....And he's making up for lost time.

THE THIEF WHO COULDN'T SLEEP
19403-9

A wake-up call is the last thing that Evan Tanner needs. Champion of lost causes and beautiful women, Tanner hasn't slept a wink since the sleep center of his brain was destroyed. And with the FBI keeping tabs on him, the CIA tapping his phone, and a super-secret intelligence agency wanting to recruit him, keeping wide awake is definitely a smart choice.

THE CANCELED CZECH
19404-7

The Canceled Czech finds the sleepless adventurer on a mission to Czechoslovakia to liberate a dying man, who turns out to be a Nazi. For his troubles, he finds himself leaping from a moving train, tangling with an amorous blonde, and playing the role of a neo-Nazi propagandist. Just another typical work day in the life of "the thief who couldn't sleep."

TANNER'S TWELVE SWINGERS
19833-6

Evan Tanner, intrepid spy, is back in the third of his original, hilarious adventures. This time he finds himself up to his neck in a dozen leggy beauties and a life-and-death smuggling assignment out in a cold corner of Russia.